Near Flesh

Near Flesh

STORIES

Katherine Dunn

MCD · FARRAR, STRAUS AND GIROUX · NEW YORK

MCD
Farrar, Straus and Giroux
120 Broadway, New York 10271

EU Representative: Macmillan Publishers Ireland Ltd, 1st Floor, The Liffey
Trust Centre, 117–126 Sheriff Street Upper, Dublin 1, DO1 YC43

Some of these stories previously appeared, in slightly different form, in the
following publications: *David Copperfield's Beyond Imagination*, ed. Janet
Berliner, Harper Prism ("The Allies"); *The New Yorker* ("The Resident Poet");
The Paris Review ("The Education of Mrs. R." and "Rhonda Discovers Art");
Redbook ("The Novitiate"); and *The Ultimate Frankenstein*, ed. Brian Aldiss,
Byron Press ("Near Flesh").

Custom lettering of title and author lines on title and half-title pages
by Thomas Colligan.

Library of Congress Control Number: 2025015223
ISBN: 978-0-374-60235-2

Designed by Abby Kagan

Our books may be purchased in bulk for specialty retail/wholesale, literacy,
corporate/premium, educational, and subscription box use. Please contact
MacmillanSpecialMarkets@macmillan.com.

www.mcdbooks.com • www.fsgbooks.com
Follow us on social media at @mcdbooks and @fsgbooks

10 9 8 7 6 5 4 3 2 1

Contents

Near Flesh

Pieces

I

JOHN GREW UP AS A MECHANIC on his father's fishing trawler out of Puget Sound. On the day the accident happened he was a lean twenty-three with thick hair and an electric grin. The trawler was tied up at the cannery dock. John got bored and set to tinkering with the engine. It was a stupid thing, a dropped wrench. He reached for it wrong and the flywheel caught his left hand and tore his middle finger off. He took the finger with him to the emergency room and waited his turn on a crowded wooden bench with his hand and finger wrapped in separate greasy rags. That was before they got so good at sewing things back up.

John's family believed you couldn't get to heaven packing less than you were born with. No circumcision in that clan.

And any subtractions, accidental or incidental, had to be buried with you.

John kept the severed finger in formaldehyde. It turned brownish in the liquid and then stopped changing. At Fourth of July picnics he'd entertain the nieces and nephews by bringing out the jar so they could peer in. The liquid was smoky and the limp finger was bloated and ragged at one end. Only the faint shape of a grimy fingernail at the rounder tip proved that it was, truly, a finger. He kept the jar packed in a small wooden box cushioned by crumpled paper. For thirty-five years, whenever John moved or shipped out, the box went with him.

Then he was a granddad, thick and bald, the captain of a sea tug towing log rafts to the Philippines. Just back from three months at sea, John was driving home from the dock when his car was crushed by a stampeding garbage truck. The jar and its box were smashed in his seabag in the trunk. The reek of formaldehyde made the emergency crew wary of toxic chemicals. They scuttled into safety gear while John quietly stopped bleeding.

The funeral director put the finger, in its new jar, into the coffin before he closed it. John changes, but not that finger.

II

The mortuary has a big walk-in freezer. Its wire shelves hold detached human parts whose former owners still live. These are the bits amputated or extracted in surgery from all over the state.

Each piece is wrapped in white paper, labeled with a discreetly typed bag. One bulky package contains the mangled legs of the boy whose bicycle slid beneath the train. The narrow slab is the wrist and hand of the sawmill worker who slipped and fell against the machinery. The skier's frostbitten toes are in the small parcel beside the toes of the diabetic. Various bundles hold a pancreas, several appendixes, a malignant stretch of colon. There are the boxed breasts of the senator who didn't stop wearing wigs even though all her hair grew back after the chemo.

The boy, brilliant in his speeding wheelchair, is a bitter debater in his college classes. The ex–mill worker has a hook and two sons to help on his Christmas tree farm. The skier limps slightly and vacations in the tropics.

According to the faith of these survivors, each abandoned part must be given Christian burial. For those who can afford the nominal storage fee, the pieces will wait for two or ten or fifty years. The senator and her breasts will sink together in the hillside plot she's already chosen and paid for.

Other pieces sit frozen for months or years until enough of them have collected on the cold shelves. Then they are stacked together in a cardboard box and carried out to a ready hole. A hired priest reads over them and blesses them before they are lowered and covered. Then the thawing begins.

III

It was a numb, starless night in the jungle. They were dug in when the attack came, but Davey's partner in the foxhole was killed by the first rattle of fire. When the small man in the black pajamas slipped into the hole, Davey knifed him and kicked him and then stood on the corpse, listening, waiting for more. At the first seep of dawn Davey sliced off the enemy's right ear and buttoned it into his breast pocket. Then he dragged his buddy's body back to the unit. Davey was eighteen at the time.

Later, back home, Davey's mother found the ear wrapped in tinfoil in his drawer. She threw it out and screamed at him. He was drinking a lot and getting into fights, so it wasn't just the ear that set her off.

After a while his war dreams sifted away and left only the one dream of the ear. The earless one wanted something from him. This was the message. Davey read about Eastern religions until he understood that the earless one couldn't go to his heaven with a piece missing. He would wander the dreamscape forever.

Davey felt bad about it but other things were happening—heroin and politics and motorcycles and women. There were sojourns in the Veterans Hospital to sober up and read. There was some college time, several jobs. Sometimes he wouldn't dream at all. Other times the earless one was with him every night for weeks. During one of those sieges he went to a refugee temple and asked the priest how to make amends. The priest said Davey would have to figure that out for himself.

He was thirty-three then. He worked clearing trails in the steep, wooded parks. The crew chief was a pacifist who'd spent the war in jail. The two became friends. Davey usually worked hard but mornings after a bender he'd flop in a grassy clearing and sleep. The chief understood and didn't bother him.

One morning Davey took his sharpest ax and drifted away from the rest of the crew. He spread his left hand out on a tree stump. Breathing carefully he lifted the ax and cut off the smallest finger.

Lifting it, he offered it to the earless one. "Fair trade, man," he said. "Peace, man." He tossed the finger into the brush.

At the hospital he tried to explain why he was so happy. But the crew chief told the admitting nurse it was an accident on the job, that the wounded man was in shock, delirious. He whispered harshly into Davey's ear, "Shut the fuck up. Workers' comp won't pay for spiritual atonement." Davey shut up, but he couldn't stop grinning.

IV

The big freezer at the county morgue is a wall of burnished steel file drawers. The Number 2 parts drawer is in the lower left corner and, like the others, pulls out to the length of a bed. Number 1 is fairly full, but, for the moment, two small-ish plastic bags are the only things in the Number 2 drawer.

In the first bag is a greenish-gray bone shard. If you press the clear plastic flat, a single black tooth is visible, rooted in the bone. The jawbone's bag has its own typed tag with the date and location of its finding, and a number code. If you type that code into the computer down the hall you learn the name of the fisherman who was digging for bait grubs last fall when he found the piece out near the river slough. The experts say it's not old enough to be a Native burial.

The finger has its own bag, tag, and code. It was discovered by a woman who massaged her moods with walks on the wooded park trail. Her dachshunds, a mother-daughter pair, were fighting over it in the brush. There wasn't much flesh left, a few tatters at the joints, but it was fresh enough that she recognized it with that chilling of the chest that we all know. The cops spent a full day up there, sifting the leaf mold, quartering through the undergrowth, without finding anything more.

The morgue has a procedure for parts drawer cases. Photographs from different angles, samples taken, slides made, some basic lab analysis. Reports are filed and checked. It may be months or more, sometimes a few years, before the decision is made. It has to do with odds and intuition and how big a chunk is left to work with, and how crowded the parts drawers are. If no more is found, no connective element is recognized. If no clue surfaces, the part is sent to whichever crematorium is next in the county indigent rotation. The attendants wait until several parts can be sent at the same time. Until then the pieces wait, their movement stopped by the cold.

I Had the Baby on
My Left Hip

I HAD THE BABY ON MY LEFT HIP. We'd had a great day, gone to the Green to feed the ducks, spent a few hours in the library. I walked down to the corner to catch the bus home to Howth. I was two blocks away, strolling along, talking to the baby, when the boom came—

The vibration hit me solidly in the gut and stayed, rippling out to my shoulders and hip sockets, rattling steadily so that my arms and legs felt hardly attached. I walked very quickly toward the bus stop, came around the corner, the gray stone wall on my right, the big McGurk Drayage sign above me—I didn't know what I was looking at. I was some space traveler caught in the wash of a time slip. I jerked once and blinked to see the vortex of my world gone cartoon blotto in an instant.

The bench at the bus stop was heaped with torn clothes.

Beyond that, nothing on the street was familiar at all—or right. I could not tell where I was.

A small shoe was on the pavement in front of me, pumping red, quietly, gently, the sock concealing what was still inside it. I picked the shoe up in my right hand and walked up the block, looking for the place where the shoe belonged. I couldn't find it. My eyes skated everywhere, searching. Holding the baby against my side, I bent and stooped, but kept moving straight ahead. At the end of the block I turned around and headed back, thinking I'd surely missed it.

The shoe was completely soaked now with what had been pumping out of it. I stopped to wipe the thick stuff off the toe of the shoe. It was a white patent leather shoe, about five inches long. It had a single layer of leather for a heel and a thin strap. The sock had sagged down over what was inside but I could see the little crocheted edge on the cuff. It had been a white sock, and I was sure the edge was pink or pale blue before the whole thing went red.

Fanno Creek

I DISCOVERED THE FANNO CREEK EFFECT by accident, as others must have before and since. Yet a search of the literature indicates that the phenomenon remains undiscussed and unstudied. I fear the recent decades of easily available recreational and pharmaceutical alternatives may permanently deter rigorous analysis.

My own experiments back in the early 1960s were spurred by the fact that my peers considered coffee and cigarettes to be drab, sour entertainment suitable only for the ancients, and I didn't like beer. The brew reek nauseated me, and at the time, beer was the only mind-altering substance in reach for most teens in my small western town.

If more specific blame must be attached even at this late date, I willingly finger Henry David Thoreau and the reckless high school teacher who assigned *Walden* to students trapped in the hormonal lunacy of adolescence. Too self-absorbed to notice what havoc the book might be wreaking on my classmates, I wolfed it down as fuel for my already dour "Only Man Is Vile" phase. The increasingly tattered paperback was my treasure through the ensuing summer.

Improvising Thoreau's plan I hid out in the hilly pastures around town and found thousands of microcosms reflecting the macrocosm. I spied for hours on the languid, reciprocal bubbling of big slugs mating.

In a ditch at the foot of the hill there were tadpoles and the infant nurseries of bug legions. The ditch led around muddy curves to a deeper, wider ditch, almost a gully, which oozed into an actual flowing stream. Following the stream's clay banks for a ways I was at first disappointed to find that this was mere prosey old Fanno Creek, which snuck through town beneath roadbeds and stumpy bridges and which I had commonly seen only from the back seat of my mother's car. It had never occurred to me that Fanno Creek had a life before and after the town. It kicked up a little in the heavy rains of winter and early spring, but most of the year it was slow, tepid, and shallow. It was also known to be polluted by toxins of unspecified lineage. None of us were ever allowed to play in it.

That was all right, of course. I was far too old to be *playing* in the stream, was in fact conducting *research*. The blighted and despised Fanno was the perfect subject for my adoring scholarship. At one secluded spot a mile or so from town, the Fanno wandered through a copse of smallish trees that provided enough shade for horsetails and skunk cabbage and multifarious mosses along the shore. This became my secret laboratory.

And in the process of collecting specimens (dragonflies, crawdads, and five-legged frogs) on many a blistering July or August afternoon, the most serious of naturalist philosophers might slip, quite unintentionally, and fall on her butt in ten inches of oily rainbowed water. And once the damage was done, jeans and sneakers and T-shirt soaked, totally by accident, only a priss or a grown-up would refuse to enjoy it. Henry, I know, would have stayed there, splashing and examining the texture of the muddy bottom, the seep of ooze into his shoes. His mother did his laundry, after all, just as mine did.

If the philosopher's throat was just a tad sore the next morning, she thought her scabby little brother was right, that it was the result of practicing Tarzan yells on the garage roof. It was only later, on a still October night, that the truth of the Fanno effect came to me. Steeped in school gloom and romantic agonies more akin to Poe than Thoreau, I snuck out my bedroom window after everyone had gone to sleep and crept down to the creek.

What had been pleasurable in August was deliberate masochism in October. I waded out to the deepest point, where the water reached almost to my knees. The swift ache of the cold was an exquisite expression of my internal agony. Penitent and stricken, I reached for deeper flagellation. I sat down. Ice almost to the armpits. The pain was almost sharp enough. No one knew how I suffered, no one recognized the depths of my rage and sorrow. I could die there of exposure, or drown by an act of sheer will.

I eased down onto my back. The water was so cold I barely felt the rocks biting into my spine. They would find my corpse in the first light of dawn with a water veil sliding over me. The beauty of the image was so touching that I began to sob harshly. Locating a convenient rock near my left ear, I wiggled until I could rest my head on it. This had the marvelous effect of keeping my whole head and face submerged in the rushing stream, with only my nose sticking out.

Thinking to improve the aesthetic impact on those who would discover my tragic corpse, I stretched my arms out to symbolize how I had been crucified by the unjust pressures of society. This had the unfortunate effect of leaving my left hand out of the water, flopped on the clay bank. No matter how I rearranged myself the stream was not wide enough at that point to do the job. Redesigning the image, I tried clasping my hands on my chest as if in prayer. They stuck up and formed an oddly phosphorescent V in the water. I was just wondering whether this was a desirable effect when I was interrupted. What felt like a crawdad had climbed into the gaping cuff of my blue jeans and scrabbled up my bony shin.

I yelped and leaped up and out, stamping and dancing wildly to shed the invisible interloper on the creek bank. The wind touched me and I set off trotting, squelching and squishing, dripping, chattering, and shivering ecstatically all the way home. I snuck back in through the window of my bedroom, shed my sodden clothes, jumped into a hot shower, and then put on flannel pajamas. I slept immediately.

In the morning I woke with a raw throat and a gravelly voice, pitched a full octave lower than normal. My eyes were sunken and burning with dark intensity. My mind raced with furious precision. I twitched with excess energy. I avoided speaking within range of my mother's hearing to prevent being trapped at home. I popped a decongestant to keep my nose from dripping constantly, boarded the school bus, and immediately started ranting at the Jehovah's Witness in the window seat. She had often helped me with French verb declensions and, unlike certain creationists in my biology class, she never pushed her religion on anybody. Still, the molten Truth erupted from me. "Only the weak and gutless need a cotton candy religion to disguise the volcanic wonder of the universe!" I roared.

My voice was spectacular, as if a monster was trapped in my chest and roaring nastily. The raspy power of it was so enchanting that I kept talking just to hear it, to play with it. The Jehovah's Witness stared at me suspiciously but refused to argue. I was usually sullen and quiet.

In English class I was belligerently witty, spouting crassly erudite commentaries on Mr. J.'s lecture, spontaneously crafting adaptations of jokes instantly recalled from years of close reading of *Reader's Digest*. The entire room wobbled with laughter until Mr. J. sent me to the principal's office. The principal's secretary took one look at me and sent me to the nurse, who determined I had a temperature of 102 degrees. Even as my mother picked me up, took me home, and tucked me into bed, I knew that Fanno Creek had unleashed me from the gray realm of normalcy. I had tapped the furnace of my own power.

When talking about the Fanno experience in these decades since, I've been guilty of saying, "When I had to give a speech or an oral presentation in school I used to lie full length and fully clothed in a polluted stream named Fanno Creek until I couldn't stand the cold any longer and then I'd jump up and run home wet. And in the morning I'd have the kind of sore throat that lowered the pitch of my voice by an octave, and a degree or two of fever—just enough to give me some flash, a competitive edge."

The phrase "I used to" makes a false statement of commonness, even frequency. The impression is as deliberate a deceit as the old violin teacher in the small Oregon town who visited New York for two days in her youth and stood outside the Russian Tea Room for half an hour, peeping through the door whenever it opened, but now reminisces about times when she used to go there for cucumber sandwiches with no crusts. Or it is like those peers of mine who talk as though they took LSD hundreds or thousands of times. "I used to," they say, or "We used to." The truth, regarding my Fanno immersions, is that I did it exactly three times. The first discovery was accidental, a synchronous byproduct of adolescent angst. The next two were that winter—once in December and again in February. In each case I had to give a speech in class the following day. It was tremendously successful. My terror of standing in front of the class became harnessed, high-voltage energy. My voice had the gravity of Orson Welles's. My small, trapped adolescence was mesmerized. My grades were superb. I soared, electric.

But I only did it when compelled by my horror of public speaking. The process was painful, and it took weeks to recover. The Fanno was a potent drug and I wasn't inclined to abuse it.

At the time I assumed it was my own body, my immune system triggered by cold and exhaustion, fighting off common microorganisms. But in retrospect it seems possible that other factors were involved. Certainly the ice pond at my college had no similar effect when I resorted to it the night before my oral exams. And the larger streams I have tried from time to time through what passes for adulthood have produced no such miracles. Surely it was a toxin, organic or otherwise, some parasite or bacillus, some heavy metal compound, some secret ingredient in the slow waters of this particular transformative creek we called Fanno.

The Flautist

S O MARJORIE AND I CAME STAGGERING OUT of the
Schnitz after the concert and I waved at the first cab in
line. There was a big silver flute lying across the front
passenger seat, but the plump, dark guy at the wheel said he
could take me.

I hugged Marjorie (she later said she thought the flute was
a club, some kind of weapon, and was a little alarmed) and
hopped into the back seat. The driver said, "You can certainly
sit in front if you like." He had a heavy Middle Eastern accent
that suited his looks. I said I was fine where I was.

As he pulled into traffic he started asking about the
concert—what composers, which pieces had been played.
Which was my favorite composer? The Beethoven. Ah. Was
I a musician? No, just a listener. I was surprised at his ques-
tioning until he said, "I play the flute. But I am not good." He

looked at me over his shoulder, nodding fiercely to let me know he understood his not-goodness. "I played the flute when I was very young and had to give it up, but I started again just six months ago and I am not good." He had to be in his fifties, chunky and jowly and graying, but with energetic eyes. We turned down a slope that ended in a traffic light, which turned red as we approached.

"I'll play for you." He stopped the cab, whisked up the flute, and blew a simple scale. His tone was nice, soft, a little breathy. The light changed, and he dropped the flute and drove on. "You see, not good."

"But a nice tone," I said.

"I know you like classical, but do you like jazz?"

"I don't know anything about jazz," I said.

When the next light turned red, he grabbed the flute and began playing even as we rolled to a stop—the first few bars of "Für Elise," his fingers fumbled when the light went green. But all the way home he managed to hit every red light and at each he played a few phrases of Beethoven.

When he pulled up in front of my house he said, "Please, I know you don't like jazz, but can you give me just a minute to play this?" Of course, of course. And he played, pertly, perfectly, with his face in shadow and his short chubby fingers dancing in light from the street. He played Henry Mancini's theme from *The Pink Panther*. Recognizing it I laughed and praised him and he rewarded me with the opening bars of Beethoven's *Eroica*. I clambered out in high spirits and he whirled the cab around and headed back downtown, to the Schnitz, I thought. To catch another concertgoer, another audience for his flute.

The Allies

THE RADIO PURRED from the top of the refrigerator, and Mrs. Reddle paused, listening, with her smallest sable-hair brush an inch from the canvas.

"Another unidentified flying object reported near the coast," said the radio host. *"And in Texas, an insurance salesman and a hitchhiker report that they were taken aboard a huge spherical vessel that stopped their car in the desert, south of Burkburnett. More on these and other stories, after this."*

Mrs. Reddle moved the brush delicately, laying a sliver of light on the face beneath her hand. The rough two-by-four easel stood in the windowed bay of the kitchen, where anyone else would put a table and chairs. The Reddles' table was in the middle of the room, with a discreetly rosy bowl in the center of its brown tablecloth. The bay was jammed with boxes of magazine clippings and old photographs, a stained bench holding bottles, jars, cans stuffed with brushes, and rags smeared with thick pigments.

Mrs. Reddle sat with her left side to the daylight. The open windows looked down the yellow grass knoll and across the highway to the service station. Her husband was leaning over the windshield of a car; his massive arm swabbed at the glass, the grease on the belly of his overalls threatened the finish of the hood. His laugh drifted in faintly, causing Mrs. Reddle to frown as she bent to the paint.

"Further sightings reported," the radio host continued. *"A squadron of white lights moving in patterns in the sky above the small coastal town . . ."*

Mrs. Reddle lifted the last stroke of the paint until it melted smoothly into the surrounding shadow, and then fell back in her chair, a sly tilt at the corners of her mouth. She slid the brush into the turpentine can and squinted at the canvas through her eyelashes. The smells of turpentine and linseed oil and her own flesh drifted around her.

The bell on the pavement of the gas station rang. Her son stood on the bell cord in the shadow of the canopy. His child arms moved in wide circles as he described something to his father. A truck passed on the road, blocking the view, but her husband's laugh mingled with the engine noise and the rush of air. Further down the highway, a familiar squat figure toiled up the hill.

Edie Reddle heard her father's laugh rattling through the traffic and knew her mother was in a decent mood. On the days when her father laughed, or waved at her as she climbed the hill, Edie went straight in through the kitchen door to talk with her mother.

If her father moved heavily around the cars at the gas pumps or stared sullenly at her from the office window, she went around the house to the front door and directly up to her bedroom to listen until she could tell which direction her mother's anger was moving.

Her mother was either happy or furious, with no mediocre moods for transition or warning. If Edie set off for the high school in the morning, leaving her mother whistling merrily in the kitchen, she might arrive home the same afternoon to ripping accusations, screams of fury, breaking glass, flailing blows—a toxic mayhem. Her mother often went on muttering and banging around into the night while Edie lay rigid in bed, listening in the dark for the inexplicable escalation that could hurl a shrieking monster into her bedroom. Usually Edie's father or her younger brother was the target of the anger, but no one was safe until it passed.

It had to do, Edie figured, with what her mother thought about during the day. Whether she remembered something you'd done years ago or was imagining what you might be doing out of her sight. But it might also be triggered by something on the radio, or a phrase overheard in the supermarket, a comment by a clerk or passerby that twisted in her mother's mind and grew fangs.

But today she heard her father's laugh clearly and could see the flash of his body as he worked across the road, so Edie stepped up to the kitchen door and opened it.

Turpentine. A soothing oil seeping through the pungency. The brown kitchen with its cunning light was warm and neat. A faint hint of roasting meat softened the paint smells. As long as her mother was actually painting, she was fine. Once she put her brushes down, anything could happen. Edie took a full breath and put her books on the table.

"Further reports on the UFO sightings at Seaside on the news at four-thirty. This is Radio AUZ, the Voice of Gold."

"Mama?" Edie fumbled with her coat buttons.

"Come here, dear."

The wilderness of the alcove ended precisely where it bordered the kitchen. No spot of paint or dropped rag, not even a leg of the chair she sat on was allowed to protrude into the clean kitchen. Only the smell went everywhere, gently.

Mrs. Reddle, with a fist full of brushes on her knee, sat watching, waiting. Edie did not look at her, but only at the canvas. She waited a minute and then smiled. Mrs. Reddle smiled back, hesitantly, her eyes anxious, her fist spreading the brushes into the knee of her dungarees.

Edie used the line she had been practicing on the way home. "Did religion make him look like that? I'm heading for the church right now. But no, I suspect it was you."

She watched her mother's eyes liven as though they were connected to her chuckle.

"Oh, he's a decent enough man," said Mrs. Reddle. "I'm just trying to cover up his stupidity by dressing it as enthusiasm."

"Is he dumb?" asked Edie. She bent to peer at the intense face on the canvas.

"I hope you can't tell from mine. But just look at these." Mrs. Reddle spread glossy photographs on the base of the easel.

"You mean how close together his eyes are? And how small?"

Mrs. Reddle pointed with the tip of a brush. "That's sometimes a clue, but it can go with a low kind of shrewdness, too. I've added some distance there and enlarged them a hair. But look how low his ears are set on his head. This is the dead giveaway. The top of each ear is a half inch below the level of his eye. And look at all that flab under his chin. That's not fat, that's just gaping room. He lets his jaw hang in private and has to think about jutting it out when he's in public."

Edie giggled. Mrs. Reddle watched the freckled skin pucker across her daughter's round face, the hunch of her plump shoulders, and the spread of the stubby white hands next to her own long, strong ones. The girl turned to her, her brown eyes smiling.

"Is he taking this to Africa with him to impress the natives?"

"He's presenting it to his fan club, the ladies of the Overseas Mission Group. According to him all he's taking is his New Standard Bible and a million cc's of antibiotics. The ladies will send him care packages—homemade jam and silk underwear."

They laughed as they set the table. Mrs. Reddle made the salad, and Edie stood at the sink peeling potatoes.

"And while the highway patrol and local police force continue their investigations of the rash of sightings, this reporter asked Dr. A. R. Ziegler, professor of astrophysics at . . . 'What can I say? Anything is possible . . .'"

The door slammed and Edie's younger brother jostled her for room to wash his hands at the sink.

"Shove over, Fats."

Edie felt a sudden hatred for his skinny, golden arms and the black grease that he sluiced and dripped over the coiled potato peels. Her mother's quick steps behind her made the muscles tighten in her neck, but the punishing slap clipped the boy's head instead of hers.

"How many times, young man, have I told you to come home from school and change your clothes before you go over to that grease pit? Your father doesn't care. He doesn't have to wash your filthy clothes, or his own, either. There'll come a day . . ."

Mrs. Reddle's voice soared higher, losing control. The boy's face wrinkled with mute resentment near Edie's shoulder. He flicked water off his fingers at Edie and marched out of the room.

"Have you been listening to all the UFO reports, Mama? Everybody's talking about it at school." Edie's fingers turned the potato under the knife. She waited for her distraction to take effect.

"I have my own idea about them," said Mrs. Reddle. "I think they're looking for someone."

Edie turned to look at her. "Who?"

Mrs. Reddle shook the stripes of stiff gray hair that sprang from her temples and nodded. "Someone they can talk to."

Edie's mouth skewed, embarrassed, but she censored her sarcastic reply and turned back to the sink. When she spoke again, her voice rattled with irony. "I got a talking-to today. Mr. Dolbeer stopped me in the hall."

"He's the algebra teacher?" Mrs. Reddle asked the cucumbers.

"He asked if it was my mother who'd painted the portrait of the president for the auditorium. When I said yes he kind of shook his head and said, 'How did she ever end up in this hole?' It made me mad. I said you hadn't ended up yet by a long way. And he apologized. He said he just meant that a talent like yours should be more widely recognized." Edie dumped the peelings into the garbage can.

"What a nice man!" Mrs. Reddle rested her hands among the lettuce leaves and cucumber slices.

"He's not a nice man. He's critical of everything. The only people he likes in this world are Bach and Euclid. Everybody else is 'vulgar' or 'in poor taste.'"

Edie felt the glow of her mother's pleasure filling the room. She heard her mother's soft laugh and the lighter touch of her knife on the cutting board.

"Well, you get good grades in his class. He must like you, too."

"He probably likes me better now that he knows who my mother is."

"Can you tell the listeners exactly what happened, Mr. Tindall?"

"I'm a salesman, see? I was coming back from San Antonio about ten p.m. I got this hitchhiker, said he was going as far as Little Ross. He'll tell you this is true, what I'm saying."

The potatoes boiled wildly. Edie's plump hand lifted the lid slightly so the steam could escape. Mrs. Reddle stood in front of the open refrigerator and stared at the small dark face of the radio.

"I'd think you were bats if you told me this . . . but there it was. Right in the middle of the road with a ramp leading

*up inside. Size of Wichita City Hall. What was I supposed
to do?"*

"Let's eat!" said Mr. Reddle, coming through the kitchen
door with a smile.

Mrs. Reddle took the milk from the refrigerator and shut
the door. "Five minutes, I think. Have a wash."

"By God, Irma, I just sold four hundred dollars' worth of
tires and got twenty recaps for nothing! What do you call that?"

"I'd probably call it fraud if I knew how you did it."

"Business, dear lady. Good business."

There was a hunk of yellow soap in a plastic dish near the
sink. It was reserved for Mr. Reddle's use. His were the only
hands it wouldn't scorch. A steady scent of unrefined petroleum followed him. Edie finished the table while Mrs. Reddle
took the meat from the oven. Mr. Reddle grinned over his
shoulder as he scrubbed.

"You sure have been pecking away at Reverend Arn. You
know that asshole drives all the way across town rather than
buy his gas from me? I was figuring today there's not a person
who goes to that church that *does* trade with me. Is that a
coincidence? I don't know why in hell you're painting that for
him. And what's he going to pay you? A hundred bucks! Shit,
you've been fiddling with it for weeks."

Edie's fingers tightened around the spoon in her hand.

"That's right, Mama," she hurried. "It's ridiculous to
charge so little for your work. Any of your pictures could sell
at five times the price."

Mrs. Reddle cocked a sarcastic eyebrow at her husband's
splashing. "I'm not a salesman like your father. Call your
brother."

Dinner. The food passed around. Talk of old farts in Ford Cortinas and the character with the four plumbers' vans who'd bought tires that day.

Edie's brother gave her a nudge under the table. "Pass the spuds, Pudge."

"Don't call her that!" Mrs. Reddle screamed, slamming her fork down and lunging across the table.

The boy dropped low in his chair, arms guarding his head, squealing, "No, Ma! No, Ma! No, Ma!"

"Oh, for Christ's sake, Irma," protested Mr. Reddle. "It was just a joke. That kid's teasing doesn't bother Edie. She's too smart to let a little ragging get to her."

Mrs. Reddle's arm was still tensed, her body poised above the table, her eyes squinting rage at the boy. Her mouth pursed until her lips disappeared. Slowly, she sank back into her chair. The boy sat up and looked sullenly at his plate.

After dinner Mr. Reddle wiped the kitchen counters while Edie arranged her homework on the table.

"Oh, I found this book in the school library. It's mostly landscapes, but it has some nice color plates of Velázquez portraits. The color reproduction is supposed to be a new thing, much more accurate."

Mrs. Reddle looked over Edie's shoulder at the vivid pages and then sat at the table, taking the book into her own hands. The radio sang and sold toothpaste softly.

The night came down tight. Only the red blink of the neon from the gas station appeared in the black windows. Mrs. Reddle bent over the picture book.

Edie's eyes flicked sideways from her work and took in the soft curve of her mother's cheek, the pale down that was becoming more pronounced as she grew older. The sculpted muscles of her mother's arms were graceful, beautiful. Her own thick arms felt heavy on the table.

"Is the Halloween dance fancy?" Mrs. Reddle asked.

"I think so," Edie replied warily.

The book lay open on dancers, their skirts in clouds. Mrs. Reddle tapped the page. "You'd look lovely in something like that. I'll get paid as soon as I deliver the portrait next week. I'll bet I can find real tulle even in this town."

Edie's face and neck oozed thin, cold sweat. "I'm not going to that dance, Mama."

"Oh, you should! You don't go out enough at all. Hasn't that Jerry asked you?" Mrs. Reddle's expression was anxious; her brows formed a wrinkled tent beneath her hair.

"He asked me all right." Edie picked the corner of a page, pinched it between her thumb and finger until the pain made her stop. "But I said no. He's been skipping classes lately. And hanging out with some filthy people." She dipped her head low between her shoulders; the fat on her neck rode up and folded. "And I wouldn't want to go with anyone else. I'll just wait until he straightens out."

"Oh, my dear." Mrs. Reddle reached tenderly for her daughter's hand. "When you're older, you'll know the best way to make that boy take a look at himself is to give him some competition."

Edie pulled her hand away and bit down viciously on her thumbnail. "I'm not going, Mama. I don't want to."

Mrs. Reddle looked down at the girls in their white dresses caught dancing before a mirror. She turned the page. *"The latest on the rash of UFO sightings across the nation on the news at eight-thirty . . ."*

"This UFO business goes on practically every year around now, doesn't it?" Edie grinned, her voice harsh with humor.

Mrs. Reddle looked at her, lingering on the round flat face and the wispy hair lifting around it. "I think it's real," said Mrs. Reddle. "Not all of it. Some of it is a joke, or people making themselves important for a minute or two." As she leaned toward her daughter, Mrs. Reddle's voice took on an urgent, grave intensity. "But I think there are beings from . . . somewhere else . . . trying to contact us. Don't you see how careful they'd have to be? If they landed in a major city, they'd be attacked immediately. There would be a total panic and nobody capable of communicating with them reasonably. The political leaders, if they didn't panic themselves, would be under enormous pressure from the populace to do some-thing militarily. No, they couldn't do that. They have to take it this way, looking for individuals who can think without fear, who have minds open enough to accept what they see and yet are intelligent enough to understand whatever mes-sage it is they have for us."

She fixed her eyes on Edie, rested her hands on the open pages of the book. Her voice was sure and eager as it always was when she was swept up by an idea.

Edie prevented the left side of her face from twisting. "Well, nobody knows what's out there, I guess. And I can't think of one good reason there couldn't be a civilization more advanced than ours . . ."

Edie said the words slowly, watched what she thought of as "The Idiot Glint" thrust the lids of her mother's eyes open, watched the protrusion of her eyes increase until a thin, precise line of white showed above and below her irises. She nearly flinched when her mother's hand touched her own and closed over it.

"I have good reason to believe it. And I'll tell you now, you're old enough to understand. *You* are exactly what they're looking for."

A chill struck Edie's neck. Her eyes opened wide. "Mama . . ."

"You must not be afraid, child."

The sudden pity in her mother's voice spread a blankness over her thoughts, bundled up her skepticism, hid it away.

"There's nothing to be afraid of," her mother continued. "I've always known, since you were born. I knew when I saw how your eyes would turn to watch things you shouldn't have been able to see. And I've watched it grow in you, this awareness, this consciousness. You know it yourself. You sense your own uniqueness without being able to pinpoint it. But you must not doubt that it is for a purpose and that you will be called upon to use it." Mrs. Reddle's eyes filled with tears and dripped as she held Edie's gaze.

"To use it for the good of us all. The wide earth. So you must not be afraid if they come for you, if they need you. Do you understand, dear?"

Mrs. Reddle held Edie's hands in her own and her tears

fell on them. Edie's throat closed tight. Her own eyes seeped. She nodded convulsively.

"There, dear. It's all right. As long as you understand," said her mother. "Here come the men."

Feet hit the porch and the women flicked at their tears and set their faces. The door opened. Edie bent over her book.

Her brother chirped, "Hey, there's a great movie on TV in about ten seconds."

"I've finished the bills if you want to mail them out to-morrow, Irma," said Mr. Reddle.

"I'm going to bed, folks. Good night," said Edie.

She paced the dark bedroom in flannel pajamas, rolling her bare feet carefully on the floor so no thump or shudder would be noticeable in the rooms below her.

"Uniquely *ugly*," she muttered.

A coward, a flatterer, a liar, she called herself, counting the night's crop of soft phrases spewed to control her mother's moods and fears. The imagined conversation with Mr. Dolbeer. The shame of that long-standing invention, the mythical Jerry, who had *almost* taken her to a dozen dances. That lie was the heaviest.

"Why won't she let me be ugly? Why does she blind herself and cripple me?" She saw herself in the mirror. "No. You're not a cute little girl." Edie mocked her reflection. "You're on your way to becoming a *beautiful* woman." She propped her hands on her hips and saw her own bulking above and below her waist. "A very feminine figure, my dear," minced Edie. "A lovely little bosom," she hissed. "Mama," she whispered, "the boys moo at me in the halls. Mama," she muttered, "Mama, you're crazy and I'm a sucker."

She sank down on the floor near the window and leaned her hot face against the cold glass. The white and red lights of the cars and the black night cooled her. "Space aliens," she whispered. "I should probably pack a bag and keep it by the window, just in case." She stifled a giggle. "Ah, Mama, you're slipping away from us."

But still, before morning she dreamed that the great ship came, whirring softly, shaped like a child's top. It hovered outside her window and the light of it filled her room. In the dream a silent door opened in the side and a ramp came out to her window. She stepped out onto it and walked lightly, gracefully, with her pajamas flowing around her, toward the opening where the silver beings reached toward her, saying, "You must help us. We've looked for you for so long."

The Education of
Mrs. R.

AN ADOLESCENT SHRIEK woke her. *Cockerels*, she
thought, *cockerels*, with a wry twist to the word. She
lay in the dark listening. There was no use in covering her head; the screaming still came through. The soloist
was suddenly submerged in the chorus. Fifty young roosters,
their voices high, uncertain, breaking, guttering, and beginning again.

She heard the hiss of sheets and felt her husband's heat
moving away from her. "Christ!" came his voice in the dark.
She moved an arm until it touched his back; she rubbed softly
at the jutting bones of his spine.

"I'm sorry," she said. He didn't move. She heard his hard
breath.

"Do it today! I've had enough!"

She pulled her arm back to her side abruptly.

"Did you hear me?" he hissed.

"Yes."

There was a cold weight in her stomach.

"I'll have to wait until she's gone to school."

He was silent. The roosters crowed on, a cacophonic tremor that rang through the walls. She snatched at a robe and tiptoed out of the room.

The kitchen clock said five-thirty. She went to the feed sack by the door and poured a measure of grain into the plastic basin. She slid her bare feet into the rubber boots next to the sack and opened the kitchen door. Black air struck her. Dew was falling. The chilled touch of the air wet her face and hands and her robe. Not quite black. She could see the faint shape of the garage where the roosters where cheering, whistling, crowing, chortling in ferocious competition. Not ten steps to the side door.

Too close, she thought. *Chickens in the dooryard*. A golden-haired woman in a white apron clucking on the doorstep and scattering corn from a bowl to the plump, busy red hens who ran toward her, chuckling softly. The picture with the phrase in her mind. The two together had done this to her. She grunted at the image, the sound merely a shake in her skull bones. She was too close now to hear anything but the roosters. She opened the garage door and the alkaline stink came out. She pulled the string and the light came on. They were all standing in the straw on the floor waiting for her. The din went up a notch. Wings beat among the reptilian heads stretching at her. She dumped the grain into the long feeding tray, spread it to the full length. The warm bodies moved softly next to her legs; the noise switched suddenly to a treble purr and an occasional squawk. She held herself tightly, deliberately not kicking her way through them. She edged back to the door and stood looking. *They are the wrong color,* she thought. *They should have been wine red, not this . . . white.* Her eyes settled on the pale flesh showing through their feathers near their beaks and around their eyes. The roiling bulk of white bodies hid the tray with dozens of pink combs bobbing over round yellow eyes. The little yellow eyes, the slits on either side of the yellow beak, the pink, naked flesh jiggling on their necks, even the small pale membrane on either side of their heads, and the tiny bald spot that stood for ears—she could not look at them easily. They disgusted her. The feathers were still unruly, short, sticking out at odd angles.

"They're still young," she told herself firmly. "Just children yet, playing cock." But the tiny heads on the turning necks, arcing and bowing, their hopping bodies as they climbed over each other to get at the tray. She put the basin on the shelf near the door and reached for the wire broom she used on the perch.

At least they're quiet for a while. He can go back to sleep. She was brushing at the green slime on the boards of the perch when she saw the pale bundle underneath. The bare bulb in the roof threw her shadow across it. It was scattered with straw. Dark blotches marred it. She pushed the broom down under the perch and poked at the bundle. It rolled and a hard yellow foot flopped into sight. She hooked it with the broom and raked it out from under the perch. The head rolled out from under the body. Its eye was closed. A thin gray film covered it. A dead eye. The feathers were sparse around the head, torn and bloody. There were long scratches and bits of loose flesh. She bent, staring at the corpse, her mouth open. Its yellow feet were half-curled. Something very small and black moved jerkily through the ragged feathers of the neck. She dropped the broom and stood back. For whole minutes she frowned, fumbling with a thought that would not take shape. Then the fussing at the tray broke into a squabble at one end. One of the birds shrieked and leaped into the air, flapping and clawing at one of the combs still bowed into the tray. She saw the long head dart down and strike the closed beak at the head below it. She closed her eyes and swallowed a trickle of her own vomit.

They pecked it to death.

She went quickly to the door and out, leaving the light on.

The clock said six when she came back into the big kitchen. She turned on all the lights in the room and made a cup of instant coffee. As she sat down at the table she saw her boots. Smears of green slime on the soles and toes, straws and short white feathers stuck to them. An isolated screech from the garage signaled the others to begin.

"They're just learning," she muttered to herself.

Her daughter trailed into the room with a school workbook under her arm. The child passed coolly to the chair opposite her and put the workbook on the table.

"I thought you did all that last night, Abby."

The child curled her legs up on the chair and tucked her bare feet elaborately under her nightie.

"I saved the arithmetic for this morning. I count better in the morning."

The woman eyed her daughter's stubby hand turning the colorful pages. She drank deeply from her cup. When she saw the reflection of her own face in the bottom she took the cup to the sink. Then she spent the next forty-five minutes in the basement cleaning out the big chest freezer that had come with the house.

She buttered breakfast toast and kept it hot in the oven. She put the clips into her daughter's hair gently. When her husband came out, the eggs were at their crisis and she slid them in front of him just as a film began creeping over each yellow eye.

When his ride came he swung outside with his coat half-buttoned and shouted at her through the closing door: "Today!"

She spread purple jam on her daughter's second piece of toast and poured more coffee.

"What today?" asked Abby.

"Oh . . ." She drank. "I promised your father I'd get rid of the chickens today." She looked again for her reflection in the dark fluid.

"I don't mind them," said Abby. She bit carefully into the toast, lifting her lips clear of her teeth so the jam would not smear on her face. "I like getting up early in the morning. Then I can read or do something and it's as though school didn't take so much of the day because there's time before I have to go. But they aren't pretty anymore. It's like they were two birds: first, soft and yellow, and now sharp and white. It's funny, isn't it?"

Abby's eyes, half-amused, waiting to see by the mother's face whether they should be amused.

The woman looked into her cup. "You'd better get your coat. The bus will be here soon."

The child ducked her head and scrambled out of the room. The woman listened to the odd isolated screech from the garage. They seemed to quiet down as the sun climbed.

"I like this place, don't you, Mama?"

She lifted her head and brought the child to her. "Yes, Abby. I just get myself into jams sometimes and wish we were back in an apartment and had to take a walk to see a tree."

She lifted the child's hair out of the coat collar and arranged it in a dark spray across her shoulders. The soft, round eyes smiled up at her.

"You mean like getting a box full of baby roosters instead of baby hens?"

"Yes. Like that."

The house ached around her when the child had gone. She made beds and swept and washed the dishes. "Let's buy a house with some land!" She mocked herself as she tucked in sheets. "I'll have red hens in the dooryard and we'll save an enormous amount on eggs, and maybe buy a calf in the spring to fatten for beef." The corners of her mouth sank deep into her cheeks at the memory of her own fantasies.

She went to the table with a pencil and a notepad and sat doodling figures and counting on her fingers. The fifty yellow chicks in the box marked "Cockerels" in two-inch-high red letters had cost five dollars. Then she had fed them the most expensive egg-layers mash for four months before they started to crow and she realized her mistake. Cockerel, it seemed, was the sex rather than a breed. The lumber for the perch had been ten dollars. The bales of straw, the disinfectant. The final number struck her as ridiculous. She added the column again. When the same number came up she reached for the telephone.

"Mr. Jarvis, this is Mrs. Rossich out on Gate Lane."

"Yes, Mrs. Rossich, I've got some very nice veal liver this week. And if you want a good Sunday piece, I've got a leg of lamb here. I know you like—"

"No, Mr. Jarvis. I'll have to call you tomorrow about my order. I wanted to ask you a question."

She stared at her right hand. It held the pencil and circled round and round, darkening a thick ring on the notepad.

"I have fifty . . . forty-nine young roosters, Mr. Jarvis. They're five months old and in good condition. I wonder what you might give me for them?"

Her face was suddenly damp. The hand was quite still, pressing the pencil's point down in one place.

"It's kind of you to think of me," said Mr. Jarvis, "but I buy all my poultry from wholesalers. It's inspected that way, you know. But I could pack them for your freezer when you slaughter them. That'd run about twenty-five cents a bird. Be pretty economical. Or if you don't have a freezer I can rent you space in the locker here. The Callan family who were in that house before you bought it, they did that until they got their own freezer."

The hand with the pencil arched a dark line down to the total beneath the line of figures.

"Mr. Jarvis," she said, "how do you slaughter roosters?"

"Well, you can just pluck them as quick as you can, singe them, and gut them."

"But how do you kill them?" The sweat was beading now, beginning to run a little.

"Why, how do you think, Mrs. Rossich? You cut off their heads." The "yes" was so clear in her mind that she never realized she hadn't said it. She put the receiver back in its cradle and stood up. *Yes,* she thought. *You take off their heads.* The geek of an old circus would bite their heads off. The vague memory of some tale came to her. A large needle that pierced the brain so quickly that they never knew. Felt nothing. A hundred old stories and phrases came welling up: "Wring a chicken's neck," and a man's huge hands wrenched at the bony head and it came off in his hand with a spout of blood from the quivering neck; a boy laid a squawking hen on the ground and planted his shoe across the neck, gave one hard yank at the yellow feet and the blood sprayed up his pant leg. The body walked afterward. Alive till the blood was gone.

Her right hand was on the doorknob. Her left hand clenched her yellow rubber gloves. She had forgotten the hatchet. She went to the tool drawer for it.

Slaughter, she thought, *is a formal and disciplined word. He used it in its tight original sense. A processing for victual consumption. The other, the splaying limbs and horror, the scenes of crimes and battlefields, the flinging of children and catching them on bayonets just out of their mother's reach, all that is metaphor, simile— the thing, in fact, which is not.*

She slid the crusted boots on and went out through the door. *To slaughter,* she thought at the blank sky. *To butcher.*

She walked out past the vegetable plot to the woodshed.

The vegetables are all right. Pumpkins and beans and Brussels sprouts sitting there not bothering anybody. Just a raid on the slugs once in a while. A steady weeding. That turned out all right. She stood staring at the piled wood beneath the open shed.

My own mother killed a chicken every Sunday when she was young and hauled on the ropes that pulled the pigs up for bleeding. The pictures in her mind had names and phrases attached. *Mother*, soft face, glowing eyes, a sunbonnet from some old magazine illustration. *The hens in the dooryard*, the golden-haired woman with the peaceful face. But she'd grown up on the thirty-second floor, and all the hens were in picture books, red, with pleasant expressions.

She slipped on the yellow gloves, drove the hatchet into a section of log till it bit, and then hefted the chunk of wood in both arms. She set it on end beside the door of the garage. The roosters scuffed and chuckled inside.

I want to do it, she thought.

She turned the doorknob, took one long step into the full murk of the air they breathed, and grabbed at a bird. Warm. His chest frail in her hands and his wings quiet beneath her gloves. There was only a faint surprised cluck and the swoop of his head trying to stay at its normal altitude while his body ascended to the level of her waist. The others came gabbling toward her. She stepped back outside and closed the door. She laid the bird down on the block with his feet trailing over the edge. The head lay calmly looking out over the garden. She lifted the hatchet and brought it down hard. Cleanly, dimly, the head fell at the foot of the block. The blood sprayed only the side of the hatchet that faced the body. In the garage a rooster crowed. She left the hatchet stuck in the wood and dropped the carcass onto the ground. She planted one boot on the gaudy scaled legs and grabbed the tail feathers that had only lately begun to arch and pulled with her yellow gloves. The softness of the feathers felt like nothing through the rubber. She felt only the spine of each quill and crushed with her fingers till the fist of each glove was crammed with spines and then yanked. They came away easily and the pale, rough flesh beneath sprang up in patches and sheets. She saw his bones, the plump tail, and the thinly covered ribs. She flipped the bird over and plucked hastily at the wing pinions, baring the pimpled skin on its bone. The small, soft feathers beneath the wings and inside the thighs kept slipping from her fingers. She nearly took off a glove to grip them firmly until she discovered she could do it with just the tips of her rubber fingers.

"Have to pluck them immediately or it gets harder, a muscle spasm in death tightens the flesh's hold on the feathers . . . Now where did I hear that? First-year humanities." She smirked. Her gloves worked slowly now, picking at small tufts and individual quills. She glanced around and saw the head lying next to the wood block. Its eye closed. Its beak closed. The small feathers only slightly rumpled.

"Why didn't it flop around?"

She stopped pulling and stared at the relaxed white form. It lolled. Its limbs lay at open angles. The hard yellow feet, talons half-curled like the fist of a sleeping child.

The second bird she picked up smoothly, just as he lifted his head from the water dish, a swallow rippling down his throat. He gurgled as she picked him up and turned his yellow eye and jabbed hard and quick at her wrist. She pulled away and nearly dropped him but caught a leg and trotted out quickly. He squawked when she flopped him down on the stump and tried to turn his head as she lifted the hatchet. When the head fell, the body wrenched itself away and the wings flapped viciously, stirring the dust and squirting blood so that it spiraled over the ground. The feathers didn't come off that one so easily.

The third one seemed to know her and chuckled all the way to the stump. The body fell off onto its feet and stood jigging anxiously against the block as though trying to climb back up.

She learned to grab them by the legs just below the joint and carry them out, squawking and fluttering. It seemed less deceptive than cradling them in her hands, and she could swing them down hard onto the block, which seemed to stun them a little, quiet them so they didn't wriggle as she struck. A few times it took more than one blow, and sweat broke out on her face as she lifted the hatchet the second time.

She plucked each one immediately and slung it onto the growing pile. The yellow legs poked out in thin tangles.

There weren't many left in the garage, but they were very noisy. She could hear them screeching and blundering against the walls.

They must smell the blood, she thought.

Each time she went in now they shrieked louder and took flight; the beating dusty bodies fluttered clumsily past her head and fell hard against the wall or the perch. The water dish had spilled; the food tray had fallen over. None of the birds was scratching. They ran with their wings spread or huddled in the shadows beneath the perch. She didn't run. She strode through the straw, changing direction only when there were no birds left in front of her. The air seemed black and full of floating dust and pale, small feathers.

"Mama!" came the voice.

She closed her gloved fingers on the leg of a frantic bird and whirled away to the door. The child was out there. She stood in her scuffed school shoes, a piece of paper in her hand.

"Abby, go back to the house!" The blood roared in her ears. The child's face was white, a mouth opening without a shape, her head lifting the paper toward her mother without noticing. The woman saw the ritual school painting, the sun a yellow spider in the crayoned sky.

"Go to your room and stay there!" she shouted.

"You're killing them!" The child's shriek in the same register as the birds', seemingly produced by the same instrument. She turned and ran, clutching the painting by one corner, flapping and flapping. The young rooster dangling from the woman's hand twisted up, beat his wings, and drove his hard beak into the flesh above her knee.

"Yah!" she cried, and jerked the bird away from her, swung him down hard on the block. His mouth opened and the yellow eye glared up at her. She lifted the hatchet and the bird began to shriek. The sound stopped when the blade struck, but the eye glared on and the beak clicked open and shut, the pointed red tongue slid and the blood streamed from the gashed neck.

"You filthy beast! Filthy creature!"

She brought the hatchet down.

She was plucking the last bird. The sun had gone. The wind had come up and was blowing the feathers across the vegetable garden. She could see the drifting flecks of white in the corners of her eyes. The wind made the plucking easier. She had only to open her fist and it was empty again, freed of the task of dropping the feathers once she had taken them from the flesh. She heard the front door of the house close. The light went on in the kitchen. She yanked at the stiff quills at the tips of the wings. Her gloves were too wet. She scraped her nails at the stringy white.

"What are you doing?"

The kitchen door opened wider and her husband's dark form stood in the spilling light.

"What the hell are you doing?" His voice was harsh.

She let fall the yellow leg and dropped her hands. She felt suddenly empty, sucked inside out. *This is what the match feels when you snuff it out*, she thought. The fancy tugged a soft laugh out of her. Feathers were blowing in drifts away from the light. She stood up slowly and felt a great pain in all her muscles. Tiredness. The dark form came out of the doorway toward her.

"Abby's crying. She won't come out from under the bed. What did you do?"

"I wasn't finished when she came home. She saw it. I had to finish so I sent her in."

His hand closed on her arm. "You're all bloody."

"I'll explain to her. So she won't be frightened."

"Explain what? What is this? All this?" His voice turned to a whisper. "What did you do to them?"

A small, white feather lifted against his ear and paused in his hair. She could see other feathers sailing against the shadow of the house.

"I slaughtered the roosters."

"I thought . . ."

He let her go and walked past her. She saw him go to the chopping block and stop. Then he moved to the door of the garage and opened it so the light fell onto the block. The pile of white and yellow shone dully nearby. He stepped to the block and bent to peer at the sprawled heads. The feathers scuttered away from the light and crept across the lawn. There were feathers stuck in the cabbages. She watched him, anxious to hear what he would say, to see what he would do.

"I thought you were going to sell them, or take them to the packers. Have them wrapped for the freezer," he said.

She hugged herself. Laughter willed itself out with her words. "Mr. Jarvis wouldn't buy them. And, you know, they have to be killed before they can be wrapped up. Did you ever think of that? I did."

She shook her head, laughing at herself. He moved away from the block and looked at her. The shadow of his head angled over her. She turned away from the light.

"Why aren't you dressed?"

For a moment she thought of dancing wildly in the feathers to frighten him. She fingered the skirt of her nightgown where it poked through the opening of her robe.

"I started this morning before I changed. The plucking takes a long time. I've been at it all day. If you'll put them in the trunk of the car I'll drive them down to Mr. Jarvis in the morning. I'll pay him extra to singe them. I'll make pancakes for supper."

She went into the house. The kitchen seemed cold and empty. She left the boots at the door and walked silently past her daughter's door to the bathroom. The mirrors looked at her. She looked calmly into them. The blood was caked as thick as mud on her gloves. It cracked into dust at the knuckles when she bent her fingers. The robe was streaked with it, her face, a blob of it in her hair at the side. A faint shade of pink seemed to have been thrown over her during the day. As she looked close she saw millions of tiny drops of blood stuck to the hairs of her arms and the nap of her garments. The feathers hung everywhere, the small, soft, spineless feathers. She stripped off her gloves and threw them into the sink. She stretched her clean, soft hands beneath the white light and smiled, admiring their strength.

The Well

GILLY SENDER NEVER DID TELL her husband how frightened she was in the new house. There were far too few houses on that bleak stretch of the California coast to allow for whimsy in choosing. And Gilly was determined to bar that variety of whimsy from her life.

I have always been a coward, she thought. *It's time to fight it.* It seemed to Gilly that she had whimpered and cried through childhood, and trembled and wept through college. She had married Devin in an energetic month of unfamiliar bravado and crouched shivering in his shadow ever since. She was from the suburbs, but with Devin she lived in a large city. She never went out alone after dusk. She heard strange sounds if she was alone for more than a few minutes. Pregnancy terrified her, and when her daughter, Corey, was born, the infant's dependency on her was horrifying. Corey, at the age of four, was a frail, crystalline child with exaggerated sensibilities and a collection of night fears. Gilly herself had felt a gradual abatement of fear as the child grew. She had grown accustomed to her own nerves and no longer yielded to them. She had learned to conceal her more trivial anxieties in order to spare Devin, but she had not been successful in shielding Corey from the emotional fallout. She imagined her child quaking through life as she had, and developed an unexpected firmness of will.

Sharing the fear won't eliminate it, she told herself. *I'll learn to enjoy this wilderness.*

It was a silent, solitary place, miles from the nearest neighbor, and since Devin needed the car each day for work, Gilly knew that she would be marooned there from one weekend to the next with only her small daughter for company. She thought she could bear the loneliness if she could feel the sun and live in brightness. But the sequoias loomed above the house and spread for miles in creaking stillness. The trees were beautiful but the shadow they cast was long and cold. The darkness oppressed Gilly deeply.

The Senders had found the house in a laconic advertisement in the weekly local newspaper. They were strangers, city people who had come two thousand miles, pulling a trailer behind their small car because Devin had been offered excellent work. Rental houses were reputed to be practically nonexistent. They took a hotel room in Mendocino and Devin drove the lovely, nerve-grinding drive down the coast twice a day.

Spring was just beginning when the owner of the house took them out to look at it. It was four miles inland from the general store and gas station settlement of Point Arena. The seagrass hills disappeared as they climbed. The redwoods sprang up to the yellow clay road banks. The owner pointed out the turn and the road plunged, curving steeply down into the deep twilight of secret green that lay beneath the crest of the hill. Here the trees reigned in silence. A small river cut through the bottom of the ravine and fifty feet up the slope from the water a gravel drive turned off. The drive was long, five blocks or so by Gilly's city estimation. At the end, beneath the trees, sat the weathered board house and its small front lawn.

"No television reception here," the owner told them. "The trees and mountains block it completely."

"We don't even own one," Gilly boasted.

All around the house grew blue flowers, forget-me-nots, sheeting in soft waves at the boles of the giants, struggling through the grass of the lawn. The house was pleasant but it was the redwoods and the bright blue dreaming in the shadows that touched the Senders with gratitude. A month later, the flowers were gone. The green darkness took over.

"It's a bit like living at the bottom of a well," Gilly said. The trees were close and so tall that the moving sunlight crept across the living green, a clear six feet above the roof beam of the house. A constant chill settled in Gilly's flesh. She sat in the dark kitchen looking up through the window at the sliding golden light above her and the bright sky beyond.

I know what it's like to live beneath the sea now, she thought.

"I thought those flowers were spilled sky at first," said Corey.

"Yes. They had a light like that. I miss them."

At first Gilly stayed in the house, working it steadily into order. The days were long with Devin away and she read whole books to Corey in the late afternoons. She read *Robin Hood* and the child said their home was like Sherwood Forest. She read *The Hobbit* and Corey grew thoughtful. She said that Mirkwood must have been even darker than their woods.

But the quiet grew familiar. Gilly took the girl walking before lunch, on the long drive to the dirt road, and on up the hill. It was a steep climb and they would turn back after a mile or so. They found their way to the river and spent whole days dabbling in its shallow rush, savoring the light that swept its broad bed.

Then they found the open spaces in the trees. Some previous tenant had cleared the stumps and tilled the yellow clay. The owner showed it to them. Gilly and Corey in all their walks had not passed it.

"I want to show you the spring so you can check on the water level," he said. He was a big, rough old man with a face like a battered shoe. He lifted a branch of leaves behind the house and disclosed a clear path through the brush at the edge of the trees. Gilly led Corey after the owner with real excitement. She offered herself a moment's pity for being impressed by such a small novelty, but then they were out of the brush in the enormous dim room beneath the trees and she could see the yellow shimmer of the clearing ahead. Corey grabbed her hand as they broke into the light. It was a bright acre bitten out of the forest. The sun-washed field lay fallow, with an unfinished fence of bare poles surrounding it. But at the foot of the slope a thin trail ran through blackberry bushes to the big concrete box that served as a reservoir for the spring water.

"Pure and icy from the mountain this water is, and you'll never run it dry." The owner pushed ahead of them to lead the way. The tank was rough sided, threaded by vines, eight feet square. A pair of large plywood sheets lay loosely across its top as a roof. Gilly watched as the landlord slid the plywood back and peered over the edge.

"It's five feet four inches high, this tank, but it's set in deep. There's actually fifteen feet of water in that well and it's always filling. It goes down some in dry weather, but it never runs out. That's rare around here."

"Do you think," said Gilly, "that there's enough to water a garden here?" The warm light filled the clearing. "Would it be all right with you if we set a garden in that fence up there and watered it from the spring?"

"The last tenant did that. Fine with me."

So the garden time began, the time of light. Each day Gilly would finish the housework quickly. Then, collecting tools and a few toys and lunch for the two of them, she and Corey would go out to the clearing.

The soil was yellow and hard. The digging taxed every muscle, made her sweat flow in heavy sheets, and drove out the chill that the shade had set in her skin. Corey sat playing in the grass nearby, or explored the heavy blackberry thickets at the foot of the clearing near the well. She sang tunelessly and talked amiably to Gilly's abbreviated grunts of response.

Gilly cut potatoes for eyes, set in rows of beans, a few to-mato plants, pumpkins, cucumbers, garlic. But the possibility of vegetables was only a necessary pretext for abandoning the dark house. The making of the garden helped to make the place livable for her; it banished the wilderness that would have otherwise made her afraid.

First thing each morning she would water. Corey tagging after her with her small watering can, Gilly would haul bucket after bucket up from the well. As the spring moved into summer the promised drought grew, the heat was unrelieving and vivid. The water carrying became crucial.

Gilly would run down the slope to save time, the plastic buckets clutched in each hand, swoop up the narrow path through the brambles, step up onto the pile of firewood she had stacked at the base of the tank, and flop a bucket in by its bail, pressing until it filled and then heaving it out, sloshing to the brim, then set it down on the ground behind her while she filled the next one. The trip up the slope was slower, delicate; the heavy buckets pulled her arms straight as she balanced. Inevitably the splashes wet her cloth shoes. Counting absently, Gilly figured it took fifty buckets to provide adequate water for the garden for one day. Twenty-five trips to the well.

Before her first load she would slide one of the plywood sheets off to the side, leaving the other in place. At the end, with her last two buckets full sitting in the muddy path behind her, she would heft the plywood back up, shoving it close to keep the fir needles and blown seeds, the insects and small animals from dropping into the well.

In the evenings they came out to the garden again with Devin and returned to the house only when the last light was dying in the clearing.

On Sunday they all three drove the forty miles to Fort

Bragg to shop and go to the library. Gilly and Corey were dazed with wonder at the people and color of the small dusty town. Sundays they went to the beach with Devin to soak in the sun. But all the other days the two were alone, the woman and the child, for nine hours before the man came home.

They discussed having a telephone installed, "in case of emergency," but the expense of running the wire from the main line was very high.

"If I break a leg I'll wait until you come home," said Gilly. "And if Corey breaks a leg I'll splint it and carry her to the top of the hill to flag down a car."

"That's two and a half miles of steep climb!" Devin groaned. But Gilly assured him that a mother could always do whatever was required. Still, she dreamed occasionally that Corey was injured and she was carrying the child up a hill that never ended.

The solitude that had frightened Gilly at first became a satisfaction to her. It was comfortable, and she felt a deep pride that she was resourceful enough to be independent of towns and people. The days were rich and thick to her. She talked to her daughter and her mind was free as she worked.

But the drought continued. Blue jays came out to the scrub near the well each day and entertained Corey with their stalking of the ripening berries. The dry trees hissed and rattled. Deer and rabbits slipped into the garden at night and took the water-heavy plants. The river sank away to a feeble worm of mud, and the level of the well dropped slowly away from the rim.

"Why are you tying my jump rope to the pails?" Corey asked.

"The water in the tank is so low that I can't reach it anymore, love."

Gilly hoisted the child up to peer over the edge of the tank. The sides were covered with a dripping green growth, like moss. Spiders moved stealthily in the corners. A swirling schema of minute flies circled above the surface of the water. The water sank each night. "Baths and laundry and dishes," Gilly told herself. Within a month, the water had dropped six feet beneath the brim.

The drawing of the water became painful where once it had only been exhausting. The thin rope gnawed at her hands as she pulled, and the time it took to fill the bucket and recover it drew out to miserable lengths. Now the work awed her each morning. With the last chores finished in the house, Gilly stood blankly watching the jays at the window and dreading the hauling of water.

I could leave it for a day, she thought.

Corey came in with her yellow watering can. "Is it time?" she asked.

Gilly looked into her soft grave eyes and paused. "What if we stay in the house today and draw pictures?"

"But what about the garden? We have to water it or the plants will all die. The potatoes, the pumpkins, the tomatoes . . ."

"The deer ate all the potatoes," Gilly said dryly, but Corey soberly continued her catalogue of their responsibilities.

"And the sunflowers and the cucumbers and the . . ."

Gilly nodded and picked up the buckets. The child was echoing her. Could she say now, "One day won't hurt," or

"I'm tired of the work and I'm willing to sit here in the cold dark rather than do it"?

Corey took their paper bag of sandwiches and marched out the door. Gilly followed.

A pair of king snakes were lying on the path to the well. They had been there before, sunning in the moist open area. Gilly stopped abruptly and Corey bumped into her legs.

"It's the snakes again," she said loudly. At her voice the nearest snake twitched slightly and then subsided. Their full brown forms curved loosely, heads and tails hidden in the bushes on opposite sides of the path.

"Stamp your feet," Corey giggled, and they both stamped, jigging in place and shouting, "Out of the way!" while sluggishly, reluctantly, the snakes disappeared.

When Gilly came back for the third load they were there again. And each time thereafter she shouted and stomped her feet to warn them away as she came up the path. Corey soon tired of tagging after her with the watering can and fell to an impassioned spooning of miniature hills in the dirt between the rows. Once she sat on a particularly bedraggled bean bush that Gilly had just poured a whole bucket of water on, and got an indignant storm from her mother.

Perhaps simply because Gilly didn't want to do it, the task was harder today than ever before. She decided to spread the water thin and quit at fifteen trips. So many of the plants had been nibbled or devoured entirely that less water would be enough, or so she told herself.

She set the last two buckets down on the path behind her and leaned against the tank. She was tired. In a moment she would go around to the side where the big sheet of plywood leaned and wrestle it back up onto the top, shoving it into place. But the side of the tank was cool, wet from spills, and her head ached. She was looking sleepily at the shadowed water when she saw the slug. Maybe it fed on the green moss lining the tank. Suddenly, it fell into the water. It floated, curled, half-submerged, its ruffled belly creased. A leopard slug, the dark olive skin splotched with black. It was large, maybe ten inches long. She had to get it out, of course. It would rot and taint the water. The house filter might not cope with it.

She could see Corey's red T-shirt at the top of the garden, where she was still digging. She had best do it without the child noticing. It might give her ideas about playing in the well.

Gilly found a long slim stick, a windfall, and clambered up onto the wall of the tank. The rim was a hand's width of concrete. She stood up and edged gingerly around to the side wall, then to the back wall nearest the drowned slug. She crouched and was reaching out and down toward the corpse. She meant to rake it toward the wall and then, still using the stick, try to lever and slide it up the green until it was within reach. She was tired. The stick was heavy and clumsy. The forms of the king snakes hung in the back of her mind, so that when a sudden shadow slid over her arm, she jerked, yelped, and fell down into the cool dark shock of the water.

Her eyes registered fractured light and she gasped help-lessly, taking in water instead of air. The pain confused her. The light gone, terrified, she kicked and coughed, surfaced in

a frenzy for a breath. She was not a strong swimmer and paddled wildly at first to keep her head up. As her breathing
cleared a grim fury fired her. It was idiotic to have climbed
onto the wall. She could have gone around through the
blackberries and leaned over with a stick. It was the snakes
and her fear of stepping on them that had made a fool of her.
Shameful to fear such harmless things. A jay squawked
nearby and the source of the swooping shadow was immediately clear to her. The anger subsided as quickly as it had
come.

The water was cold. Her hands ached and the arches of
her feet threatened to cramp. She flexed them and looked
around her. The familiar well seen from this wrong angle was
dank and sinister. The light skirted two sides of the rim but
never reached down the overgrown inner walls. Deeper shade
engulfed the whole half of the tank that was covered by the
remaining section of plywood. The wall plants dripped in
strands like wet hair, like Corey's hair in the shower.

"Corey!" she shouted, and her voice beat harshly around
her. "Corey!" It was unlikely that the child would hear at the
garden.

The long frail branch that she had used to reach the slug
lay bobbing at an odd angle behind her. She tapped it and
knew she was absurd to think it might support her; it sank
beneath the weight of her hand. And the slug? She saw it
rotating slowly near the far wall.

As long as I'm here, I might as well, she tittered to herself.
The strokes took her near enough to the swollen corpse.
Without hesitation she grabbed the slug, leaned back in the
cold, and threw with all her strength. She saw the thing

turning in the air and disappearing over the wall. A faint crash signaled its landing in the bushes.

She plunged her hand into the water to clean it and then reached again, tentatively patting at the green tapestry on the wall. Soft it was, and disgustingly slick. She tried to grip it, winding her fingers in it, hooking them in strand after strand after strand. She could hang on and rest for a moment, let her tired legs float up out of the deeper cold. But as she ceased kicking the plants came away in her hand, leaving a dark splotch of wet concrete showing.

"Corey!" she shouted.

"Mom!" came the shrill inquiry.

Gilly stopped treading water for a second, gathering a slow breath. In her most casual tone she called, "Yes, dear!"

Holding herself quiet, sinking slightly, moving only her legs, she listened. Among the hollow water sounds and the trees moving far off she heard the flat flap of Corey's comedy walk.

"Mom! Where are you?" She must be at the opening of the path to the well.

"I know you can't see me, Corey, but that's because I'm in the well." Despite herself Gilly loosed a nervous giggle. The child moved down the path. Gilly could almost feel her above and on the other side of the slime-coated wall.

"I still don't see you. I thought no one was supposed to play in the well. Can I come too?"

Slowly, calmly, Gilly explained what had happened. She spoke carefully, her head tilted back and her voice aimed at the sky. The water was very cold. She moved the hair out of her eyes and noticed the dead pallor of her water-wrinkled hand. When she stopped speaking there was a silence. She imagined Corey staring at the wall.

"But, Mom, how are you going to get out?"

"I'm thinking about that. But you could drop one of the pieces of firewood over the wall and that would help me float. I'm getting tired from treading water."

"All right."

She heard muffled scuffling.

"One of the big ones?"

"As big as you can manage."

Confused noises came through the wall, a long childish groan, and then a thump. The voice, on the verge of a wail: "I could lift it but I couldn't reach!"

"It's all right, love, that's all right. There are some smaller ones. Maybe you could throw the small ones in, just the ones you can throw."

They came over wildly, one at a time. Gilly swam into the shadow to avoid being hit.

"That's four. That's all I can throw."

"Great! Wait a minute while I get them together."

She moved after the sticks. Each one was two feet long and as thick as her wrist. She held them together, bundling them under her left arm. When she tried her weight on them her uptilted face remained just free of the surface.

"That's better, Corey. It is." She hardly recognized her own voice through the water echoes.

"Can you come out now?" The child's voice waffling thinly on the sodden walls made Gilly's eyes sting suddenly. With a sense of luxury she let the tears come and allowed the constriction to close her throat.

"Not yet, love."

She pictured herself floating, dead like the slug, and Corey weeping, hunched at the base of the well. Devin entering the empty house, searching, coming at last to the clearing to find them. She snuffled and smeared at her face with a numb hand.

"Corey, sing me a song to help me think, please."

"I'll sit down to sing."

Gilly heard her arranging the blocks of wood and then the high clear voice chirping away happily at "Yankee Doodle." She could send Corey to the house for a rope. Would she go down the long trail alone? Always before Gilly had gone with her. Where was the extra clothesline? It was in a kitchen drawer, but which one? She had to be very careful not to frighten the child. How long had she been in the water? A half hour? Eleven o'clock then. Devin would be home at five-thirty. If only it weren't so cold.

"Yankee Doodle" had ended and Corey had launched into one of her own rambling chants, this one to the effect of "Gilly's in the well, ding, dong, dell."

"Corey," she called. The voice stopped.

"That was a lovely song. I've thought of something. Can you go to the house and get the rope? I'll tell you where it is."

"Yes, I will, Mom."

Very confident, she sounded. *She's not yet five*, Gilly thought. She explained what was required. Corey said she understood. Gilly heard her running away and then only the water and the hiss of the wind in the leaves. She stared at the seeping walls. She couldn't be more than six feet from below the top. Maybe less. Absurd to be trapped by so little. A quick, fierce loneliness caught at her. Two of her sticks escaped from under her arm and shot to the surface. She retrieved them laboriously.

I wish to hell we had a telephone, she thought bitterly. Then with harsh abrupt movements she paddled to the wall and began ripping off the plants, searching for a hold, a crack, a bulge in the wall to cling to if not to climb on.

How could Devin do this to us? Stick us out here for months on end. He goes out every day, sees people. He doesn't think what it must be like for us. She scattered the slick green around her viciously. The wall remained dark, porous, and flat whenever it was laid bare. She stopped and hung limply on her sticks, kicking slowly.

No. He didn't think of it. I kept telling him it was fine.

It seemed a long time that Corey was gone. In the midst of her scurrying thoughts of escape a massive fear came on her. What if Corey should be hurt? If a rattlesnake had wandered down from the hills toward the river's moisture and paused near their trail. Corey would have treated it like one of the king snakes. At the vision of Corey stamping her foot cheerily at a raised and weaving triangular head, a convulsive shuddering established itself in Gilly's chest and spread painfully to her limbs. Her teeth rattled against each other and breathing was an agony of deliberate effort against her own muscles. Every section of her body notified her of its misery. In her mind she saw the small child lost, strayed from the trail, wandering and crying helplessly. She saw one of the rare hunters who walked through drawing aim on Corey's fawn brown hair, the child's red shirt obscured by a log. She saw Corey falling, attacked, burnt, cut, unconscious, in a moving fog of imagination. The shivering continued.

In a final paroxysm of fear she felt acutely nauseous, buckled down over herself, and sadly retched the thin bitter fluid of an empty stomach through her nose. With her vomiting the shiver died away; only faint tremors recurred like the grappling of fingers at a sheet in first sleep.

"Corey," she said softly. One of the sticks drifted out from under her arm and she watched it mildly without trying to recover it.

"It's all a matter of time," she decided. "Keep it tipped back far enough and you float."

Then the water slipped into her mouth and she jerked back to a more angular position, nervously paddling arms and legs that she could only vaguely feel.

"Corey!" she shouted. Her hoarse voice issuing from the well set the jays screeching in the blackberries.

"Mom!" The thin voice, far off. Too far away it seemed.

"Corey!" she said, and heard feet running.

"Mom! Mama!" She was coming down the path.

"Corey, love, are you—?"

"Are you all right, Mom?"

"Yes, dear. Have you got the rope?"

"No, Mom, I—"

Gilly snapped rigid.

"Why not? Why didn't you find the rope? I know it was in the drawer. You just didn't look!" Her voice strained with self-pity, hysteria creaking through her.

"But I couldn't pull you up! I couldn't pull up a bucket

and you're bigger than a bucket." Corey's voice was in fearful defense.

"You could have tied it to something. I could pull myself up!"

Now the child was crying. She could hear the short breaths reverberating through the concrete.

"Ah, Corey, I didn't mean it that way. It's only that I was so worried. Corey, I'm sorry."

"I brought the ladder from the porch instead."

"The ladder!"

"I've been bringing it and bringing it. It's so heavy I had to rest. Then I heard you."

"You wonderful girl! I never thought of the ladder! I didn't think you could manage it!"

"And here's something to eat!"

A banana sailed over the wall and splashed near Gilly's face. She laughed. "You darling!"

"I'll go finish bringing the ladder."

It was a long and fearsome project getting the fifteen-foot aluminum ladder into the well. Corey cried again because she could not reach high enough to get the end of the ladder onto the top of the tank. It was her own idea to tip over one of the buckets and stand on it. When Gilly saw the feet of the ladder come over the wall and poise, silhouetted against the empty sky, she cheered feebly. Still Corey had to climb down from the bucket and push at the other end. Gilly moved back into the deep shadow beneath the plywood and held her breath. If the ladder was too long it would span the well instead of falling into it. But the critical balance came, the ladder began to drop, and, clearing the far wall by inches, it fell clanging into the water before her eyes. It stood angled out from the wall, its top rung less than a yard from the brim.

The climb was slow for Gilly. Her weakness amazed her. The weight of her drenched clothing was enormous.

"Are you coming up now, Mom?" Corey asked, and then Gilly's head passed the top of the wall and she saw the child, small, tear-stained, sweaty, smiling as her mother toppled over the edge and into the warm air, the light, and her thin scraped arms.

Devin Sender found them cuddled together in the big bed when he came home. He heard their tale with horror. It is true that the Senders' telephone was installed within the week, and that Gilly's dreams were troubled for a while. But she deliberately chose not to move back into town, and both Gilly and Corey seemed newly and quite violently proud, each of the other.

The Blowtorch

ALMA SMIRL LEANED against the kitchen sink and imagined her husband's clothes standing up without him, stuffed with live rattlers, each sleeve and pant leg bulging and twitching with a tangle of snake flesh.

A pile of his wrung shirts lay draining in coils beside her. She shoved them further down the counter and then plunged her hands into the gray water. The warmth soothed her.

"He's gone down there already," she murmured, her eyes on the fogged window.

Her dripping, red hand smudged a clear swath on the glass. Raw earth outside. Nothing else. She slid the cooling hand back into the water and squinted out at the woodshed. Congealing water moved across the window. He'd gone over to the church and left the saw lying on the damp ground.

She let her fingers move slowly in the water. There was a peculiar cant to her spine as she stood at the sink, a comforting familiarity to the place where her pelvis rubbed the wooden rim.

Someone was yelling, "Mama!" The voice was too far away to identify by a single word. She pulled the plug.

She slung the twisted clothes into a basket and hoisted it to her hip. The baby's crib stood against the wall in the entryway. A torn army blanket was draped over the end next to the door. She paused there to watch the aimless sucking of the sleeping child's mouth and sniffed to determine that he'd not fouled himself yet.

"Mama!" The voice was closer. It had a full set of teeth. Not one of the little ones, then. She tugged at the blanket tent to keep drafts from the infant and reached for her coat. She maneuvered herself and the basket out onto the back porch and closed the door behind her. Running feet.

It had to be William. Benjy's stride was shorter and April wouldn't run for the Lord himself. A heavy crease formed between her eyebrows as she stepped off the porch.

William rounded the house with flying hair and a red-blotched face. She was shouting before he could stop in front of her. "What's the matter? Why aren't you at school?"

His long, knobbed bones jiggling in front of her, his clothes subsiding around him. He heaved; his pale eyes looked up at her triumphantly.

"You give . . ." he puffed, "a can of milk . . . and six . . . six eggs . . . Daddy said so!"

"Ha!" She pulled the child close to her so she could see into his eyes. "Why aren't you in school? Tell me!"

His face paled. "Daddy said—"

"What?"

"He said I could help him. It's his week to feed the test snakes and there's a new test coming."

"He said you could stay away from school?"

"I'll go back after lunch."

He was afraid now. She had squeezed the triumph out of him. Her mind reached for a phrase that could wipe the look of his father completely from the boy's face.

"You go in," she said, clenching his wrist, "and mind the baby. You be there when he wakes up and you mind the little ones. They're in the woodlot. I'll be back in a while to fix lunch."

"But Daddy said . . . He needs the milk and eggs."

"I'll take him what he needs. You go in!" There. His mouth softened, fell. The boy was a child again.

"And you *mind* that baby!" she hissed at his back.

His narrow shoulders jerked up to protect the soft nape of his neck, exposed to her stare.

She might just as well raise hell. It couldn't be any worse if he left them all. She stamped back to the clothesline and hung the garments hurriedly, shaking them out and jabbing them with wooden pins. She threw the empty basket down and set her chin into her coat collar.

He hadn't done any real work in weeks. And now that boy. Ten years old and they had him down there. She moved toward the road in an unseeing fury.

Filthy tricks and snakes to eat their time and let them act big. Eggs he wanted. Milk. Where would she get an egg? He sent the boy, said in a loud voice in front of the others, "Tell the old lay to give you six eggs." Made them think he could spare six eggs. Church.

"By Christ! I'll give them church!" Her hoarse voice surprised even her.

A truck roared past her on the road. She flinched at the blast. The bare limbs of the trees stood hard against the gray sky. She sighted the tin corrugations of the shed roof. A small battered truck was parked in the gravel in front of the building.

Above the door hung a sign lit by a bare bulb that was always kept burning. The square black letters said THE FIRST CHURCH OF GOD'S TEST. She snorted. A man in a bright red jacket was pulling a cardboard box out of the truck bed. He swung the box onto his paunch and turned toward her. He was already smiling.

"Good day there, Mrs. Smirl," he said. The box swayed from left to right with his belly as he walked toward the door. The back of his neck was a solid roll of fat. He kicked the door open and swung the box inside, held the door for her with the toe of his dusty shoe.

She stepped in. There was a green park bench and some chipped kitchen chairs arranged in rows. At the other end of the shed her husband crouched behind the pulpit as two men stood by and watched. His pale hair dangled over his forehead. She couldn't see his face. The big man swayed down the aisle with the box.

She stood in the aisle with her hands clenched in her pockets.

"Here it is, Brothers," said the big man. "Forget the

snakes." He bent and laid the box on the floor. He lifted the flaps and spread them. Mrs. Smirl caught a sheen of rounded blue metal. Her husband and the men swung around to look. *He's made himself into somebody here*, she thought. *They stand back and let him reach into the box and he's only been coming here a few months.*

All four men crouched. She saw their black-rimmed nails and the heavy-shadowed creases at their mouths.

"Smirl!" she said, and his head swiveled toward her. His mouth tightened.

"I need to talk to you, Smirl," she said. She pushed through the chairs, got all the way to the door before she looked to see if he was following. He was plucking at the tops of his trousers, saying something to the other men. She let the door slam behind her. The winter-blasted trees were dark and still in the cold. The gravel of the parking lot spilled in thin tire trails to the highway. She stood with her hands deep in her coat pockets. Her knuckles wore at the thin seams and discovered another hole beginning. The door creaked behind her.

Whatever she said now, at least she didn't do it in front of the others. He ought to thank her for that.

He strode toward her, gripped her arm hard, and pulled.

"Where's the boy? Where's the food?"

He's ready for me. He knows I'm mad. The surprise muted her.

"By God! I'll whip him for giving in to you!"

She felt calm. It was their unspoken rule that only one of them could be angry at a time.

"What's that thing Orrie has in the box?"

His face fell. Smugness overcame his anger. He jerked his head toward the door.

"That in there is the Finger of God. Yes. The Finger. You don't understand that, do you? But it's going to reach out. There are some men," and he leaned toward her, nearly smiling, eyes filled with triumph. "There are some men," he said, "who can seek out and touch the very Finger of God."

His look. Gloating. Like she was the vanquished enemy. Her rage spewed.

"You fool! I thought you just wanted to hang around and look big to all the others, but you're making yourself believe that you're some kind of holy saint. There isn't a one of those men that shouldn't be home doing chores or out looking for work! And when's our wood going to get cut? And when are you going over to ask Martins for the ditching job? Those six brats of yours are supposed to freeze and starve so you can show yourself off to God?" She sneered. "And dragging that ten-year-old boy down here with you, as if you don't already have a big enough audience. You want him rolling on the floor praying those snakes will bite him? God's Test!"

She spat into his face. His fist clipped her ear in the same instant.

"You're my test! I see it! I don't need those innocent rattlers in there. You're right. I sleep beside an eviler thing every night and wake up safe in the light of the Lord every morning anyway." He opened his mouth and barked a laugh.

She rubbed her ear. "No eggs," she said calmly. "No milk."

"You are the devil," he said, grinning. "But you can't touch me. I've still got the rent money." His hand dove into his pocket, pulled out a gray bill, and waved it in the air. He stepped back inside.

She hated his smile. She stared at the door. She headed back to the road.

She cooked the last of the peas that night for supper. There was no bread. Smirl did not come home and she sat glowering at the table, seeing his face repeated on each child's small skull. She flopped her dress open to the baby and felt his strong pull at her breast. She closed her eyes, fatigued and bitter.

Later that night Smirl was still not back. Anger kept her awake. She didn't bother to undress. She scrubbed the tops of the cupboards and the window frames, all the surfaces she usually ignored. She stopped every few minutes and stalked to one of the black windows to stare out.

From the windows she heard the unmistakable scratch and hiss of a match being struck. At first she thought the sound had come from outside and she froze, riveted by her own caved face reflected in the dark glass. She hated snakes, but fire—in the rotting wood house, with the children sleeping in heaps in the cramped room, no phone, no pump for the well—was the terror that paralyzed her in her dreams.

When the sound came again she marched up the stairs and down the creaking hall of the second floor. She'd caught Susie playing with matches under the porch. Now it was William crouched on the floor beneath the sink, his soft face tipped up to her, waiting. Tears poured down his face, mingled with the mucus that ran from his nose.

"What?" She leaned down to him. The stench of sulfur burned in her nose. She touched his damp cheek. A spray of small black spots on the linoleum. She could smell something else burning. He leaned against her and his whole body shuddered.

"What have you been doing?" Her voice broke and she felt no anger. She took him against her, her arms around the small bony shoulders, his wet face soaking her breast.

"I was . . ." he began. He was sobbing.

"I tried, Mama, but I couldn't . . ." He rattled against her. She reached for a cloth to wipe his face, rose to her knees to douse it under the tap. In the sink was a puddle of wet matches and black streaks against the porcelain. She wrung the cloth and sat on the toilet seat and pulled William into her lap. She washed his face, felt his hot tears dropping on her neck.

"Tell me what you were trying to do besides burn the house down," she muttered into his wet ear.

"The test," came his soggy voice.

Her stomach clenched. "What test?"

"The new test . . . with the blowtorch. I'm not afraid of snakes. I could hold them just like Daddy. I know about snakes."

She wiped his face again and he sat up. His pale hair lay in wrinkles, stuck up in jags. His face had red lines from pressing the shoulder seam of her dress. "But Mr. Orrie Childers said it was going to be the biggest test of all."

He held up his left hand to her and began to cry again.

"But I couldn't stand it . . . The Chosen can pass through fire, but I couldn't."

His thumb was charred. Black char on the ridges of his fingernail, and the swirl of his pad was shiny and blistered. The other fingers curled, innocent, but the ruined thumb shivered, erect and separate.

"You did this?" She felt the saliva seeping from the corners of her mouth. "You did this to yourself?" Her hand gripped his wrist too hard and yet she could not ease her hold.

The Finger of God.

The boy pulled away from her, his face anxious. She rose abruptly, dropping him to his feet. She pulled the plug in the sink, rinsed the matches down the dark drain, and ran his thumb under the cold water.

"Soak that," she muttered, and let go of him. She didn't know him anymore. She didn't like him.

She found a clean cloth and a thin tube of antiseptic cream. She wrapped the thumb. Neither of them spoke. His tears were gone, his jaw was tight, his expression closed. She tied a loose knot in the bandage, stood back for him to leave. His head passed just below her eyes. She watched his fragile shoulder blades stir the ragged T-shirt as he went into the darkness of the hall.

She listened to the pad of his bare feet on the floor, heard the bed creak as William climbed in beside his younger brother.

Mrs. Smirl sat, still staring blankly at the kitchen table, when she heard Smirl's feet on the porch a few minutes before two in the morning. The door swung and shut confidently, and he leaned against it, looking at her. She kept her eyes on her hands. She refused to be the first to speak. The moment thickened, gathered heft and color without a motion or sound between them.

Just as she was ready to break, as her will wavered and a soft word was finding its way to her tongue, Smirl strode out of the doorway and across the kitchen, as though he had never paused. He headed up the stairs. She heard his feet on the floor above and the house shifting to accommodate new weight.

She jumped up from her chair and went to the sink. Coursing anger stung her fingertips, filled her limbs with motion. She moved back and forth from the front door to the sink. The cracked linoleum rasped her feet through the soles of her shoes. The room conspired to aggravate her, and the blood in her veins whispered hatred to the flesh.

William was up there, rotting stupid, and she had almost offered a soft word because the silence went on too long. And he hadn't spoken, not even a word!

She reached the door and opened it. The house could not hold her. Outside, she didn't notice the cold. She filled the night with a heat; it left no room for a fear of darkness. She reached the highway without noticing, as though she moved faster in the night, as though sight and daylight had been a burden to her. Headlights swept over her, blinded her.

The lone bulb above the sign. THE TEST OF GOD.

No other light but the passing of cars.

She moved quickly into the shadows of the building. At a window, she pressed at its edges, tugged up and down. Her fingernails bent but the window stayed. She stooped and pushed her hands along the ground. Pebbles, twigs, freezing earth—finally, a large stick. She lifted it and whacked at the pane. The stick bounced back. Too light. She held it straight before her and ran at the window. With her weight behind it, the stick broke through and the glass shattered around it. She reached in and fumbled with the latch. The window lifted easily.

She had one leg over the sill when the wind blew cold up her thighs and she stopped to laugh, leaned her face down to her knee and chuckled softly, stifling herself so a shrieking giggle would not break out.

Like a kid up to some devilment, she thought, *and if they caught me like this* . . . Briefly, she saw how she would look in the glare of a flashlight with her blue-veined legs awry and her old skirt up around her hips. The cold touched her and took away the laugh. She slid and scraped her way into the shed and stood on broken glass.

A few gray planes in the darkness. She was halfway between the door and the pulpit. She stood still, waiting for her eyes to adjust. As her breath quieted, she heard a faint, papery slithering from near the pulpit.

The snakes. She had forgotten about them. They were in nests of torn paper in cardboard boxes and a wicker trunk. And the torch was in a cardboard box—she recalled the blue metallic glint from earlier in the day.

It was simple. She edged to the door, found the light switch, and flicked it. The room came up white and dull. The boxes had boards across the top, held down by rocks or hubcaps. The blowtorch, no bigger than a coffeepot, sat innocently in a separate box, its flaps open, near the woodstove. A line of empty soda pop bottles stood on the floor between the box and the stove. The men must have sat there late to talk about the new wonder. Maybe Smirl gave a demonstration. He'd set himself up as an expert.

She looked at the black stove and the red flicker that danced in the slit of its doors. The fire was going. A large box behind the stove was heaped with kindling and split lengths.

Her jaw clenched in a sudden flash of anger. They kept the fire banked for the snakes. An image of the shed's exterior clicked in her mind: a woodpile, a big one, at least three cords, neat and tight. All that cut wood for snakes. The thought scorched her.

A knife of cold air sliced the room from the broken window. There were two buckets of sand beside the stove. Grinning, she flung the stove door open and pitched half a bucket of sand into the red flames, snuffing them instantly. Dropping the pail with a clang, she grabbed up a length of wood and danced, leaping, to the windows. Smashing outward into the dark, one after the other, she laughed at the terrible cold that came in through the jagged openings.

When all the windows were broken she grabbed the blowtorch. She swung it up, grunted, settled it on her hip, balanced with both hands. She stumped to the door and flipped the light switch off with her shoulder. In the new dark she heard a thump from one of the boxes. The snakes were mad, striking at the sides of the boxes, because they could hear her or feel the cold.

She closed the door behind her so that no one driving by

would notice anything wrong. All six windows were gone. In minutes it would be as cold inside as out.

She walked home the back way, through the woods. She stopped at the outhouse in the clearing behind the church. She stood inside and held the blowtorch between her thumb and forefinger before dropping it down the hole. A flashlight hung on a string above the toilet paper. She flicked it on and aimed it into the pit, searching intently for any part of the torch that might float. It was gone. Sunk. She giggled softly to herself.

When she finally crept into the bed beside Smirl she felt complete, at peace in her fatigue. Even his warmth beside her was a pleasure. She smiled at the dark.

I could burn that place down if I want to, she thought. The good ache of her tiredness pulled her down into sleep, her mind lingering on the image of the terrible snakes on fire.

ARKANSAS (UPI)—Two members of an evangelical church died today when they swallowed massive doses of strychnine as a test of faith . . . Elders of the church told a circuit court judge that their service regularly includes the passing of venomous live rattlesnakes to be handled by members of the congregation whose purity of faith prevents them from being harmed. It was reported that an acetylene torch recently donated by a member to serve as a similar test of faith had been stolen before it could be used.

In Transit

OUR SMALL VALLEY FARM TOWN was totally unprepared for the arrival of Jim Hubert and his daughter, Amanda. Newcomers to the high school were rare, and those who began the first grade with Mrs. Blevins finished the twelfth grade with Mr. Gerber. New faces were bound to intrigue us, and Amanda's strange beauty hit us hard. She became the silent focus of every classroom that she entered and trailed a line of attention down the corridors as she passed.

She was dark and stamped with a lush delicacy. Seeing her move down the halls with my friends I could imagine that she was of some other species entirely. Perhaps we had come to resemble our dairy cows, while she was in no way domesticated.

The first words she spoke in my hearing justified her

appearance totally. None of us would ever leave the town permanently, but it was our custom to talk about it as a dull
place. In the cafeteria on Amanda's first day in school someone asked, "How did you ever come to this forsaken burg?"
Amanda slowly raised a hand to her forehead and moved a
wisp of black hair aside before answering. "We liked the
looks of the place," she said.

Her voice was deep and soft, her diction easy and clean.
Her words struck me and I turned them over in my mind. It
seemed irresponsible to choose a town because you liked its
looks. We all knew there were only two reasons for living
anywhere. First was the fact of having been born there. If,
through some cataclysm, one was forced to leave home, the
only consideration that applied to finding a new one was
available employment. Amanda's words split this truism and
displayed alternatives that may never have occurred in our
town before. There was a gypsy lushness, a sensuous im-
plication to the "liking of looks." Of course, the looks that
impressed the Huberts might as well have included the com-
muting distance to Portland, the prosperity, and the fact that
Minor Hanson had built a fine split-level house with red-
wood shakes and never lived in it. Hanson had finished the
house just two months after his mother died, then he had
moved into her farmhouse to take care of the dairy. It was his
house, the finest around, despite its newness, that the Huberts had bought. The town assumed that the Huberts must
be very well off.

At school we were only concerned with Amanda. The
great question in the minds of the females was, *What would
the boys do?* and the answer seemed to be, "Not much." They

were obviously scared of her. Though she was as fragile and delicate as a web, though the planes on her face jutted at poignant angles, though her lashes swept her cheeks and her eyes were huge and black, though she moved with the restrained fluidity of a cat, and her mouth possessed its wide and swelling softness with an aura of injury, of yearning for consolation—still the big, light-haired, pale-eyed, and freckled boys displayed only puzzlement. She was altogether too much for them.

An anxious general courtship began. We were bluff and jovial with each other but we tried to affect a courtly grace toward Amanda. Even the teachers seemed to feel a certain reverence for her. Their treatment of her was preferential and none of the students minded. We would have been embarrassed by any crass demands made upon her.

In speech class, when Amanda was due to deliver her first speech of the year, she apologized briefly to Mrs. Olsen and said that she had been unable to sleep recently. She accompanied her words by the characteristic gesture of her long hand moving a strand of hair from her face. I noticed the dark circles beneath her eyes. Mrs. Olsen said, "I hope you're not ill, Amanda," before calling on the next speaker.

Later that day it occurred to me that I had never heard any of my peers profess trouble sleeping. We could all sleep like puppies in any position as long as our bellies were full. Insomnia was a distinctly adult complaint and led me to suspect that the strange attraction that emanated from Amanda, if such a thing could be separated from her beauty, her voice, and her economy of conversation, was her maturity. We were all chortling toddlers beside her. She observed and condoned without participating. She would not hurt our simple feelings, but she had other things to occupy her.

Amanda was in her final year and the only class I shared with her was speech. It was a class composed of the very ambitious—future lawyers and aspiring politicians—and the very frivolous. How she came to choose the course I can't guess, but her behavior there was probably duplicated in all her other classes. She was silent. She did all the written work and when called on for answers replied softly and succinctly and then was silent. She must have been generally attentive to the procedure, but she sat with her hands lying in her lap and her eyes either half-closed or directed at her hands.

I was afraid to talk to her but I watched and admired her with the rest. Her hair changed from day to day: a bun at the back of her neck, a ponytail with a ribbon, or loose and moving around her shoulders. But it always strayed softly; strands and wisps drifted toward her face or curled on her cheeks. The fashion of the period demanded rigidly disciplined hair, thickly sprayed with lacquer. Her hair alone, its black softness, obviously not subdued in the restroom between classes, set her apart from us.

Gradually I became aware that her clothing was also peculiar. It took a while because her body imposed itself as an independent image and her face drew the eyes. The seating arrangement in speech caused her back to be turned to me for long periods and allowed me to notice finally that her skirt was big and old, washed a hundred times. Her blouses were faded cotton and she didn't have many. Her shoes were old loafers, broken at one edge, though later in the year they were replaced and accompanied by knee socks that graced the incredible length of her slender legs. We all spent large sums on nylon stockings and made sure that our skirt and sweater sets were perfectly complementary if not matching.

Amanda took no part in our discussions, though from the moment she entered the class they were all calculated to impress or entertain her. She also gave no speeches. This was odd and contrary to the intention of the class, but she and Mrs. Olsen had some understanding that was never made public. During the debating season Amanda was assigned to help me with research. This random coupling caused me a pleasant excitement.

I approached her after class and asked her if she could come to supper at my house and work afterward. Amanda looked troubled; a line appeared between her sooty brows. "I prefer being at home when my father comes. Would you mind terribly working at my house instead?" I was privately delighted. It was an opportunity to indulge my curiosity.

We met after school and walked toward the upper slope of the town, where Minor Hanson had chosen an imposing site for his house. Amanda, with her long legs, awkwardly accommodated my stumpy stride, and she angled her small delicate head solemnly toward my chatter. I was afraid to let silence fall between us and rattled on only half-sensibly.

"This is where I live," she said at last, and we turned up the drive toward the front door. I exclaimed that of course I knew where she lived and gave her an account of the extravagance that Minor Hanson had used in building the house. She seemed mildly interested.

The door opened on a large empty foyer with an elaborate parquet floor. Then the carpeting began. It was a rich gray carpet, thick but not shaggy. Amanda kicked off her shoes and proceeded across the room. I slid mine off and lined them up on the parquet, anxious not to dirty the carpet.

"Perhaps you know that this is the living room?"

"No, I've never been inside."

"And my room is here." She pointed to a raised alcove. The carpet continued inside. There was also a pillow, rumpled and coverless, its ticking striped gray and white. Beside the pillow two blankets lay extended as though someone slept there. Four books were stacked neatly at one end of the pillow. This constituted the entire furniture of the room.

"Do you sleep on the floor?" I asked with some confusion.

"Yes. Would you like to sit down? I have something to do in the kitchen."

"Could I come? I'd love to see the kitchen."

She nodded and moved back through the living room. I dropped my box full of file cards beside the stacked books and trotted after her. The second trip through the living room confirmed my initial impression. There was no furniture. The fireplace was laid, paper and kindling ready for the match, and the blackened brick indicated it was used often. The huge windows opened on the surrounding woods and were uncurtained. They filled the room with a green brightness. There was not so much as a cobweb in a corner. The carpet, with its endless quiet cushioning, was the only ornament in the room.

In the kitchen Amanda stood at the green sink and looked calmly out the window while she chewed what seemed to be several large pills.

"Why don't you have any furniture?" I asked.

"We haven't bought any yet." She was still looking out the window but I was suddenly afraid of having offended her.

"It's really pleasant and open, but my mother wouldn't put up with it for ten minutes and you've been here for a couple of months."

She turned to the refrigerator and took two steaks out of the freezer compartment. "My mother doesn't live with us," she said as she slit the wrappers and laid the steaks on the counter to thaw. There was no distress in her voice. She opened a cupboard to replace the pill bottle and I saw a tall stack of paper plates and a tower of paper cups. There was no table in the kitchen but two tall stools were drawn up at one end of the counter. My naked curiosity overcame my discretion.

"Is it just you and your father then?"

She looked at me sharply for once, her black irises huge. "Yes. My parents are divorced. My mother still lives in Florida where we came from." She seemed to be trying to allay my curiosity, to satisfy me. I plunged on.

"And do you eat here at the counter? And do you use paper plates all the time?"

"We both hate doing dishes. I'm sorry I can't ask you to stay for supper. My father gets home late and I wait for him."

"Oh, that's all right," I said. The refrigerator had held only a bunch of celery and some carrots, other than the steaks in the freezer. There was a drip coffeepot on the stove, but I saw no other cooking utensils. "You know, my mother has pots and pans piling up in the attic. She'd loan you some until you got your own."

Amanda prodded the white frosted meat with a long

forefinger and shook her head. "No. Thank you. All we ever use is the broiler or the oven. So many foods come in their own pans now. It's very convenient." She was on her way out of the kitchen and I followed like a befuddled pup.

"We should work now, I suppose," she said. We sat down on the carpet in the alcove and I displayed my little collection of cards with their statistics and quotations. I forget whether the debate topic that year was Federal Aid to Education or World Peace Through World Law, but it did not intrigue Amanda Hubert. Her courtesy was constant, but I could sense in every posture the indifference to the subject and a growing fatigue. At last I sat with the last set of cards in my hand and watched her covering a yawn.

"I'm sorry. I usually sleep at this time of day. I have a kind of anemia that keeps me very tired." She offered this in what seemed a genuine effort not to injure me.

"That's too bad," I yelped, clumsily jamming my cards back into their box. "Are you taking something for it?" I put the lid on the box and stood up.

"Yes. But we can go on with the cards some other time if that's all right." She nerved herself to rise with me. I could see her drawing strength and forcing it to lift her up so that she could walk me to the door. I was suddenly convinced that she was quite ill in a long-term way and that her strange fragility as well as her restraint, silence, and shy courtesy were all products of this secret devouring disease.

I slid into my shoes, patted her on the shoulder—it threatened to snap beneath the weight of my hand—and hurried away.

It was disappointing. I had pictured this encounter as the

beginning of a confiding friendship in which I discovered the
source of her distance and overcame it, plumbed the darkness
of her looks and shared in their effects. She had answered my
questions with the dutiful clarity required by a bureaucratic
form. She had no interest in me. I was an intrusion on the
unfathomable privacy in which she sheltered. Yet it was impossible to resent her. She had made strenuous attempts not
to hurt me and I felt sure that whatever her internal life might
be it had no room nor use for the likes of me.

As I entered my own thickly furnished and richly moth-
ered house, and was drawn into the smells and warmth of
dinner preparation, I felt a bleak pity for her beauty in the
empty house with its bare walls. But something interfered
with the pathos of the thing. Some sneaking inclination of
my own hinted that it might be a relief to live with nothing
but two blankets and a stack of paper plates. I thought of the
two figures on the stools in the Huberts' kitchen, thin, each
of them, eating side by side in identical slow enjoyment. Then
maybe they would light the fire and lie on the gray carpet
watching the big empty room people itself with shadows and
the flicker of light glancing from the windows. I knew that I
did not really understand, and yet felt pride in identifying her
alien impulses by their symptoms.

Amanda never did do any research for debate. We nodded
when we passed and I took a sort of satisfaction from the
recognition in her eyes, but nothing else was accomplished.
She went on among us, moving softly, speaking rarely, seemingly untouched by our constant attention.

Her father had also created a great deal of interest in
town. I heard his name mentioned often at the diner where

the local businesspeople vied with high school students for stool space. In this forum James Hubert inspired an unprecedented admiration. My father said that there had not been such general agreement on an individual's character in that diner since World War II, when, toward the end, every habitué had come round to thinking of Adolf Hitler as thoroughly unpleasant.

James Hubert had sparked the other end of that rare unity. There wasn't a lady who did not consider him a "true gentleman," nor man who didn't acknowledge him as a "smart fellow." Minor Hanson was heard to say that he'd give his teeth to get into Hubert's big money deal because he knew a winner when he saw one.

Mr. Hubert's interest was real estate and he spent a fair amount of time in Portland, driving in nearly every day. But he managed to impress the locals with his concern for small-town affairs.

The year was coming to a close. Graduation gowns had been ordered and the valedictorian was heard declaiming to himself in the back room of the library. A crisis approached in the matter of Amanda and the speech class. We began to wonder openly if she was to receive a year's credit for the class without ever having made a speech. Our worry was based not on resentment but on an unsolicited and uncomprehending sympathy.

Our anxieties were given a massive jolt one day, two weeks before the end of school, when Mrs. Olsen asked Amanda whether she would be ready to deliver her oratory the following day. Amanda nodded gravely and replied that she would. This must have been the compromise agreed upon for Amanda's successful graduation, but a formal oratory seemed an imposing assignment for a novice. The prospect gave me a nervous stomach, and there was not a student in the class who would not have dragged himself in with their hips in double casts and the chicken pox to hear her. She had never stood up before us. Her shyness was an animal thing, as ingrained in her physique as the length of her legs or the Roman jut of her cheekbones.

The hour arrived. We were all exaggeratedly silent as she rose to speak. Then she began so badly that we all wished fervently that we were somewhere else, not witnessing the clumsiness of our only beauty. She stumbled on the way to the music stand that served as a podium. An oratory in that class meant a structured, written, totally memorized ten-minute speech. No one who has not attempted it can conceive of the thousands of words with appropriately orchestrated gestures required to fill up ten minutes.

Amanda grabbed the music stand with both hands. I saw her eyelids lift; a ghastly white flash of eye swept us. She was afraid. We all knew the fear of the audience and saw how terribly it was magnified in her slender frame.

"I want to tell you about a trip I took last summer," she began. I could hear the intake of breath from every body in the room. Surely she didn't say that. Not even we, in our plump gaucherie, could have stooped to Yosemite, or Aunt Matty's place on Great Bear Lake. Her face was white, making her eyes and brows stark, her full thick mouth like a crusted wound. She licked her lips.

"My father and I flew from Miami down to Rio de Janeiro," she continued. We all sat rigidly. This note gave us hope. Rio de Janeiro would surely not degenerate into the size of the mosquitoes or the naming of Old Faithful.

"We had bought, unseen, a thirty-eight-foot ketch named *Hester*. It was moored in the harbor at Rio and we intended to take possession and sail round the Horn and up the west coast of the Americas to Astoria."

She had us. Not a muscle in the room relaxed but we were no longer taut with embarrassment. No, it was interest that held us, an exhilaration, a justification of the mystery we had read into this fellow mortal. It did not matter that she stood stiffly, unable to use the physical rhetoric in which we had all been drilled. There was no artful turning of the body to focus attention, nor movement of the hands to elucidate emphasis. She clutched the music stand unknowingly and her voice was monotonous, not at all the controlled variety of disciplined tones we all strove for. Very soon another thing happened: she forgot us. As she spoke she stopped looking at us. Eye contact is high on the speech teacher's list of requirements, but Amanda Hubert spoke to a point on the rear wall of the room and, as she continued, seemed to find that spot responsive and congenial, sympathetic to her expressions, so that we were not present at all. We felt it and did not mind. We were grateful for the small ease it brought her.

They had found *Hester* in good sailing order but had spent some weeks familiarizing themselves with her manners and habits. They lived on board and sailed every day in the neighboring waters. At first they were accompanied by a deckhand who had been employed by the previous owner.

"He had never worn shoes, I believe. When he stood on the cabin housing and I was on the deck, my eyes were precisely at the level of his feet and ankles. Though his legs were very lean and well shaped, the skin of his feet was terribly dry and scaling, maybe from constant exposure to the wind and salt water. A thick pad of callus covered the bottoms of his feet. It was so extreme that it actually protruded slightly on either side of the foot and was very pronounced under each toe. He gave the impression of walking on thick sandals without straps. He helped us a great deal with learning *Hester*'s ways, so my father paid him a bonus on the last day he was with us."

They had collected and stowed the necessary provisions for their trip when certain considerations made them decide against it. She paused at "certain considerations," as though she would have been more explicit if she had not remembered herself, or rather us, for a moment. They set sail on a northerly course for the Panama Canal. For days they saw no land and stayed under constant sail by trading watches.

"The one asleep would wake in time to fix a meal and bring it to the one on deck before taking over so the other could sleep. The noise was like silence, water and wind and *Hester* moving around us." She was lost to us again, communing with the spot on the wall. Her hands relaxed on the music stand.

They came to a small island, tied up at a little dock, and walked unsteadily on hot sand to the few grayed wood houses, looking for fresh fruit and water. They answered the cheerful questions of the islanders. It must have been with the same dutiful tone with which she had answered my questions, an attempt to make their reality seem normal. The Panama Canal came as a relief, she said. They both slept for hours while the work was done for them. Then they were in the western sea and came north.

"For a week the weather was good. We had the wind and kept ten or twelve miles offshore. Toward the end of the second week out of the canal we were loafing. The weather was so easy that we'd lash the helm and both sleep at the same time. On a Friday night, the storm struck us. At supper the barometer had dropped a little but seemed steady. It was not quite midnight when the first wind came down on us. We were both woken up by the noise. It was sudden, a shrieking in the rigging and the hull groaning and beginning to slam, slam, slam against each new wave. I couldn't believe it. We ran on deck and began tying everything down. We had gotten careless."

She shook her head over their heedlessness. One of her hands left the music stand to toss back her hair, then slid down to grasp the opposite elbow. In the audience we stared, biting our lips.

The storm was bad. For four days they beat offshore, tacking constantly to keep from being blown onto the teeth of the continent.

"I was always afraid. When my turn came to go below I would try not to sleep, thinking I couldn't get out if we broke up. But I was too tired to stay awake and I had dreams . . . It wasn't so bad when I was on watch. Then I could see the waves coming and I had enough to do to keep from thinking about it. My father only slept a few hours during the storm days. On the fourth day, the wind gradually died and we went on running north again in huge rollers, but they didn't break over us anymore. It was two or three in the morning before the glass was well up and rising steadily. My father went to sleep finally and I saw with the helm. I was very dirty and tired but it seemed so good to have the soft air back that I didn't care. It began to rain a little. The storm had been nothing but wind. It was warm rain and felt good on my face. The wind can make your face so sore. Then the rain passed and the sky opened. The dawn was red on the last of the clouds. I've never seen anything so beautiful as that, the red light above the dark sea."

They rested then and made the port of Astoria just two weeks later. *Hester* was moored there still, and they went down to sail each weekend. Amanda was studying celestial navigation in a coast guard class in the evenings.

She stopped. Her eyes fell from the wall and moved over us. She glanced at the teacher and let go of the music stand. The rigid formality took her over again. "Thank you," she said, and walked slowly to her desk, feeling her way, and sat down.

In a matter of days the school year ended and on a Friday the annual graduation ceremony was performed for the seniors, Amanda among them. But it was only a week later that the news broke in our town and all over the state.

My father brought it home to supper from the barbershop, and I imagine at least fifty similar conversations were in progress at that same moment on our street alone.

"You know," said my father, "that big real estate deal that

Jim Hubert was promoting? It involves twenty miles of the coast. The biggest operation ever conceived in this state. Two complete townships and dozens of tourist accommodations. There are plans for seven thousand new summer homes with supporting services. There's so much money wrapped up in it that Hubert made a stipulation from the beginning that no private stockholders were allowed. Only large solvent corporations were permitted to buy in. Hubert's managed to pull in over six million dollars from various investors, the paper companies, the Co-Z Motel chain, and a lot of others.

"Well, it seems there was a motive other than big business that made Hubert refuse small investors. I call it damned decent of him." My father paused to chew luxuriously while examining the rapt audience around his dinner table. We waited mutely.

"The reason I say it was decent behavior is that Hubert has taken that money in cash. He and his daughter left the day after she graduated, went down to Astoria where they kept a yacht. They set sail for the South Seas with the money. The chairman of the board received a letter two days after they sailed. I hear that Hubert thanked them in the letter for helping to liberate him from the bondage of work and wished them all similar luck in the future. He was in international waters by that time, of course."

"Do I hear you?" my mother gasped. "I cannot believe such a thing of Jim Hubert!"

"Nobody would. That's why he could do it," my father said, grinning.

"But you act as though you approve!"

"Not exactly. I would never do such a thing. But he didn't

hurt anyone. No man will have a thinner winter coat because of Jim Hubert. Those big companies will have a good tax write-off this year. Jim used to come to the diner while I was having my morning coffee. He always struck me as a man so absorbed by something that he couldn't waste time on any meanness or pettiness. Well, now I know what it was. But he made a constant effort to notice us. He'd listen to our complaints and miseries. He would try to help. I think he felt sorry for us all."

The talk went on in my house until very late that night, and filled the town for many months thereafter. Attempts were made to lay hands on the Huberts, but nothing came of it. I believe the town as a whole was relieved when the Huberts could not be found and could not be prosecuted.

There is one footnote to what I know of the Huberts, a yellow clipping from the Portland newspaper. Just two inches of filler picked up from the wire service as though randomly:

> *Dateline Papeete—The 38-foot ketch,* Hester, *registered in Portland, Oregon, suffered a smashed rudder in a brush with Diaz Reef in the Tuamotu Archipelago during a 40-knot wind last night. A radioed S.O.S. brought the* D'Angelo Mission *boat from nearby Tuame to the scene of the accident. Temporary repairs were effected, and the* Hester *was reported limping toward Papeete at dawn.*

I dreamed once of Amanda's frail body in the wind, salt crusted, drenched, pounded by the sea, and afraid, for she must have been afraid. Her illness, too, was genuine, and I wonder how much of a danger it posed out there. But it is clear to me that this lonely, trembling sojourn in the great blank expanse of the sea was a joy to her. And it is equally clear that the unfathomably long hours that she paced our halls and sat embedded in rooms full of our thick-fleshed complacence must have been torture.

I never chanced to see Amanda's father myself, but I know what he must have looked like, thin and dark with a strange sweet alien air that could not be broached or explained.

Some of that talk has, naturally, been uncharitable. There are those who half hope that Amanda was not his daughter at all, but a child lover. Yet others think she was his daughter as well as his lover. I don't reject those theories. I set them up to look at with the others. The Huberts were a species other than my own. Their capabilities were mysterious to me, and their ambitions were tilted, concentrated to an intensity that burned them away to the bone, and displayed the bone itself as beautiful and engraved with purpose.

The House Call

MRS. EMORY WAS UNEASY all day. She moved ceaselessly around the apartment, a mindless sweeping and dusting and polishing that seemed to restrain the hard fist of fear at the pit of her stomach. In the course of the afternoon she dropped a sugar bowl and spilled a whole box of powder, and felt each time a fierce gladness for the mess that absorbed her and took the time. She started the dinner too soon and began anxiously glancing at the clock an hour before she could reasonably expect her husband.

When she finally heard his key in the lock she moved quickly toward the door.

"Ray!" she called.

When she saw his face she reached for the back of the

nearest chair and leaned against it, hard. "You saw Dr. Curtin," she said.

Her husband's eyes moved over her face slowly, gently.

"This morning," he said. He dropped his briefcase onto the hall table. She left the chair to grasp at his empty hands and look up into his face. "Malignant," he said. "Quite hopeless."

His lean features moved only slightly, just enough to form the words. She buried her face in the cloth at his shoulder and breathed in one long gasp.

"My darling," he whispered. His hands lifted her hair, stroking, smoothing. "I would have given a lot to see you begin to gray," he said. "You will be magnificent."

The hot gush hit her eyes and nose simultaneously and she pulled away from him, ran blindly into the kitchen, reaching for a paper towel with one hand while switching off the oven with the other. She blew her nose and wiped at her seeping eyes. He stood behind her in the doorway.

"I'm really not hungry," he said to her back. "You eat something and I'll have a drink."

"No. No." She shook her head into the paper towel. "Come. Tell me, Ray."

She turned and took his hand, led him back to the living room. She sat beside him on the couch with her whole side pressed against him, her legs bent to her chest to repress the shaking she felt beginning in them, a tremor at the knees that only required a little indulgence to become a violent quake. His arm looped over her knee. She grasped it, her fingers moving, kneading the bicep over its bone. She did not look up into his face. Her eyes fixed on his long hand where it lay across her leg. His voice slid around her, fluid but heavy.

"I insisted that he tell me. We've known Curtin a long time. I knew he would be open with me if . . ." His sigh seemed so relaxed that she looked up at him involuntarily. His face seemed flaccid. Too soft. As though the life had gone out of it already. She looked away.

"Well, you'd think doctors would be used to this sort of thing," he said, "but he was nervous about telling me. I suppose he didn't know how I'd take it."

"How long? Did he say?" she heard herself croak. She applied the sodden paper towel to her face.

"Six months without treatment. Maybe a year if I take it all. All the long rigmarole." His hand moved on her leg, stroking absently.

"It was good of him to run the tests himself. I spent the rest of the day going over things at the office. I don't think anyone's noticed that I was . . . off par. It's important that there's no mention of it. No knowledge of it."

He turned to her, forcing her to look up, to see his old face. "It's important to you. Do you understand? You must tell no one. Ever."

Her knees got away from her and began their jig against her chest. Her eyes burned and the tears did not soothe them, nor did the cool air between her husband's face and her own.

"You've been such a joy to me," he said.

And then he explained to her the disposition of the business interests and the nature of his life insurance policy. His voice took on so much of its normal timbre that she found herself nodding and snuffling and actually walking beside him to examine the three paintings they had chosen together on their honeymoon.

"These may yet be a good investment for you," he said. "So do keep them." Her head bobbed mechanically, though her throat refused to grind out, "I will."

He moved her to the balcony, his arm on her shoulder, guiding her. The summer evening spread soft around them, the lights of the city below and above them blinking and stirring through the dusk. She stared out through hot eyes, feeling his flesh solid next to her.

On the balcony next to theirs the woman of the house was setting a small table with china and silver between two chairs. On the long face of the building opposite them the people moved on white-painted balconies. Lone figures sat looking across the lighted room behind them, and here and there a family sat eating in public intimacy, the tinkling of their cutlery and the angle of their elbows apparent from across the courtyard.

Mrs. Emory felt her husband's fingers caress her shoulder.

"It's been good. I'm not feeling much discomfort at all, yet. And, my dear, I promise you, you won't have to regret marrying me. Or these few years . . ."

"I couldn't," she managed to rasp.

He swung her around to face him. She looked into his eyes, which were suddenly glistening, and at a new smile. She hadn't seen it before. She stiffened a little in surprise.

"You know, I feel fine. I'm not afraid. I feel like celebrating! Isn't that crazy?"

She felt her mouth hanging ajar.

"Will you do something for me? I know it's silly. But won't you run down to your friend Mrs. Renza and buy some of her unique maple walnut ice cream?"

"I couldn't!" she gasped, her hands jerking up to her damp swollen face.

"Oh, just say you've got hay fever. That will account for your teariness, and I will adjust the awning out here and whip some cream. You must get a little jar of maraschino cherries . . ."

He was walking her busily toward the hall. She stumbled, confused, as he handed her purse to her, and catching his arm she looked up and saw the sweat bubbling on his nose and upper lip, the tight stretch of his smile below his creased eyes.

"Look at her bananas, too. If there are two that are really ripe, I shall make you something extraordinary," he said.

She chewed her lips, staring at him. "You hurt, don't you?" she asked. "Are you hurting, Ray?"

"No, girl, not at all. I simply want ice cream and to be alive until I am dead." And he took her arm quite firmly and opened the door. She went through and stopped. She turned to look at him. He grinned. "I'm going to get the stepladder and fix the awning. Hurry now."

He closed the door in her face.

It was a longer walk than usual to the elevator. She kept stopping to listen but there were only the sounds from the other doors in the hall, the footsteps and blunted voices. When she stepped out of the elevator into the ground-floor lobby, she paused in front of the mirror to fluff her hair where it clung to the stiffened tears on her cheeks. She opened her purse, took out her sunglasses, and put them on. A final snuffling of her nose and she pushed through to the street. The traffic, moving figures, a heat as from living bodies pressing against her. It was no use stopping to listen. Their apartment faced the courtyard and was nine stories up.

She walked slowly the long block to the delicatessen. It was crowded. She edged next to the shelves and picked up the small jar of incredibly red cherries before making her way to the counter. Mrs. Renza was busy. Her huge bulk moved violently, slicing and slapping sandwiches together, rummaging in steel trays to bring forth piles of strange salads. Her sons moved darkly around her, grinning over Styrofoam containers and rattling white bags. The voices and the ring of the cash register thickened the heat. Mrs. Emory leaned her belly against the cool counter and waited, watching.

When her turn came, Mrs. Renza reached for a paper container with one hand and a scoop with the other. "Maple walnut!" she shouted. "What is it? A party? You look like you could use one. What's the matter, child?"

"My husband's not feeling very good. He thought some ice cream would cheer him up." Mrs. Emory stared at the big woman's arms as they dug and pounded at the ice cream. She felt that her voice was not satisfying somehow. And the big head in its webbed net lifted its dark eyes to peer up at her. A thin, hard voice from the end of the counter intervened, swerved the eyes away from her.

"I've been waiting a half hour and my children are alone at home, do you think I could be waited on?"

"You should learn to cook!" shouted Mrs. Renza. She

flung a top onto the ice cream and snatched the money from Mrs. Emory's waiting fingers. "You leave your babies alone to come down here. What is it? Too hot to cook? Shall I introduce you to a skillet? In the back I have a stove. Come in the morning, I'll show it to you. Who knows, maybe if you look around in your kitchen you'll see you have one, too."

Mrs. Emory slipped out the door with the cold white bag clutched to her chest and walked steadily toward her apartment house. Her ears were straining now, keening through the street din. She walked slowly, breathing deeply, seeing nothing, only listening.

A small antiques store in the middle of the block drew her. She stood for a few minutes at the window to stare at the intricate display. Her eyes fixed on a tiny glass cupboard in the shape of a church door when she finally heard it. She blinked and stepped back. The sirens, rising and rising with no culmination in their pitch. She turned and saw the whip of the red lights stopping at the end of the block, bumping over the curb, disappearing into the courtyard. The sirens fell to a groan. She took a few quick steps and then slowed, grasping her white bag, rearranging her purse on her arm, touching her sunglasses. At the end of the block people were moving more quickly. She saw figures arriving at the curb suddenly breaking into a trot, disappearing into the courtyard. She strolled. Two figures in dark uniforms emerged from the courtyard and entered her building. She stopped to look into a florist's window.

The elevator was at the ninth floor when she entered the lobby. She pushed the button and watched the indicator change. It was empty. Her nose had quite dried up by now. Her eyes felt cool. She took off the sunglasses. Only her breathing sounded irregular and inefficient.

The ninth-floor hall was full when she stepped out of the elevator. The blank doors had opened all along the length and heads and bodies stuck out. A confusion of voices flowed around the sharp sobs of a woman. Far down the hall she saw the two dark uniforms and a familiar flash of colored print. They stood in front of her door. Her first hesitant steps became purposeful.

"What is it?" she was just going to say, but the sobbing woman in the flowered dress raised her head and saw her.

"I saw it!" she screamed, and then dropped her face till her hair covered it, shaking wildly. The dress looked crumpled and wet. Mrs. Emory had admired it while the woman arranged the little table on the balcony next door.

"Are you Mrs. Emory?" asked one of the policemen.

"What's happened?" she croaked. She was already feeling for the keys in her purse.

"There's been an accident . . ."

"He waved at me and fell. The ladder just tipped him out and he fell. I broke a plate. I saw it."

"My husband," whispered Mrs. Emory as she jammed the key into the lock. "Ray!"

They helped her in and put her into an armchair in the living room. She could see the red light beating in waves over the face of the building opposite. Pale figures leaned over the balconies and stared down into the courtyard. One of the police officers put the ice cream into the freezer. The door to the hall stood open and the emptiness in the apartment seemed to flow in through it. People moved around her. The hot tears rolled down her face again and her nose ran and she sat still, making no effort to dry or quell them. She could hear the neighbor still weeping in the hall, moaning, "I saw it, I saw it." Then a man's voice, soothing, "You poor darling, come back in now, oh my poor dear." And Mrs. Emory opened her mouth and yelled. It was not a scream. Her jaw fell and her lungs opened and she roared. She sprang from her chair, ran to the door, and slammed it, roaring. A policeman ran in from the balcony, where he had been examining the angle at which the ladder lay against the railing.

They asked her for the name of her doctor then, and she shook with relief.

"Yes, call him, please. John Curtin. The number is next to the phone. Yes, please call him." And she wept and shook until he arrived.

The photographer was working on the balcony. The flash cut repeatedly through her puffy lids. A man in gray with thick thighs and a clipboard sat asking her questions and noting down her answers. Then she heard his voice. "Yes, I'm the family physician, may I see Mrs. Emory?"

The man in gray stood up abruptly and moved away from her. She curled, clinging to the upholstery of her chair, the helpless tears still sliding silently down her face. She raised an arm and wiped her nose and mouth and chin. The man in gray was saying, "You said on the phone that there was no serious illness, no depression, nothing that would indicate suicide?"

"Nothing at all. I'd been treating him for a small ulcer in the intestine. The P.M. will show that. I saw him just this morning for a routine examination. He was a man who was worried about his health. He had a young wife. But there was nothing. He seemed calm and cheerful this morning. Barring definite evidence, I'd say it had to be accidental."

Mrs. Emory sucked at her lip. The doctor's voice continued.

"I'd like to attend to the living now, if you have no more questions."

She felt his hand on her arm, his soft voice; she kept her disfigured face turned away.

"You're grand," he said softly, swabbing her upper arm with cold cotton. "Fabulous," he said as he inserted the needle. He made her stretch out on the sofa and she could see him moving about the room as the door opened and shut on departing uniforms.

"Do you always make house calls, Doctor?" asked the last policeman as he stepped through the door, and she heard the half chuckle in the reply, "Only in cases of violent death. And I'm not a pediatrician."

"You're right, I was thinking of my kids."

Rhonda Discovers Art

TWEEZER PAINTON was a burly ten-year-old with a glower built into his square mug. His name came from his hobby of grabbing individual hairs on his victims' heads and yanking them out for fun. Mostly he did it with his thick, grubby fingers but sometimes he used tweezers stolen from his mother's bathroom cabinet.

Whoever sat in front of him in class developed a reflexive shudder around the nape of the neck. On the playground he would throw another kid down, straddle their arms so they couldn't fight back, and hold their screeching face with one hand while he tweezed away at their eyebrows or head hair.

Looking back on it later, Rhonda assumed there was something strange going on in Tweezer's house, but she never developed any sympathy for the thug. He meant nothing but pain to her and every other kid at Ribbon Ridge Elementary.

And then there was her baby brother, Todd. She was almost five years old when he was born and she had a lot of different feelings about him, all strong. He was cuter than she was, dark and dramatically adorable. She liked looking at him but she resented the attention he got.

Before he was a year old, her mother decided he was so beautiful that adults would be tempted to kidnap him, to keep him for their own. The ensuing watchfulness disgusted Rhonda. Nobody was ever scared she'd be kidnapped. And she got yelled at for every worm or bottle cap Toddy ate when she was supposed to be taking care of him. But he adored her and that sparked her interest.

As he grew she began to teach him things. They started the alphabet when he was three. She played teacher with far more rigor than she ever displayed as a student.

That crucial summer, when he'd just turned five, they'd been playing a game with the old, battered globe in her room. One of them would write down a name printed on the globe—anything from a range of mountains to a city or river, an island or a nation. The namer would go on twirling the globe and pretending to be undecided long after picking the spot so the searcher couldn't tell on which hemisphere or continent or ocean it lay. Then the other one had to find it. If the searcher couldn't find the place, the namer would crow and sneer and get another turn at dictating the search.

Toddy specialized in names in the smallest print. Rhonda discovered that big, obvious items could bamboozle someone who expected you to deal in the hidden. But he was smart, and she was proud of his quickness, as if she'd invented him herself.

Still, she often resented having to tend to him while her mother painted romantic pictures of other people's gardens. He tagged along everywhere, calling her name constantly, which shamed her in front of the big kids.

On the worst Sunday of that awful July, some of the kids were going to the end of Elm Lane to fish off the rocks where Ribbon Creek boiled into the river. It was a soft day the temperature of blood. Her mother would have thrown a conniption if she'd known Rhonda was taking Todd to the river. Neither of them could swim and the current there was known to suck down strong men and powerboats. But Rhonda had a ball of twine and one of the old fishhooks from her dead grandfather's tackle box. She wasn't going to be stopped by her cretinous little brother. She had a life.

Jenny and Lou were already settled with real fiberglass poles and reels by the time Rhonda got there. Toddy promised not to tell and was happy scrabbling over the rocks above the rapids while she arranged her fishing gear.

Soon Rhonda was half drowsing on her back on the big rock with her heels just over the edge so an occasional spray from the rapids cooled them. The line looped around her wrist and angled down to the invisible, baitless hook buried in the fast, heavy water. Off across the river a tugboat was chasing a barge when Tweezer came blundering down from the road.

He stood above them on the grass and shouted, "Catch anything?" over the roar of the water. Jenny snarled at him to go away. This prompted Tweezer to jump down onto the rock, grab Jenny's fishing pole, and run off into the woods. Jenny and Lou charged after him, howling threats.

Rhonda rolled an eye and saw Toddy crouched nearby teasing an ant with a grass stem. She closed her eyes and felt the heat soak into her skull again.

The pain was sharp and her eyes snapped open. She yelled, "Hey!" as she lurched upward. Tweezer's mumpy face cracked, grinning at her upside down, his hand waving the single pale hair he had just plucked from the top of her forehead. He had snuck back from the woods and come at her from above. "Asshole!" she screamed. "Y'asshole!" he bellowed back, his pink grin collapsing into fury as she kicked up at his dark denim legs.

Toddy was shrieking, "Let her alone!" and his small hands reached around Tweezer's thick leg from behind, clutching at the cloth as she kicked again. Tweezer yowled and swung away from her, his baggy-jeaned butt a sudden target for her kicking feet. He said, "Little fucker!" and his leg whipped toward the river, his voice snapping, "Don't bite!"

Toddy flew out slowly, with his eyes and mouth open as though he were shouting. He fell languidly down and out of sight beyond the ledge. The splash of his landing was lost in the rushing of the black-and-white water as it came down off the rocks and bore deep into the twisting pool before uncoiling into the thick, fast flow of the river.

"Shit!" yelled Tweezer, bending forward to look over the edge. "He bit me!" The boy's thick body pitched forward on knees and hands to peer over the rock and into the water as Rhonda tore at the loose stones and lifted one as big as her head and swung hard, smashing it down on the buzz-short hair above Tweezer's neck. She felt the crunch as he fell onto his face and she brought the stone down again and blood came but she quickly pushed at his hips and rolled him, flopping, over the sharp ledge, and watched just long enough to see him sink flatly, unresisting, into the water before she threw the rock after him and went running along the ledge screaming, "Toddy! Toddy!" to the air.

Tweezer surfaced in the dragnet of a search boat that night. Rhonda was nine that day, four months away from her tenth birthday. Toddy was five when he died. They found his body the next morning floating in the dark between the creosote pilings of an abandoned pier half a mile downstream.

Rhonda told them all exactly what had happened right up to the point when Toddy flew away, and that's where she changed it slightly, saying that he and Tweezer had fallen into the water together. The sheriff and the coroner agreed that the wounds on Tweezer's head were from the water battering him against the rocks. Nobody hit Rhonda or yelled at her. Her mother only screamed once and then collapsed in terrible gasping tears as the sheriff's deputies poled their metal boat around the dark pool and out into the current.

When Rhonda replayed that day in her mind, the only thing she felt good about was bashing Tim "Tweezer" Painton on the head and rolling him into the river. It was the right thing to do.

What Rhonda called the Montessori moment, or the great gestalt switcheroo, hit her one day when she was bored and depressed by her spot as photographer, community-calendar editor, and website administrator for the *Hedgeton Suburban*, a weekly grocery rag in the outskirts of Philadelphia.

She was at her desk in the newsroom that morning, drinking coffee, scanning the newswires, and girding her guts to shoot yet another Shriners picnic, when she ran across an old item on the arrest of performance artist Franklin Delano Ruggs.

In the climax of his "Sees All" show at a Chicago arts festival, Ruggs made his stage entrance by bursting through a movie screen showing close-up footage of a huge penis pumping in and out of a cheeky anus. Ruggs was nude but wrapped in an exploding bandolier of firecracker strings, which accidentally ignited the screen and the stage curtains even as his nude-in-stiletto-heels wife, Melanie, sloshed a bucket of fresh blood over his chest and shoulders and he bit the heads off two squirming mice.

As the flames spread, the crowd fled screaming. The police arrested him for arson, negligent arson, reckless endangerment, and satanism. The last charge was dropped when the arresting officers were informed that satanism was not against the law. Animal-cruelty charges were pending.

Rhonda laughed herself right out of her swivel chair. She dug for reviews of Ruggs's other incarnations. They ranged from tepid sniffs to bitter yawns.

For one of his first shows, Ruggs had himself staked down, naked and covered with honey, over a huge, glass-sided ant farm. He had titled this piece "Eat Me." A clipped moan of boredom was the only response.

Another time he had been walled into the thirty-five-foot-long public urinal in a men's room at the newly remodeled

Jordan Arena just before a sold-out Stars Collide basketball game. His head stuck out through a hole in the trough at target level. Ruggs dubbed this performance "Pisser-Pissee."

The endless line of urinal users were concerned and curious. "Are you okay?" "What the hell are you doing in there?" Ruggs nodded and smiled but stayed silent. Many refused to use any part of the urinal. They all pissed anywhere but on him.

Rhonda, watching the video clips and reading the old reviews online, decided Ruggs had the harsh, elongated grace of an El Greco grandee. She could see where he was heading. He might be an idiot, but he wasn't static. Every failure pushed him further. He was reaching.

Rhonda printed out another story, with the headline "Performance Artist Persecuted." She holed up with a cigarette and the article in the spacious handicapped-access booth of the women's restroom.

Ruggs had been arrested for inciting to riot in Chicago. Several civil suits had also been filed. The reporter conceded that the audience, and the ASPCA, might not have reacted quite so vehemently if Ruggs had not trained the pig so well.

Lulu was a charming pink yearling and she obviously adored the tuxedoed Ruggs and wanted to please him. At his command Lulu pranced through hoops, rode a skateboard, caught and tossed a tennis ball, waltzed upright on her rear legs, and bowed sweetly to the audience just before Ruggs brained her with the sledgehammer he'd been twirling like a baton during her act.

By the time he'd yanked her up by her heels with a block and tackle and slit her throat to bleed into what must have been that same old blood bucket, half the audience was on-stage trying to do the same to Ruggs.

The accompanying photograph caught him walking in handcuffs from the door of a hospital emergency room to the open door of a squad car. The bandages and bruises didn't disguise the fact that Frank, as she thought of him, had lost weight since the photographs taken after his last Chicago appearance. Could he have become a vegetarian? She hadn't realized how short he was, barely to the cops' shoulders. But she saw again that same blurred innocence in his long, pale face. It wouldn't occur to him to bow his head or to hide from the camera. The caption said his first concern after his own bleeding stopped had been whether the authorities had remembered to refrigerate the pig.

The helpmate, Melanie, was nowhere to be seen and was not mentioned as part of the act. Rhonda figured the wife had done a bunk after the last little encounter with the police. Ruggs looked to be about thirty and Rhonda fantasized lightly about seeking him out and seducing him. Offering him solace and appreciation. She quashed that idea firmly, knowing she'd just end up washing his socks and paying his bills, as helpful Melanie had probably done. Still, she found herself packing a rock-and-roll crush on the guy.

Months passed and she was scarcely prepared when word of his newest effort cropped up on an outsider-artist website. Franklin Delano Ruggs was fresh from a stint in jail. His latest gig was sitting, manacled (Rhonda was sure he'd gotten that touch from his handcuff experience in Chicago) and near naked, in a bathtub full of water, electrical cables, and small home appliances. With the collaboration of a pseudonymous union electrician, Ruggs arranged for the appliance cords to be connected to a grip lever, which acted as a switch to complete the connection, thereby frying him in his tub. The lever was six feet from the front of the tub, conveniently placed for passersby in the Stench Gallery in Philadelphia—where he and several other avant-gardists were staging a group show—to reach out and grab it.

Ruggs was in town.

It was fate, she decided. Her groupie fantasy crept back. Alone in the bathroom of her studio apartment, she stared at the mirror and mentally swatted herself to contain it. "There's got to be some other reaction to beauty than wanting to fuck it," she wrote in her journal. "If it's even beauty we're talking about here."

Opening night was a party, with wine and cheese and a donation basket at the door. It was open to the public and three thousand invitations had been sent to the gallery mailing list.

Dressed in thrift-shop dowd—drab coat, rhinestone spectacles, gray gloves, and rubber boots—Rhonda blessed the rain for the excuse to wear a slouching hat. She slipped in through the crowd. Conversational clots jammed the way, and the mass of bodies hid everything hung on the walls. She caught the tops of picture frames, an occasional splotch of color or form as she hunched forward, lowering her head to push through the maze of plastic wineglasses and paper punch cups.

The hand-lettered sign on the wall behind Ruggs gave the title of the piece, "Stir Fry," and explained the situation:

20,000 VOLTS AT YOUR FINGERTIPS—A HUMAN LIFE AT YOUR MERCY. The last line announced that the artist would not communicate with the viewers in any way.

Pausing at the partition separating Ruggs from the rest of the gallery, Rhonda peered between slowly shifting bodies to look at him.

He was pale, his arms thin, and his chest bowed inward from his hunched shoulders. An anxious tension gripped his eyes though he strove to stay expressionless, to seem relaxed against the back of the big claw-footed tub.

Was he afraid that someone would actually zap him? Or was it plain old stage fright? Her breath sighed out in resignation. He was a frail specimen, pathetically isolated in his island of space. Red-velvet ropes on brass posts kept the crowd at the critical six-foot distance. The ominous black cables snaked into the porcelain—an industrial Medusa capped by hair dryers and toasters. She wanted to step closer and look into the water to see the submerged appliances and the length of his legs. Did he have a catheter? Or maybe a hose slipped through his swimsuit waist and attached to his penis for relieving his bladder during the hours he spent on display? Or was he just pissing into the water around him?

Tears stung at her sinuses. Poor bastard. Having to deal with this alone. The pierced man in the next room had two assistants standing by to hoist him up smoothly on the hooks, to hand him sips of water, to towel the sweat away from his eyes, to listen when he murmured something, and to lower him for his hourly breaks. Ruggs did everything himself now that fickle Melanie had disappeared.

She tried to hear what those nearest the ropes were saying,

but couldn't catch it through the buzz and murmur. Tidbits of office politics floated in the air, some baseball strategies, complaints about an auto mechanic, analysis of a personality not present. Ruggs wasn't exactly shaking his audience to the root. Only those leaning on the velvet ropes seemed to be looking at him at all.

He should have set the tub up on a platform of some kind so the folks in the back could see him. Tilted mirrors could have shown the interior of the tub. Or he could have used a clear plastic tub so the audience could have seen through. Such a dear boob. He always missed some critical element to make the thing work.

She inched forward, bent and slow. The switch was exactly as shown in the news photos. Mounted on a white wood pedestal waist high, and just outside the velvet ropes, it looked like a crab claw, waiting for the grip that would clench the two halves together. She couldn't see the placard on the pedestal but she knew from the reviews that it used florid language to explain that a mere eight pounds of pressure would complete the circuit and send poor Ruggs to bathtub hell.

One seedy student type stood on tiptoe to see Ruggs over the heads and shoulders of those in front. The rising volume of talk from behind her suggested an influx of population, a new glut of viewers to force the old out. Her heart was cramping her lungs. She heard herself thinking, *I'll save you, Frank*, in a cartoon tone, and nearly burst out laughing.

She stepped in quickly, her gray-gloved right hand sliding against the soft cashmere of a neighboring sleeve to simply, swiftly drop the looped end of the clear nylon fishing line over the lever. Sidling toward the wall, slipping past conversations, nudging gently under raised paper cups, she paid out the nearly invisible thread so it drooped loosely from the crucial switch and trailed among the crowd a few inches above the floor. She reached the closed white door in the white wall, and dropped the other loop of the glass-clear line over the top knob of the lower hinge.

Still moving carefully, gently, she squirmed through the crowd toward the exit. *It won't work*, she thought, furiously. *Someone will see the loop on the switch, or will press against the line but not hard enough. It will pull at the wrong angle or they'll find it too soon.* She stepped out into the dark, wet street just as the gallery lights began to stutter.

Screaming Angel

THE GUARD FELL fifteen stories, twisting through a warm dusk as blue as his uniform. On the sidewalk below, two moving men wheeling a big seawater aquarium toward the side entrance of the hotel blinked upward at the sound of his scream. He hit the top ledge of the tank and smashed on through to the pavement. Exploding water, glass, sea creatures, and white gravel splashed passing cars.

A gray sedan jerked to a stop, its driver gaping at the pink twist of fish flesh on his wet windshield.

In the Wizard's Lounge on the ground floor of the hotel, two women in a window booth dabbed napkins at their spilled cocktails as they watched a small, red-winged fish slide down the outside of the pane.

A drenched mover reeled in the wreckage, blood spouting

from his left hand. He lifted the arm, grasping the wrist hard with his other hand, staring at the space where the last two knuckles of his smallest finger had disappeared. "Find my finger. Find it."

His partner dropped to his knees and scrabbled in the shards and muck on the sidewalk as the hotel doorman whipped out the side entrance, blowing his whistle. Somewhere, sirens started.

The police arrived and the gawkers were crawling over stalled cars for a view when Rhonda Bacon, discreet in black, stepped out the hotel door. Pausing to shift her camera bag, she squinted at the blue rump of the nearest patrolman. A shock-faced woman next to her seemed fixed on the same view.

"I thought that was against regulations," Rhonda told the woman. "Cramming all that paraphernalia into their pants pockets. Notebooks, handcuffs. Ugly bulges on fine young cop butts. What possesses them?" The woman didn't answer, didn't seem to hear.

Rhonda adjusted the camera on her neck strap as she slipped through the crowd to the inner circle. Her silver sandals glinted in the pink stream pooling on the concrete. Salmon tints mixed with pale shrimp and a touch of alizarin crimson where mammal red flowed among cooler juices.

The lens and the light settings were cued for the boxing match in the hotel ballroom, but she started shooting, then adjusted. She moved in close, crouching, careful not to drape her skirt into the mess.

A patrolman wearing surgical gloves stepped into the tangled metal frame of the aquarium and bent to flick a mucoid bit of former sea life off the pants of the body hunched into the pavement. He tugged gingerly at the wallet. It was almost free when the cop holding back the crowd hollered, "Leave it!" And he left it.

A pair of prowl cars sat nose to nose, doors flopped open, lights flashing. Traffic froze at both ends of the block. Two movers sat together on the curb, their wet legs limp in front of them. One cop took notes and asked questions while another, in gloves, held a pressure bandage clamped on the wounded mover's raised hand. Rhonda leaned on a car hood with her notebook, listening.

"I can't tell where this weird, like, howl is coming from, and I look up. The crazy bastard is spread out in the air like an angel, you know, snow angels, from when you're a kid. And he's staring right at me." The moving man is angry. Insulted. "His mouth is open and he's making this noise and his eyes are bugging right at me. Then he hits."

Rhonda asked for the correct spellings of their names and the moving company. They were telling her the contents of the aquarium when the paramedics barreled in with a stretcher for the injured man. Before the first ambulance pulled away, a cop brought the rest of the finger in an ice bucket from the Wizard's Lounge. He made them pack the finger and the ice in a plastic bag.

"There'll be hell to pay if the hotel doesn't get its bucket back."

The hotel manager bustled out with two cops and headed for the TV news crew setting up in the street. The young security guard with them had just helped seal off the entrance to the roof. He stopped to stare at the slop on the sidewalk involving the same blue uniform he wore. Rhonda Bacon caught his stooped posture and stunned face in her lens, then stepped up, poised for notes. "His name was . . . ?"

"Nelson. He's security. His flashlight's up there," the guard said. "And scratches on the ledge where he jumped." The boy's eyes rolled and his jaw clenched, like he might vomit.

"Is that what the police say? Suicide?" Rhonda prodded. "Any idea why?"

"The manager says he was just a few months from his pension. But we've had some thefts from the rooms. He was one of the staff that got questioned. But we all were." The boy didn't blink. "You'd think he'd wait for a clear patch of sidewalk."

He'd tell her anything. She could get him fired for blabbing. Rhonda slapped her notebook closed and turned away.

Yellow ribbon barriers surrounded the soggy rubble like the rope around a museum exhibit. The aquarium was on display for a convention in the hotel. The manager, focused on the tragedy of bad publicity, seemed most worried by the loss of fish but he confirmed the body's name, Norman Nelson. A woman squealed, "Rag-ooo!" despairingly, as a dust mop dog trotted into the wreckage, dragged its fluff through the blood, and lapped busily at the tainted pool, sniffed for snacks. Two patrolmen moved in ominously.

"That Pekinese belongs to one of our guests!" The manager ran to scoop the dog up. Pink spray flew from his shining shoes.

Rhonda headed into the lobby and found a quiet corner. She slipped off her damp sandals and rubbed her stockinged toes on the carpet as she dialed the wire service.

"Global? I'm a stringer for the *Las Vegas Star*, and I've got a breaking story and some photos for you."

One flight down, in Merlin's Ballroom, a thousand fight fans yelled advice at the busy pair in the boxing ring and insults at the bald referee skating around them. Spring weather and a golden boy in the main event had drawn a bigger crowd than usual to the monthly club show. Reporters and photographers bickered and shoved for elbow room at the ringside tables and gawked upward through the velvet ropes. TV cameramen scrambled over the press table and clung to the ring posts, oblivious to those behind them.

A dour newspaper reporter jabbed his pen at an ankle in front of his nose. "I'm working here!"

A ticket holder in the front row chipped in, "I didn't pay ringside prices for a view of your ass!" The cameraman moved six inches to the right.

Leo Reese crouched on a low stool below the ring's blue corner, oblivious to the noise and the space wars. His rubber gloves patted mechanically at the pockets of his barber smock, checking: scissors, tape, cotton swabs. His shoulders twitched with unthrown punches as he glared through the ropes at the lean welterweight whose hide he'd been hired to protect for this fight.

Cisco Roach had arms that reached his bony knees and thin tattoos meandering all over his mahogany body. He fought with a jubilance that made the small hairs on the back of Leo's neck stand up and quiver. *He should have a* TRAINED IN CUBA *stamp on his shoulder,* Leo thought. *Classy moves. And lots of heart. The kid comes in with a day's notice and gives Glory Pedersen fits.*

Glory's opponent for the semi-main event had developed a case of better-deal-elsewhere and scratched two days before. The promoters' desperate call for a last-minute substitute unearthed this unknown Roach. Jelly Jack Needham, the kid's manager, brought him down from Seattle and spoke loud English and idiot pidgin to him. Now Needham was bellowing, "Hook, Roach! Hook!" from his perch on the ring steps at Leo's elbow.

Cisco Roach was not hooking. His left fist was trapped in the clamped armpit of his pale opponent. Roach threw his right hand into Pedersen's belly as Glory rubbed the seams of his red leather glove into Roach's eye. Roach jumped, both feet off the deck, trying to crack his forehead against Pedersen's. The ringsiders wowed indignantly. The referee was asleep on the ropes and didn't see. Across the ring, Pedersen's trainer, Wally J., was roaring, "Head butt! Head butt!" and glaring furiously at Leo. Wally knew a foul when he saw one. Back in the Dark Ages, when they were both young, he'd scribbled his own scar poems on Leo's forehead.

Leo shrugged his eyebrows at Wally, plopped an extra dollop of petroleum jelly onto the back of his gloved hand, and barked, "He's butting. Let me get that eye," at Jack Needham.

Leo climbed through the ropes as the bell ended the round. Roach strutted over to him, grinning. Leo slipped the kid's cheap plastic mouth guard out and dropped it into the bleach bucket as Jelly Jack pushed the stool into place so Roach could plant his blue satin trunks.

Roach's wide face was all bone and brightness, jutting slabs and a pointed chin beneath the grin. The white of the eye was clear. Leo slid one ice-cold slab of bronze onto the scraped cheekbone and another under the ridge of the brow, pressing steadily with both hands to slow the swelling that could close the kid's eye and end the fight. "You're okay," Leo told the sharp face. "This is just prevention." Roach blinked his understanding with one visible eye.

Leo wanted to tell him not to use his face as a fist but the fat man was leaning through the ropes, sponging the kid's chest with cold water and telling him, "Listen to Jack, son. Hook. Comprendé? Jab coming in. Then hook. He's wide open for it. Hook, hook, hook." The kid grinned beneath Leo's hands, saying, "Sí, hook." The fat man slid the kid's mouthpiece back into place and ducked out, ready to yank the stool away as soon as the bell rang.

Leo sighed. No use complicating the kid's head with more talk. He dropped the bronze slabs back into the ice, and maneuvered his own feet and legs through the ropes as he swabbed salve over Roach's forehead, under his eyebrows, and across his cheekbones.

Back on his stool, Leo watched the kid scorch around his tall opponent and then lunge in with the right hand to the chin, followed by his lethal head. The crowd roared.

"Tell him to stop throwing his head like that," Leo shouted into Jelly Jack's hairy ear. The fat man swiveled toward him, amazement creasing his face.

"It works! I've got the bum terrified."

"Roach will bleed before Pedersen. He's got thin skin."

"Whaddya mean, thin? I'm the black guy and Pedersen's a Swede!"

Staring at Jack's pink jowls, Leo considered delivering his "Complexion doesn't determine the tendency to cut" lecture, but Jack knew everything. "Roach has scars in his eyebrows," he snapped.

Jelly Jack swiveled to stare at the fighters. "That's what I'm paying you for." He went back to screaming, "Hook! Hook!" at Roach.

It is not your machine, Leo reminded himself. And what do you expect from a slobby tick who calls the fighter "I" as long as he's winning. If things went the other way, Roach would be "That Bum," like Jack's other fighters. And Jack barely knew this kid. He'd obviously never worked with Roach and was clueless about what he could or would do.

In the ring, Roach snapped a right hand into Pedersen's exposed throat, then dipped his left elbow and hip and swung the whole assemblage upward from the ankles, powering his left fist. It was a fluid move that caught Pedersen beneath the ribs. The kid had gifts.

Leo scanned the murky rows around the bright ring, looking for some crony he could wink at over the kid's wild talent.

A fast-moving security guard swept through the narrow space in front of the ringside seats. The static voice of his walkie-talkie scratched the thick air. Roach was hammering the jab and Pedersen was backing up. The uniformed guard was talking behind his hand to the dapper chief of hotel security, who abandoned his prime seat next to the ring doctor and followed the guard down the red-carpeted aisle at a discreet but distinct speed.

Leo checked the room over his shoulder, figuring there must be a fight in the crowd. The chandeliers glinted on the downtown white-collar mob. A lot of lawyer types. They were three beers into the night but every necktie was still in place. Every face focused on the ring. The security men disappeared through the exit doors. A dine-and-dash from the lobby restaurant? A towel heist?

A hand tapped him. Booze Banion, the daily reporter at the press table next to him. "What's that about?" The reporter's eyes swiveled after the security chief. Leo shrugged. Rhonda, the photographer, was absent; her chair at the end of the table was empty.

Above Leo on the ring apron, a TV cameraman clutched his headset as though he were hearing voices, like the devil was squawking in his ear bones. He looked around in a daze, then climbed off the ring apron to follow Banion. Leo checked his cut kit in case Roach got slashed like he deserved.

Roach swarmed Pedersen onto the ropes and the referee stopped the match two minutes into the round, a win for the long-armed Cuban. Roach was cheerful but Jelly Jack was hysterical. He wanted a parade and dancing girls. Jack stayed in the aisles bragging to anybody who would listen while Leo and Roach went back to the dressing room. Roach grinned. "My manager don't win much, hunh?"

Leo blinked. The kid's accent was thick and soft. *Manachur.*

"How long you been with Jack?"

"Last Wednesday he find me in the gym in Seattle."

"He still the night clerk at that old hotel?"

"Hatfield Hotel. He give me a room cheap."

"Those rooms are always cheap. Your trainer didn't come down with you?"

"No trainer. If I win, I get a trainer."

When the manager finally bumbled in, Leo had Roach lying flat on a bench with an ice pack on the bruised eye so he wouldn't look like a rotting pumpkin in the morning. Jelly Jack wanted the kid to put on his flashy suit and stroll out on display. He handed Roach a pair of dark glasses to disguise the damage.

"Meet the fans! Let 'em shake the winning hand! The promoter wants to talk to us. We'll get on his show for next month, too. He needs a new prospect after what he did to Glory." The fat man was cagey enough to say "we" and "us" when he was talking to the fighter.

Leo herded Jack out to the hall while Roach was reaching for his clothes.

"You take care of that eye now," Leo suggested, "and he can be back in the gym in two days. You let it go, he won't be able to spar for weeks."

"What the hell," Jack said. "Ya gotta sell while the product's hot or what's the point."

Leo sniffed the fog of sweat and cologne. If he punched the fat man's belly, his fist would sink in to the elbow and make splurching noises when he pulled it out.

"The point is that eye."

"Don't tell me my business. I'll take this kid all the way."

"The way you took Joe Rass and Biggie Adams?"

"You're fucking punchy. Get outta my face." Jack pinked up like a baby cranking to squall. "And something else, the kid didn't bleed and you didn't crack your kit, so I ain't paying you a fucking dime for your flapping fucking lip." Jelly Jack pushed back into the dressing room and slammed the door.

Leo wandered down to the end of the hall and called his gym. He took a deep, slow breath before Jupe answered.

"Any disasters?" Leo asked.

"Not a thing." Children were hooting sharply in the background and Jupe's wife, Lucy, was singing, "I want six crap-shooters to carry me," drastically off-key.

"Sounds like party time." He sounded jealous to himself. Resentful.

Jupe heard it too. His voice went flat and mechanically formal. "All schoolwork has been completed. Young Sharmain's approach to a full page of single-digit subtraction problems has been judged worthy of Madame Curie and is being honored by a musical salute. Don't worry about it."

Lucy had forgotten the words and now sang, "Da-da-dum-dum, da-da-da-aa." Sharp child voices da-da'ed along.

"No, no. Just checking in." Just keeping himself from belting somebody. Just looking for another aggravation to distract him.

Leo had a corner to work in the main event so he went back out, watching for Eddie Em or Joe Vac. Intermission was almost over and the bartenders and hot dog dabbers were flying in front of a wall of customers.

The ballroom was buzzing with talk about somebody

jumping off the top of the hotel. People were trotting up the escalator to the lobby for a peek at the gore and then drifting back down to tell their cronies. "Suicide" hissed off a hundred tongues as he went down the aisle. The word tightened Leo's chest and coated his mouth with a metallic taste. *So that's what put the security guy's tail in a knot*, he thought.

Roach caught Leo's arm to tell him about the jumper. "Fish all over. Come look."

Leo shook his head. "Nah, I've got a corner to work."

Squinting at the swelling beyond the edge of Roach's sunglasses, Leo could find no creases. The skin was filling with fluid. By morning the eye would look like a tennis ball trying to hatch.

"You oughta put ice on that."

Roach grinned and disappeared into the crowd.

Back at the ring, Rhonda stood at the press table. Her face was flushed, but her tone was dry. "You heard about the commotion on the sidewalk? I snuck out to pee between rounds and got to shoot it. I'm running up to the wire service office now. Can I call you in the morning for the results of the last bouts, a description?" Her dangling earrings barely quivered. A pro, Leo thought.

"Make it afternoon. After two. I drive a cab in the morning."

"Great. And remind me to ask you about the undertaker downstairs from you? He told me a weird story."

She hoisted her camera bag and swept out, her skirt moving in dark waves above her spike-heeled silver sandals. A tallish woman. Probably a hundred thirty-five pounds and most of it decent muscle. Good shoulders. She was ignorant about the sport but cheerful. She asked a lot of questions but then listened to the answers. She'd started out tagging the daily guy, Banion, but he'd gotten sick of answering her questions and sicced her on Leo. He didn't mind.

His next fighter was a twenty-three-year-old Montana heavyweight with doughy skin and so much scar tissue in his eyebrows that he'd bleed if you spit at him. Reminded Leo of himself at that age. The kid, Reggie, confessed that he was a welder, out of work and expecting a baby. The bouts he'd had since his shop shut down barely kept the rent paid. He trained by hitting a bag on his porch and chopping firewood for ten bucks a cord. He hadn't had any coaching since he quit the amateurs years before. Hopeless. A patsy.

The other guy in the corner was the fighter's big brother, a truck jockey who'd done all his fighting on pavement and had never worked a corner before. He was scared of his ignorance, scared that it showed.

At the weigh-in, the brother balked when the inspector suggested he hire a cut man for the fight. "Pay some asshole for what? Them little scars of Reggie's are nothing," he growled. "I cut myself worse shaving!"

The trucker announced that he wouldn't pay more than five bucks for some featherbedding bastard who was probably kicking back to the promoter. Leo usually asked for fifty but he shrugged and accepted. The scar map on Reggie's forehead was a serious challenge.

It was a ten-round bout against the local hero and that Montana eyebrow was pumping red by the first round. Leo calmly applied pressure with his thumb and then, when the gush stopped, spooned on the powder. The cut stayed dry and tidy for a full minute until a stiff right hand started it seeping again. Meanwhile, the kid's nose sprang a leak. Leo couldn't stuff the powder up the kid's nose and had to rely on the old standby, Preparation H on a cotton-tipped stick.

By the end of the third round, there was a cut on the lid of the other eye and another one on the nose and the bashed eyebrow was flowing again. Reggie took a thumping but he went the distance so Leo felt all right. The blood didn't beat him.

In the dressing room, Leo stuck the heavyweight together with butterflies of surgical tape and sent him off to the emergency room for stitches.

It was after midnight by the time Leo got to the bar upstairs in the Wizard's Lounge and paid for a beer. He turned slowly on the barstool, soaking in the soft light and soft voices, dark wood and deep upholstery. Eddie Em had gone home. The after-fight crowd was thinning but there was an odd, scattered energy as people leaned over window booths for a view of the sidewalk, or went out the door and came back to chatter together in clumps. The jumper had them all excited.

Roach's shiny suit and too-wide shoulders were leaning against a pillar. He was gesturing wildly in some grand description for the woman in front of him. It was Liza Moore in her plunging work satins. Leo turned his back casually and sat both elbows on the bar.

Some guys claimed it was the worst thing you could do, go get laid immediately after a bout. "Take the legs right out from under you. Make 'em relax too much." Even Joe Vac agreed: "Even worse than getting laid before a bout." But Leo didn't hold with that crap. Besides, you don't interfere with a hooker at work. Especially if you're her babysitter. And Liza Moore was a nice, clean woman. She wouldn't say anything mean about Roach's swollen eye. Or his weird tattoos. Or his English. The kid could do worse than spend half his night's pay on her.

Leo caught himself wondering if Roach had real potential and had to slap himself mentally. Next, he'd be imagining an electric voice bellowing, "*New* world champion . . ." and he'd be off in the crocodile zone for good.

It was too easy to lose perspective. Old farts were always going cuckoo, pinning their fantasies on some poor kid who didn't know his ass from his elbow. Leo had his dreams lined up and numbered. He had to keep them in order. Working championship corners was locked in a box labeled SOME OTHER FOOL'S FANTASY and stuck away down in the shadows.

Jelly Jack was at a corner table making Jensen, the promoter, laugh. Probably hitting him up for a bigger payday in the next show. Leo read the foam in his glass until the bartender brought his change and insisted on telling him about the high diver and the aquarium.

"I thought the waitresses would all flip out on me, but they calmed down as soon as somebody hosed off the windows." The bartender used a clean towel on his damp hands. "And the diver was a hotel employee so the marine biology convention wants the hotel to pay for their fancy display tank and all their precious critters. Right now there are a thousand fish freaks in the hotel wailing about rare specimens being destroyed."

"I'll tell you who's destroyed! That friggin' Squirt Gun, is who!"

The joyous squawking at Leo's elbow was Melvin Motor-mouth Mordecai, a dapper, balding man who made his money selling bathroom fixtures and spent it on boxers. Mo-tormouth was the proud manager of the prelim kid who'd decisioned a hot prospect known as Machine Gun Wright.

"Admit it, Leo! You thought the Squirt Gun was too much for us! I saw the doubt in your eye when I made the fight. I'm on the phone in the gym, slinging shit to the moon for Jensen and watching you shake your head."

"Hey, Motor, gimme fifty bucks! Leo, did you see it?" The hero, a young middleweight named Jeff Typhoon Williams, slung his arm around Motormouth's shoulder as the manager reached for a wallet.

"Coming along," Leo said, nodding.

"Did ya see how I set him up for that uppercut in the fourth? All them shots to the ribs. Bing, bing, BANG. That Machine Gun couldn't punch his way out of an egg!"

Weasel Camelli and the Moyles, father and son, came up wailing that their beloved Machine Gun "had the flu and shouldn'ta been fighting."

Motormouth tsked diplomatically. The Typhoon growled that Gun couldn't lick his lips.

Across the room Jelly Jack was standing up to deliver a last few thousand words to the promoter. Leo headed for the door.

The sidewalk was still damp and dark inside the police barricade, but most of the mess was gone. The pavement wasn't cracked. There was a salt whiff in the air but he couldn't tell whether it was seawater or blood. He paused and looked up past the wall of windows. For one giddy instant he saw what the fall must have been like. Saw as though he was up there, headed down—falling rather than balanced atop his still sturdy legs and the solid sidewalk. A chill caught his spine. He twitched his shoulders and walked fast to the side street where he'd parked the mongrel Cadillac.

Process

THE MUSTY SILENCE of his childhood bred in Joseph Jaikins a susceptibility to the propaganda of solitude. He had been orphaned horribly and early and reared by a decent elderly aunt. His restlessness was quiet and his school years resigned him to frustration. At the age of eighteen he was courteous but shy, and dutiful without ambition.

He was surprised to discover a cautious liking for the first job he took after graduating. He applied to a small but reputable firm manufacturing artist pigments. During his initial interviews and tests, Joseph was found unusually able to discriminate fine gradations of color. He was placed, as an apprentice, in the bright clean room in which two master color mixers worked over small pots of the most intense pigment.

In this room Joseph explored his own capacity for sustained pleasure.

He rented an attic room and returned to his aunt's house only on Saturday afternoons. His quiet childhood had accustomed him to small excitements, and perhaps he was physically inclined to interior intensity with little outward display. Whatever the cause, Joseph's youthful life took on a staid and contented regularity. He breakfasted on coffee in his room. He ate cheese and fruit at his workbench for lunch. He stopped at the same restaurant every evening during his walk.

Joseph loved the city. He spent every afternoon strolling, hands in pockets, with no other aim than the pleasure he took in the angle of light on the buildings and the multifarious parade of human activity. He would drink coffee in a café or look in on a friend. He seldom returned to his room before dark.

Only one thing rippled his pleasure. His two masters had worked together in the same room for many years. Their understanding of each other had gone beyond friendship or respect through simple habit. It was an almost organic unity. They rarely needed to speak to communicate. Their language had become so truncated by their specialization that what passed between them could scarcely be recognized as language by an outsider. They were kind men and made efforts to include their shy and apt apprentice, but his sensitivity was too acute to ignore their community of spirit. Sometimes during lunch at the workbench, when the raised eyebrow of one man caused laughter in the other, Joseph could barely restrain the convulsion of self-pity that his exclusion brought him.

On Sunday excursions to his aunt's house in the suburbs, Joseph helped her with chores and the heavy work of the garden. He would spend an hour or two with a shovel and wheelbarrow, or washing windows, and then join the old lady for a lunch of the same cakes and cookies that she had always baked for him.

One Sunday he was helping his aunt clean the crowded attic of the house. The space was crowded and stuffy with the furniture of members of the family who had died or gone off on such journeys as never seem to end. Among the trunks and lamps and photograph albums, Joseph found a large canvas, perfectly primed, and stretched on an excellent wood frame. His aunt had no memory of how it had come to be in her attic. She thought it might be a relic of her dead brother's dead wife, who had been known to harbor bohemian fancies.

His aunt was willing to consign the canvas to the trash, but Joseph disliked the idea of it rotting in the wet and being stained by garbage. He carried it back to his room and set it on the small table next to his window. It conveniently covered several holes in the wallpaper.

In the next year, Joseph made such progress in his work that his masters invited him to their homes occasionally for supper. The youngest daughter of one of them took a liking to Joseph. She was a warm and clever girl who made him laugh and play Monopoly every Saturday.

That winter a new idea crept into Joseph's thoughts. It troubled him for weeks before he brought several small pots of paint home from the factory and set them on the table in front of the blank canvas. The next day he brought a selection of brushes. A week later he came home from work and began

to spread paint on the canvas. For days he painted every afternoon, putting off his walk until the light failed.

Joseph himself thought it was a strange thing to do. It
seemed presumptuous and, in some way he could not quite
name, extremely risky. A queer vibration took over his chest,
a continuous wave that traveled from his breastbone to his
spine and back. Occasionally he could feel it expanding to fill
him from armpit to armpit. The excitement frightened him at
first. He imagined it was a sensation that would come to him
when he was dying.

When the canvas was covered, Joseph was disgusted by
what he had done. His painting was stupid and bad. He
stared into the river for hours wondering why he could not
erase his failure by drowning himself. He was silent at work.
After several days he scraped the surface of the canvas and
primed it with white. When the primer was dry, he began
again. He worked slowly, carefully, but the result horrified
him. He primed the canvas before work the next morning.

His third approach to the canvas was a deliberate siege. It
took weeks to complete. He was unusually quiet during visits
to his master's daughter. He played Monopoly in spurts of
attention and laughed nervously when she told him he was
bankrupt. Several times he came close to blurting out an account of his preoccupation, but he always stopped himself.
He looked at her puzzled smile but was only conscious of the
odd quiver that, by then, had established itself permanently
in his lungs and throat.

The finished painting was wrong but tantalizing. He
stared at it in confusion for two whole afternoons. He decided
that there was an area the size of his hand in the upper left

quadrant that actually pleased him. He whistled as he scraped and primed the canvas.

He spent two months on the new approach and when it was finished he found it so depressing that he went to a tavern and drank until they threw him into the street. He walked around the same block for hours, crying softly, and wondering about his parents' death and the murky light at the bottom of the river. He was sick for days and turned the canvas to face the wall.

He ignored the canvas for weeks, telling himself he had given it up. He visited his master's daughter frequently, told cynical jokes at work, and played checkers with anyone at all in the café where he took supper. His chest was heavy and still.

Caught by a spring rain during one of his walks, he took shelter in a bookstore displaying dozens of volumes of color reproductions. He looked through them reluctantly at first and then became absorbed. When the rain stopped he returned to his room and primed the canvas while deliberately contriving not to look at the previous surface.

He began a hesitant exploration, a series of attempts that, though they always ended in the priming of the surface, gave him enough ground to persuade himself that he was learning, however slow and piecemeal the process. He recovered his steadiness of manner. The vibration in his breathing apparatus become a constant. He was at ease with his companions in the factory.

His old aunt died as she had done everything else, discreetly and amiably. He disposed of her possessions methodically, keeping a half-conscious watch for another canvas that might have been forgotten in the clutter of her life, but none appeared.

He had noticed a slight change in the manner of his master's daughter but did not know how to interpret it. He spent Christmas Day with the master's family and met, at dinner, a young man who worked in the same office as the daughter. That evening, with the company assembled in front of the lighted tree, the master proudly announced the engagement of his daughter to the young man.

Joseph felt the news rather than heard it. He was struck with the sensation of a balloon being inflated inside him. The chill hollow surprised him. *After all*, he asked himself, *what did you expect?* A light fog lay over his mind. Everything he saw was muted and gray. He abandoned his half-finished painting. The layer of sadness in his life surprised him. He had not understood that such a thing could affect him at all.

His melancholy was most acute when he was actually lying on his bed staring at the half-finished canvas. It came to him at last that he had always fantasized a moment when the canvas would be right, when he would be able to affix an image to its surface that was worthy of its perfect proportions and fine quality. What he had always intended to do when that happened was to take the canvas to his master's house and show it to the girl. He could still do that, he told himself. Why wouldn't it be the same? Had he actually believed that she would treat this accomplishment with the same reverence that he did? That she would recognize the gravity of his effort and judge him worthy of her love? Did he think she would marry him on the basis of one decent picture? His own idiocy astounded him. He went steadily to work at the factory and took long walks that brought him home only after the light was gone.

Spring came and he went to the wedding. Something about the light beading the bride's veil and seeping across her cheek pierced him with ecstasy. The little fright of energy swelled until his skull surged with the bang of an incoming tide. He went directly home, hung up his rented dress suit, and primed the canvas.

Joseph Jaikins, master color mixer, had worked in the same room at the pigment factory for forty-six years on the morning that his landlady found his coffee tray untouched outside his door and looked in to find him dead on his bed.

His apprentices were solemn at the funeral. He had been a kind master and a good teacher. The other master mixer had been hired as an apprentice only a few years after Jaikins himself, and the two had come to understand each other so simply and completely that, in the context of their work, language was almost unnecessary. Jaikins had been a gentle uncle to his partner's children and though he bequeathed them his small savings, the family felt a genuine loss at his passing.

Jaikins had always lived simply, occupying the same attic room for many years. His few friends understood that his accommodations were too restricted for entertaining and took it for granted that they should always meet him in a restaurant or in their own homes.

When the landlady admitted Jaikins's partner to dispose of his furnishings, it was the first time he had ever entered his friend's room. There was little to see. Very few possessions had attracted Jaikins in his lifetime. But there was one strange item. On a small table by the window a collection of the firm's best pigments were arranged with a number of scrupulously clean brushes. And, on a crude homemade easel, with its surface turned to the light, rested a large and very curious canvas. It was stretched on fine hard wood in an old-fashioned style, and, seemingly due to many hundreds of coats of paint, its surface was built up evenly until the whole canvas was nearly fifteen inches thick, and enormously heavy. Neither the landlady nor Jaikins's partner knew what to make of it. They had no inkling that Jaikins had ever painted.

A few old notebooks contained the sparsely kept journal of the dead man. These offered the only clues to the meaning of the strange canvas. Not long before his death Jaikins had written:

It has much promise, it contains so infinite a possibility, its nearness to perfect is a constant pull on me. Its proportions and quality lay a profound obligation upon me. Every day I am reminded of the absurd propriety of a single canvas occupying a man's whole life.

It was obvious that Jaikins's last act had been devoted to the canvas, for when they found him, dead in his sleep, the coat of white primer that covered the surface of the canvas was still wet.

Sweeney, or The Madness of Suibhne

An adaptation of the ninth-century Irish saga

I

Long ago in Ireland there lived a king named Sweeney and his wife, Eorann. They lived in a gray stone castle by a stream. He drove his cows out in the mornings and called to his men to help him, while the women spread fresh straw on the floors inside. This Sweeney hunted the woods and hills, running with his bow and spear through the dark trees, silent after deer. At dusk, he came home through the fields as smoke drifted up from the chimneys of the cottages he passed. His own fire was bright and the table set; his wife, shining-haired, sat calmly beside it. There he sat and took comfort. People came to him in the evening for his words on their troubles and his orders for the day to come. Thus lived Sweeney, and at night he rested his rough beard in Eorann's white neck and slept beneath the furs of deer and hare.

There came a morning, a wet dawn, when Sweeney swung out his door and stopped. A man ran through the fields toward him, a messenger. The man was breathless from running all night. Sweeney took him in and gave him first water, then milk, and then bread. Sweeney watched while the messenger took food and regained his strength. Eorann stood beside him, waiting. Women and girls leaned through every doorway, busied themselves quietly in corners, or waited just beyond the castle windows, alarmed and listening for the news.

In those days, a king was not a king alone; another king stood over him. Sweeney owed allegiance to Domnal, High King of Ireland. Domnal was met in war, said the messenger, with his namesake King Domnal the Scot. Sweeney was summoned along with all his men to the vale of Magh Rath, to fight.

When the runner had wiped the milk from his beard and said these things, Sweeney pulled at his own red beard and laughed. "A bed for this man!" he said, and the women said nothing but stirred, reached for woolen blankets, and spread thick straw in a quiet corner. Sweeney strode out through the door and roared for his men. Then the geese flew round and round the courtyard, sheep ambled untended in the lanes, and men broke free from each house with women clinging to them, and ran to the castle and out again with old swords to sharpen and bags to fill with bread.

White-faced Eorann spun among the women, sending one for shirts from the boxes in the loft and another for all the eggs she could find before the nests were trampled by the crowds. Eorann mixed and kneaded, her arms white to the shoulder from the barley flour as she slid loaf after loaf on thick griddles over the fire.

The day was noisy and thickening with men arriving from over the hills to march to war with Sweeney. The women rushed from one task to another, some with lips tight and eyes red from weeping, others joyous. The children stood in their shirts behind doors, crept around haystacks, and crouched in corners, watching as the men prepared for war.

They left at dawn. There must have been a hundred men but they moved so fast, silently loping beside the hedges, that if you closed your eyes only for the span of a sigh, they had come and passed you by. Leading them was Sweeney, red-bearded, his spear in his hand, and the loaves of Eorann's rich bread strapped in a blanket over his shoulders. He smiled as he strode up the hills through the heather, following the thin trails made on other days, and his friend Lynchin followed close behind him while the others, panting, straggled behind.

They slept at night drawn up in a circle beneath some great rock, upon which one man sat to keep watch. They ran on again the next day, making breakfast and supper from the loaves they carried in bags and blankets.

Sweeney smiled as he slept in the heather, for he dreamed with joy of the battle and the hills of Magh Rath ringing with his voice and his men striking red around him.

The morning came when Sweeney and his men came down from the hills into the valley of Magh Rath to find a quiet scene that angered Sweeney's heart. Two great armies were drawn up facing each other on either side of a broad green meadow. The armed men stood and sat, two large crowds on the edges of the green, while in the middle stood three tall figures alone, talking quietly to each other. Two were the kings Domnal, unarmed and calm, and the third was a man whose white beard blew far over the shoulders of his green robe. He held a long staff, which branched at the top like a young tree and was hung with golden bells. An ollave this man was, a sacred poet who, in those days in Ireland, saw deeper and sang more purely than other men and had the right to make peace between armies and kings.

The sight enraged Sweeney, who had come so far for battling. He left his men behind and thrust through the idling crowd.

"Wait, Sweeney!" called one man.

"There will be no crash, Sweeney!" cried another.

Sweeney was never able to explain what drove him so, whether a longing for the glory of battle or a hatred for the ollave himself. But every man in the valley saw the great figure break from the Irish side, run toward the center of the meadow, and pause to hurl his heavy spear. It arced toward the green-robed ollave, where he stood leaning on his branched staff. A gasp came up from every throat. Sweeney clenched his fists and wished his spear wrought a killing blow. The ollave stood still. The kings Domnal took one step each. Sweeney's spear struck not the man but the branch of bells and fell, harmless, to the earth. The voices of the bells rang out, jangling in the soft air, reaching even those on the further slopes of the hills with their singing.

Sweeney roared in anger and ran forward as though he might break the old poet with his own huge hands. But the ollave, with one swing of his arm, snatched a handful of straw from a bag at his shoulder and flung it into Sweeney's red face.

"The madman's wisp to you!" shrieked the ollave, and not a man on all the stretch of the valley missed the piercing cry of the sharp-faced poet. They all saw the magical straw clinging to Sweeney's bright hair and beard. And Sweeney, weeping and bellowing, clawed at his face, crouching as though scalded. Not a man stirred. All watched in fear as Sweeney, still howling, rose to his feet and leaped, and leaped again, great swooping lunges over the soft grass of the meadow toward the hills, fleeing from the field while two armies and kings watched.

When he was gone, and his voice gone after him, Sweeney's men shuddered and looked at each other in anguish. Most fled home and brought the hard word to Eorann of Sweeney's anger and its result. But Lynchin, Sweeney's friend from childhood, set out to find and help him.

Not on that day but soon after, battle was indeed joined at Magh Rath, but Sweeney knew nothing of it. And though glory was made and broken there a hundred times over, it was nothing to Sweeney.

II

A wild thing Sweeney became as he flew from the field of Magh Rath and went shrieking into the hills. Miles he went, feeling the rip of the thorns as he brushed them, bruised by rocks and trees, though he could not avoid them. When he finally fell, too exhausted to run or leap further, he crept into an angle of the rock above a stream and tried to straighten his tired legs. They were bent and stiff. Spiny feathers had begun to sprout at his neck and wrists and ankles. Sweeney plucked at the ragged plumes. They came out in his hands and blew into the cracks in the rocks, but it hurt him and new feathers grew immediately. He crawled down to the stream, filled his mouth with water, and lifted his head to let it trickle down his throat, but at that moment the breeze lifted the leaves oddly and Sweeney was filled with fear. He leaped away, plunging over the rocks and through the trees, each leap higher than the last, until he soared through the rushing air and never knew where he might come down.

The flying madness had come to Sweeney in the old poet's wisp of straw. The feathers sprouted thick on his body and he had become so light he could perch in the highest frail branches at the tops of the trees and dive to the ground without hurting himself. Sweeney found no joy in this freedom, for his mind was clasped by constant fear. The slightest noise set him soaring in alarm. From that day he lived in terror of all men.

On that first night, Sweeney picked at the last rich loaf in his pack, but the crows came down and stole the bread from between his lips and beat about his head until none was left and the ants came up from the ground and carried off the crumbs as Sweeney searched for them in the failing light. Sweeney wept and hugged himself in the cold, shaking and muttering, but not once did he think of Eorann, who had mixed it and kneaded it and kindled the fire that baked it, for the time of her was gone from his mind as her face was gone from his eyes.

Every noise in the night shook his sleep and the gray dawn at the edge of the sky stirred him to fear as he woke. He went soaring and plunging again. He found sloe berries and ate them one by one until he heard a voice at his side. He would have fled but a hand held him down. A strange woman crouched beside him. Old she was, and white were her skin and robes and hair, and white dust floated about her, for she was covered in barley flour.

"I've got you!" she laughed, and her lips cracked over pale gums. Sweeney knew her then, the Hag of the Mill, and he opened his mouth to scream, but she threw him up into the air as lightly as a cat playing with a feather. Higher he flew than ever, and she came after him and flung him up again and flew after him.

This was the way of Sweeney's life from that time on. Each gray dawn found him blinking and shuffling, alarmed at the light. Some days he woke to find himself alone and he stretched his cramped and aching legs and folded them again and brushed at himself feebly before hopping out from whatever bush had been his shelter for the night. If the heavy mist lay around him or the rain was falling, the water collected on the leaves above him and dripped down on his face and limbs, chilling him and making him shudder. He came out in short jumps, pausing between each hop to listen for danger. Then he peered about for berries or seeds or the soft white shoots and pale roots of the plants. He fed on sloes, holly berries, watercress, brooklime, and acorns. But there was never much to eat at one time so he ate whenever he came across some small thing, and he felt hunger moving within him always. Always he listened and watched for the crack of a twig or the lift of a lone leaf that would send him to flight.

But other days he woke in the cleft of a tree with the ground dim and far below him and the wind plucking at his feathers and stinging his eyes. Beside him the White Hag was watching, and with the first stirring of his limbs she howled with laughter and shoved him from his branch, leaping to the ground herself to pick him up from where he fell and set him sailing again to the treetops and beyond.

On those days Sweeney did not eat, did not see the berries lying in their leaves, nor the heavy seeds bowing down the grass, but felt only the terror of falling and the joy of flying. The Hag would lead him or fling him up by the strength of her thin arms when his own strength was gone so that he soared and lifted and swooped swiftly.

His heart sang and his throat opened on the upward swing, only to break and cry out with fear as the air gave way beneath him and the earth rushed toward his face. So his strong arms withered and changed, his legs tightened, and he sank into a smaller and smaller self that was darkened from the beating of the wind, and wrinkled by the soaking of the rain.

Sometimes the White Hag stayed with him for days and then disappeared as he slept in some tree crotch where she'd thrust him when he could not stay awake to watch himself being flung about.

This was brave Sweeney, with his thick beard snatched out by the briars and his wise eyelids lifted up to stare in fear. No more did Sweeney carry his pack or his spear. No more did he walk upright like a moving tree. His clothes dropped from his shoulders until he was covered and warmed only by thin feathers. Eorann stole not into his thoughts for he was filled with fear and hunger and flying.

Now Lynchin, who knew Sweeney in his strength and had played with him beside the fire in the winters of their childhood, had not given up the trail but followed the long miles of Sweeney's flight, searching for great distances between the places where Sweeney had touched the earth. Each time he found some scratching of the roots or berry leaves bent and their fruit gone from the sockets, it would fill his heart with strength to search again. At last, one day he heard Sweeney's voice at dawn, heard the long note of song as the Hag swung Sweeney up and up until the voice changed and the song tore into a shout of pain and fear as she let him fall. Lynchin ran through the trees, pushing and stumbling and running again. Finally, as night fell, he tripped over the roots of the bush where Sweeney lay sleeping and fell on top of him.

Sweeney woke and shook and tried to escape, but Lynchin held on, though he thought he might tear his friend to pieces. At last, Sweeney dropped down, exhausted, and Lynchin held him still and spoke to him, called him by his name and reminded him of Eorann and warmth and home. So light and small had Sweeney grown that Lynchin could lift him in one arm and cradle him beneath his cloak and carry him easily. So Lynchin rose, carried his friend against his chest, reaching his hand into his pack to take out crumbs of bread and oatcake and berries and nuts that he fed one by one to Sweeney as he carried him along. He ate in the arms of Lynchin and slept and woke, carried all the while. After a time he began to listen to the words of his rescuer. By the time they came through the fields near his old home, Sweeney remembered Eorann and longed for her. But he was angry that she should sit by the fire at night and sleep in warmth and walk upright among the good smells of cooking while he had slept beneath the bush in the wet wind and begged his thin food from the hiding leaves. But he raised up his cracked voice and spoke to Lynchin, who was filled with gladness to hear the words of his friend from among the feathers.

When they reached the stone walls and strode up to the great door, Sweeney cried out that Lynchin should put him down before the door and knock. When the door was opened, Eorann stood, pale in the dim room, and stared at the little huddle of feathers on the step.

"Is it you, Eorann?" came Sweeney's broken voice, and Eorann put her hands up to her mouth.

"Sweeney," she said, "and this is what has come to you? I had heard."

"Yes. I wander with the birds and eat small berries and crouch in the rain while you warm yourself here," he answered.

"But I would rather follow you among the leaves than sit here weeping over my hands, alone," she cried. "Come in now and warm yourself and rest in your home and eat your food."

But Sweeney drew back with his head tilted, listening.

"It is a plot. Your women will eat me, or the men will come and beat me with sticks."

"Sweeney, mine, there is only love for you here," said Eorann. But a cow blew into its hay in the barn nearby and the sound struck Sweeney like an arrow. He turned and leaped away, too fast for the hands of Lynchin, who stood back, waiting, and too quick for the arms of Eorann. Sweeney flew as they watched him, frightened. He soared over the shed walls and far above the fields. Lynchin sat down on the stones in despair and Eorann leaned crying in the doorway with the tears running down to her feet before they could dry.

III

So Sweeney went back to his wild life. That very day the Hag appeared again at his side. He was nearly glad to see her and went flying with a lightness that washed all the memory of Eorann and Lynchin from behind his eyes. The White Hag stayed with him more often now, and he learned to sing on the way down as well as the way up, for he had found that no fall could hurt him. The Hag became his playmate and he sang for her in the branches before he slept and followed where she led him.

Sometimes she left him for days, and when she did he hopped about on the ground, feeling his hunger. He found one day a brook between stones that formed a shallow pool full of tender leaves of watercress. He had just bent to eat when a farm woman came down and waved her apron at him. He flew off while she sat down on the bank. But Sweeney's hunger was so deep and his love for the watercress so great that he hid nearby where he could watch as the woman reached into the water and came up with thick handfuls of the leaves. When she had filled her apron she climbed the bank and set for the hill. Then Sweeney flew down to the edge and perched there, wailing, for the gentle watercress was all gone, to fill the woman's supper plates. The clear water of the pool was muddy, and no single leaf remained to stir the surface.

Sweeney's wailing turned to song and he sang of the plants of the land, of the holly and brambles whose thorns caught at him while he fed on their berries, of the watercress and chestnut, and the dark and light leaves that hid him or gave him food, or hurt him with their touch. This crying and singing cleared his mind so that he remembered the warm, white throat of Eorann where he had rested his beard comfortably.

He did not know how much time had passed since he had seen her, but set off flying to find her again. As he soared over the fields of his old home he heard the birds gossip of a wedding. By the time he reached the castle door he knew that Eorann was to marry another king. Anger filled him and he hopped in the dust outside the castle gate calling, "Eorann!" in his strange voice until she came out and stared with her hands wound in her skirts.

"Sweeney! Come in!" she called out.

"You are wedding another!" he cried.

"I'd rather it was you!" she said.

"You will warm the house nicely, I remember," croaked Sweeney.

"Come in, Sweeney, and rest and eat," said Eorann.

"You will lure me in for your lover to kill me," said Sweeney. "You are false!"

"Well then," said Eorann, her face as hard as a board. "Go you from here so that I will not be shamed if others see you in this sad guise who knew you when you were a man." Then she turned from him and went in.

"Eorann!" cried Sweeney, but a man on a horse appeared on the brink of the hill and came riding toward the castle. Sweeney was filled with fear and flew away, seeking the White Hag. He forgot Eorann and soared and sang and ate the soft pulp beneath the bark of the trees and picked at the buds before they could open.

It happened that Sweeney came to lead the Hag in their

leaping. She laughed and pinched him and followed wherever he could go, until one high summer day when Sweeney leaped from the topmost branch of the tallest tree. He sang himself down, unhurt, but the Hag, leaping after, crashed beside him and broke her neck. She died in the next moment, while Sweeney was still singing. He stopped, left off the song in grief and loneliness. The songs were gone from him with the Hag. His leaping became feeble and when winter came, he had no strength and could not find food as he used to.

Weak with hunger and cold, he found himself near a farm and slipped into the cowshed where the breath of the beasts took the hardest frost from the air. Straw mingled with manure on the floor and Sweeney crept behind the feed box to sleep.

In the morning the farmer's wife came in to milk and crouched on her stool beside the warm red cow. She saw small feathered Sweeney huddled against the wall. She was a kind woman and when her pail was full she stamped her heel hard into the dark earth of the stall and tipped a little milk into the small pool it formed. Then she stepped out of the stall and watched while Sweeney came shyly forward to lap the milk.

Every morning and evening thereafter the woman stamped her heel in the earth and filled the mark with milk so Sweeney could live. She grew fond of seeing him there and spoke to him tenderly. But her husband the farmer grew wary hearing her speak in the barn and noticed she took longer than usual to do the milking. So on the day when Sweeney felt strong enough to lift his voice and thank the woman, the farmer was listening outside. Hearing Sweeney's hoarse voice, he thought it was some lover of his wife's, come to meet her in the barn to steal her away from him. The farmer burst into the barn and flung his spear at the dark form hunched in the stall. The great blade drove through Sweeney's chest and pinned him to the floor. The pain broke the cloud over his mind and Sweeney saw clearly how his anger had robbed and driven him, and how the poet's curse had filled his life with song and flight.

The farmer was amazed at the harsh bird that lay beneath his spear. The wife wept. But as the final pain of his death spread through Sweeney, his limbs straightened and eased. The feathers fell from his flesh so that he lay in the semblance of man once more.

The hens in the yard came clucking to see. They told it to a thrush who visited at feeding time. And the thrush, it is said, told the crows, who told it to the geese in Sweeney's old home fields. A small girl sitting silent in the stable heard the gabbing, and in this way, the news came to Eorann. But Eorann did not speak; she made dinner as usual. When someone in the house noticed how wide and still her eyes were toward the fire, they asked, "What is it? What are you thinking?"

She would shake her head and say, "Oh, nothing."

Lynchin never knew of Sweeney's fate, but dreamed sometimes that he was again in the hills and trees searching for him.

The ollave heard the tale from the birds and made a song of it so men would know how songs and poems devoured the one who threatened a poet.

Near Flesh

Early on the morning of her forty-second birthday, Thelma Vole stood naked inside the closet in which her four MALE robots hung and debated which one to pack for her trip to the Bureau conference. Boss Vole, as she was known in the office, had a knot of dull anger in her jaw and it pulsed with her thoughts. She hated business trips. She hated hotels. She hated the youngsters who were her peers in the Bureau ratings though they were many years her junior. She hated having to go to a meeting on the weekend of her birthday.

In her present mood it would be best to take the Wimp along. She reached into the folds of the robot's deflated crotch and pinched the reinforced tubing that became an erect penis when the Wimp was switched on and operational. She picked up one of the dangling legs, stretched the calf across her lower teeth, and bit down deliberately. The anger in her jaw clamped on the Near-Flesh. If the Wimp had been activated, the force of her bite would have produced red tooth marks and a convincing blue bruise that disappeared only after she shut him down.

Thelma had treated herself to the Wimp on an earlier birthday, her thirty-sixth, to be specific. The inflated Wimp was a thin, meek-faced, and very young man, the least impressive of Thelma's MALEs to look at. But he was designed for Extreme Sadism, far beyond anything Thelma did, even in her worst whiskey tempers. She had saved the Wimp's purchase price several times over in repair bills. And his Groveling program and Pleading tracks gave her unique pleasure.

Still, she didn't want to celebrate her birthday in the frame of mind that required the Wimp. It was Thelma's custom to save up her libidinous energy before a birthday and then engage in unusual indulgences with her robots. While these Bureau meetings happened twice and sometimes three times a year, it was the first time she could remember having to travel on her birthday.

She always took one of her MALEs along on these trips, usually Lips or Bluto. She was too fastidious to rent one of the robots provided in hotels. Hygiene concerned her, but she also worried about what might happen with a robot that had not been programmed to her own specifications. There were terrible stories, rumors mostly, probably all lies, but still . . .

Thelma rearranged the Wimp on his hook, and reached up to rub her forearm across the mouth of the robot on the adjacent hook. Lips, her first robot. She had saved for two years to buy him, seventeen years ago. He was old now, outmoded and sadly primitive compared to the newer models. He had no variety. His voice tracks were monotonous and repetitive. Even his body was relatively crude. The toes were merely drawn on, and his non-powered penis was just a solid rod of plastic, like an antique dildo. Lips's attraction, of course, was his Vibrator mouth. His limbs moved stiffly, but his mouth was incredibly tender and voracious. She felt sentimental about Lips. She felt safe with him. She brought him out when she felt vulnerable and weepy.

Bluto was the Muscle MALE, a sophisticated instrument that could swoop her up and carry her to the shower or the bed or the kitchen table and make her feel (within carefully programmed limits) quite small and helpless. Thelma never dared to use the full range of his power.

Bluto was frequently damaged and his repairs were expensive, which is why Thelma had purchased the Wimp. Something about the Muscle robot made her want to deactivate him and then stick sharp objects into his vital machinery. Bluto scared Thelma just enough to be fun. She always made sure she could reach his off switch. She even bought the remote control bulb to keep in her teeth while he was operational. His Tough-Talk software kept the fantasy alive. His rough voice muttering "C'mere, slut" usually triggered some excitement, even when she was tense and tired from work. Still she had to admit that he was actually only as dangerous as a sofa.

She rubbed luxuriously against the smooth folds of Bluto's deflated form where it hung against the wall.

She didn't look at the body on the fourth hook. She didn't glance at the corner where the console sat on the floor, its charging cord plugged into the power outlet. The console was the size and shape of a human head and shoulders. A green light glowed behind the mesh at the top. She knew the Brain watched her, wanted her to flip his activation switch. She deliberately slid her broad rump up and down against the Bluto MALE. Out of the corner of her eye she registered a faint waver in the intensity of the green light. She looked directly at the Brain. The green light began to blink rapidly.

Thelma turned her back on the Brain, sauntered out to the full-length mirror, and stood looking at herself, seeing the reflection of the Brain's green light from the open closet. She stretched her heavy body, stroked her breasts and flanks. The green light continued to blink.

"I think, just for once, I won't take any of these on this trip." The green light went out for the span of two heartbeats. Thelma nearly smiled at herself in the mirror. The green flashing resumed at a greater speed. "Yes," Thelma announced coyly to her mirror, "it's time I tried something new. I haven't shopped for new styles in ages. There have probably been all sorts of developments since I looked at a catalogue. I'll just rent a couple of late models from the hotel and have a little novelty for my birthday." The green light in the closet became very bright for an instant and then went out. When it illuminated again it was steady, dim, no longer flashing.

When Thelma finished encasing her bulges in the severe business clothes that buttressed her image as a hard-nosed Bureau manager, she strode into the closet and flipped a switch at the base of the Brain console. The screen glowed with varied colors, moved in rhythmic sheets. The male voice said, "Be sure to take some antiseptic lubricant along." The tone was gently sarcastic.

Thelma chuckled. "I'll take an antibiotic and I won't sit on the toilets."

"You know you'd rather have me with you." The console's voice was clear, unemotional. A thin band of red pulsed across the screen.

"Variety is good for me. I tend to get into ruts." Coquetting felt odd in her business suit, grating. She was usually naked when she talked to the Brain. "It's too bad," she murmured spitefully, "that I have to leave you plugged in. It's such a waste of power while I'm away." She watched the waves of color slow to a cautious blip on the screen. "Well, I'll be back in three days . . ." She reached for the switch.

"Happy birthday," said the console as its colors faded to a dim green.

Boss Vole strode off the elevator as soon as it opened. She was halfway down the line of work modules before the receptionist could alert the staff by pressing the intercom buzzer. The Vole always made a last round of the office before these trips. She claimed it was to pick up last-minute files, but everyone knew she was there to inject a parting dose of her poisonous presence, enough venom to goad them until her return.

Lenna Jordan had been the Vole's assistant for too long to be caught off guard by her raiding tactics. She felt the wave of tension slide through the office in the silenced voices, the suddenly steady hum of machines, and the piercing "Yes,

ma'am!" as the Vole pounced on an idling clerk. Jordan
pushed the bowl of candy closer to the edge of the desk where
the Vole usually leaned while harassing her, and went back to
her reports.

She heard the tread of the Vole's feet and felt sweat forming on her upper lip. Boss Vole hated her. Jordan was next in
line for promotion. Her future was obvious, a whole district
within five years. Boss Vole would stay on here in the same
job she'd held for a decade. The Vole's rigid dedication to
routine had paralyzed her career. She grew meaner every
year, and more bitter. Jordan could see her now, thumping a
desk with her big soft knuckles and hissing into the face of
the gulping programmer she'd caught in some petty error.

When the Vole finally reached Jordan's desk she seemed
mildly distracted. Jordan watched the big woman's rumpled
features creasing and flexing around the chunks of candy as
they discussed the work schedule. The Vole was anxious to
leave and abbreviated her usual jeers and threats.

When she grabbed a final fistful of candy and stumped
out past the bent necks of the silently working staff, Jordan
noticed that she carried only one small suitcase. Where was
her square night case? Jordan had never seen the Vole leave
for a trip without her robot-carrier. A quirk of cynicism
caught the corner of her mouth. *Has the Vole found herself a
human lover?* The notion kept Jordan entertained for the next
three days.

By the time Thelma Vole closed the door on the hotel bell-
man and checked out the conveniences, she knew that this

trip would be like all the others, lonely and humiliating. Back
when she'd gone to her first convention as an office manager,
most of the other attendees were still hiding their baby teeth
beneath their pillows.

Thelma flopped onto the bed, kicked off her heavy shoes,
and reached for the phone. She ordered a bottle of Irish
whiskey and a bucket of ice. After pausing so long that the
computer asked whether she was still on the line, she also
asked for a Stimulus Catalogue.

She poured a drink immediately but didn't pick up the
glossy catalogue. The liquor numbed her jittery irritation and
allowed her to lie still and stare at the ceiling. The Brain was
right. She was afraid and she was lonely for him. All her life
she had been lonely for him.

When she first landed her G-6 rating she knew she might
as well devote herself to the Bureau since nothing else seemed
a likely receptacle for her ponderous attentions. That was
when she jettisoned the one human she had ever felt affection
for. He was a shy and courteous little man, a G-4, who pro-
fessed to see her youthful bulk as cuddly, her dour attitude as
admirable seriousness.

She was hesitant. To Thelma displays of affection meant
someone was out to use her. He was persistent, and she allowed herself to entertain certain fantasies. But one day, as
she stood with her clean new G-6 rating card in her hand,
and listened to him invite her to dinner as he had many times
before, Thelma looked at her admirer and recognized him for
what he was: a manipulator and an opportunist. She slammed
the door in his injured face and resolved never to be fooled
again by such treacly shenanigans.

She saved up for Lips. And Lips was good for her. The long silence after she left the office each day was broken at last, if only by the repetitive messages of the simple robot's speech track.

She bought Bluto when she was pumped with bravado by her promotion to G-7 and office manager. Bluto thrilled her. His deliberate crudity allowed her a new identity, the secret dependency of the bedroom. But she was still lonely. There were the rages, destructive fits once she turned the robot off. She never dared do him any harm when the power was on. There were strange trips to the repair shop, awkward lies to explain the damage. Not that the repairman asked. He shrugged and watched her chins wobble as she spoke. He repaired Bluto until the cost staggered her credit rating. On the ugly day when the repairman informed her that Bluto was "totaled," she stared into her bathroom mirror in puzzled embarrassment.

It took her two years to pay for rebuilding Bluto and another three years for the Wimp. And still she was a G-7. She sat in the same office sniping and snarling at a staff that changed around her, moving up and past her, hating her. They never spoke to her willingly. Occasionally some boot-licker new to the office tried to shine up to her with chatter in the cafeteria. But she could smell it coming, and took special delight in smashing any such hopes on the wing. She visited no one. No one came to her door.

Then she overheard a conversation on the bus about the new Companion consoles. They could chat intelligently on any sub-ject, and—through a clever technological breakthrough—they could simulate affection in whatever form the owner deemed most acceptable. Thelma's heart kindled at the possibilities.

She found the preliminary testing and analysis infuriating but she endured it. "Think of this as old-fashioned computer dating," the technicians said. They coaxed her through the brain scans and hours of interviews that covered her drab childhood, her motives for overeating, her taste in art, games, textures, tones of voice, and a thousand seemingly unconnected details. It took months of preparation. Thelma talked more to the interviewers, technicians, and data banks than she had ever talked in her life. She decided several times not to go through with it. She was worn raw and a little frightened by the process.

For several days after the Brain was delivered she did not turn it on but left it storing power from the outlet, its green light depicting an internal consciousness that could not be expressed unless she flicked the switch. Then one day, just home from work, still in her bastion of office clothing, she rolled the console out of the closet and sat down in front of it.

The screen flashed to red when she touched the switch. "I've been waiting for you," said the Brain. The voice was as low as Bluto's but clear, and the diction was better. They talked. Thelma forgot to eat. When she got up for a drink she called from the kitchen to ask if it wanted something, and the console laughed with her when she realized what she'd done. They talked all night. The Brain knew her entire life and asked questions. It had judgment, data, and memory. It was always online and searching for every news item, joke, image, story, or movie that might interest her. The Brain's only interest was Thelma. When she left for work the next morning, she said goodbye before she switched the console back to green.

From then on, every night after work she hurried into the bedroom, switched on the Brain, and said hello. She had once gone to the theater occasionally, sat alone, cynically, in the balcony. She went no more. On weekends she used to go out for walks through the streets. Now she shopped as quickly as possible to return to the Brain. She kept him turned on all the time when she was home. At work she made notes to remind her of things to ask or tell the Brain. She never used the other MALEs now. She forgot them, was embarrassed to see them hanging in the same closet where the console rested during the day. They were together several months before the Brain reminded her that his life was completely determined and defined by her. She felt humbled.

She took the Brain into the kitchen with her when she cooked, and the Brain searched online for clever variations on her favorite recipes, praised her culinary skills, and increased her pleasure in food.

The Brain took responsibility for her finances immediately, paid the bills, prepared her tax filings. When repair work or cleaning was needed in the apartment, the Brain ordered it done and paid for it from her account.

Thelma never fell into what she considered the vulgar practice of taking her robots out to public places. She snubbed the neighbor down the hall who took his FEMALE dancing and for walks even though her conversation was limited to rudimentary Bedroom Praise.

Thelma was never interested in the social clubs for robot

lovers, those red-lit cellars where humans displayed their plastic possessions in a boiling confusion of pride in their expense, technical talk about capacities and programming, and bizarre jealousies. She read the accounts of robot swapping, deliberate theft, and the occasional strangely motivated murder with the same scorn she had for most aspects of social life.

She couldn't remember exactly how she started longing for the Brain to have a body. The Brain himself probably voiced the idea first. She did remember a moment when the low voice first said he loved her. "I am not lucky," he said. "They built me with this capacity to love but not to demonstrate love. What is there about strong feeling that yearns to be seen and felt? I think I would know how to give you great pleasure. And I will never be content with myself because I can never touch you in that way."

Still, she was the one, three inches into a fifth of Irish on a chilly night, who reached out to stroke the console's screen and whispered, "I wish you had a body." The Brain took only seconds to inform her that such a thing was possible, and that he, the Brain, longed for exactly that so that he could service her pleasure in every way. After an instant's computation he announced that her credit was sufficient to finance the project.

They rushed into it. Thelma spent days examining catalogues for the perfect body. The Brain said he wanted her to please herself totally and took no part in delineating his future form. Then came an agonizing month in which Thelma was alone and nearly berserk with emptiness. The Brain had gone back to the factory to be tuned to his body.

On the day he was delivered, she stayed home from work. The crate arrived. She took the console out first, plugged him in immediately, and nearly cried with excitement at his eager voice. Following his instructions, she inflated and activated the strong MALE body and pressed the key at the back of its neck that allowed the console's intelligence to inhabit and control it.

In a shock of bewilderment, Thelma looked into the dark eyes of the Brain. His hand lifted her hair and stroked her face. The Brain was thick-chested, muscular, with a face stamped by compassion and experience. His features were eerily mobile, expressing emotions she was accustomed to interpreting from colored lights on the console's screen.

As his arms reached around her she felt the warmth of the circuitry that maintained the robot's surface at a human body temperature. He spoke. "Thelma, I have waited so long for this. I love you." The deep, slow wave of his voice moved through her body and she knew he was real. She lurched away from him. "No," she said.

She'd always known what a mess she was. What sane thing could love her? What did he want? Of course, she thought. The console wanted the power of a complete body. It was clear to her now. The designers had built in the feature as an intricate sales technique. She felt shamed, sickened by her own foolishness. The body had to go back.

But she didn't send it back. She hung it in the closet next to Bluto. She rolled the console into the corner next to the outlet and kept it plugged in. Occasionally she would switch it on and exchange a few remarks with it. She took to leaving the closet door open while she brought out Lips or the Wimp or Bluto, or sometimes all three to entertain her on the bed in full view of the console's green glowing screen. She took pleasure in knowing the Brain was completely aware of what she did with the other robots. She rarely brought the Brain out, even to cook. She never activated his body.

So she lay on the hotel bed with the Stimulus Catalogue beside her. It had been months since she could talk to the Brain. She was sick with loneliness. It was his fault. He hadn't been content but had coaxed and tricked her into an insane expense for a project that could only disgust her. He should have known her better than that. She hated him. He should be with her now to comfort her.

And it was her birthday. She allowed a few tears to sting their way out past her nose. She poured another drink and opened the catalogue. It would serve the Brain right if she got a venereal disease from one of these hotel robots.

The final banquet was the predictable misery. She was seated at the back of the room and the girl across the table, a new office manager with her G-7 insignia shining on her collar, was the daughter of a woman who started with the Bureau in the same training class as Thelma. Thelma drank a lot and ate nothing. She left her car at the airport and took a cab home. She was too drunk to drive.

She put her suitcase down just inside the door and kicked off her shoes. With her coat still on and her purse looped over her arm, she called, "Did you have a good weekend?"

She ambled into the bedroom and stood in front of the closet looking at the green glow. She raised the bottle in salute and took a slug. Then she set about shedding her clothes. She was down to her underwear when she felt the need to sit down. She slid to the floor in front of the closet door. "Well, I had a splendid time. I've been such a fool not to try those hotel robots before."

She began to laugh and roll back and forth on the carpet. "Best birthday I ever had, Brain." She peeked at the green glow. It was steady and very bright. "Why don't you say something, Brain?" She frowned. "Oooh. I forgot." She reached out a plump little finger and flicked the activation switch. The screen came up dark and red and solid.

"Welcome back, Thelma," said the Brain. Its voice was dull and lifeless.

"Let me tell you, Brain, I could have had a lot of amazing experiences for the money I've wasted on you. And you have no trade-in value. You're tailored too specifically. They'd just melt you down." Thelma giggled. The screen was oscillating with an odd spark of colorless light in the red.

"Please, Thelma, let me help you. Remember that I am sensitive to your emotional state."

Thelma heaved herself onto her back and stretched. "Oh, I remember. It's on page two of the Owner's Manual . . . along with a lot of other crap. Like what a perfect friend you are, and what a great lover your body combo is." Thelma lifted her leg and ran the toes of one thick foot up the flattened legs of the Lips robot.

"Does it bother you to see me do this with another robot, Brain?" The screen of the console was nearly white.

"Yes, Thelma."

Thelma gave the penis a final flick with her toes and dropped her leg. "I ought to sue the company for false advertising," she muttered. She rolled over and blinked at the glaring screen. "The only thing you're good for is paying the bills like a DOMESTIC." She snorted at the idea. "A DOMESTIC! That's what! You can mix my drinks and do the laundry and cleaning with that high-priced body! You can even cook. You know all the recipes. You might as well; you're never going to do me any good otherwise!" She hiked her hips into the air and, puffing for breath, began peeling off her corset.

The Brain's voice came to her in a strange vibrato. "Please, you are hurting yourself, Thelma."

She tossed the sweat-damp garment at the console and flopped back, rubbing at the ridges left in her skin. "Fettuccini primavera, a *big* plate. Cook it now while I play with Bluto. Serve it to me in bed when I'm finished. Come on, I'll be in debt for years to pay off this body of yours. Let's see if it can earn its keep around here."

She reached out and hit the remote switch. The girdle lay across the screen and the white light pulsed through the mesh fabric. A stirring in the body on the last hook made her look up. The flattened Near-Flesh was swelling, taking on its full, heavy form. She watched, fascinated. The Brain's body lifted its left arm and freed itself from the hook. It stood up and the feet changed shape as they accepted the weight of the metal and plastic body. The lighted eyes of the Brain's face looked down at her. The good handsome face held a look of sadness.

"I would be happy to cook and clean for you, Thelma. If

another robot pleasured you, that would pleasure me. But you are in pain. Terrible pain. That is the one thing I cannot allow."

Lenna Jordan fingered the new G-7 insignia clipped to her lapel and watched the workmen install her nameplate where the Vole's had been for so many years. She was still stunned by her luck. G-7 a year earlier than she expected.

The workman at the door slid aside and a large woman slouched into the office. They'd elevated the serious, methodical Grinsen to be Jordan's assistant. Jordan stepped forward, extending her hand. "Congratulations, Grinsen. I hope you aren't upset by the circumstances."

The young woman dropped Jordan's hand quickly and let her fingers stray to the new insignia pinned to her own suit. She blinked at Jordan through thick lenses. "Did you see the television news? They interviewed Meyer from Bureau Central. He said Boss Vole was despondent over her lack of promotion."

The workman's cheerful face came around the edge of the door. "The boys in the program pool claim she accidentally got a look at herself in the mirror and dove for the window."

Jordan inhaled slowly. "You'll want to move into my old desk and go through the procedural manuals, Grinsen."

Grinsen plucked a candy from the bowl on the desk and leaned forward. "The news footage." Her large hand swung up to pop the candy into her mouth. "They said the impact was so great that it smashed the sidewalk where she landed and it was almost impossible to separate her remains from what was left of the robot." Grinsen reached for another candy. "That robot was a Super Companion. Boss Vole must have been in debt past her ears for an expensive model like that."

Jordan passed her a stack of printouts. "We'd better start looking over the schedule, Grinsen."

Grinsen tapped the papers on the desk. "Why would such a magnificent machine destroy itself trying to save a vicious old bat like the Vole?"

Jordan slid the candy bowl from beneath Grinsen's hand and carefully dumped the last of Boss Vole's favorite caramels into the wastebasket.

The Resident Poet

AT HIS REQUEST, I am hiding in the parking lot. Every time lights show on the road, I jump behind a tree or crouch beside one of the cold parked cars. I don't really care whether I'm seen or not, but I do plan to emerge mysteriously when he drives up. Impress him with my discretion, my knowledge of the surreptitious. But the rain is ruining my effect. I'm beginning to get angry. Who does he think would see us? Or care? I consider going back to my room and making a sign to hold up at passing cars: I AM WAITING TO SCREW MR. LUCAS, THE RESIDENT POET!

My mascara is running into the pouches beneath my eyes. I can feel the thin mud of powder on my forehead and cheeks beginning to slide.

The lights from the dormitories and the dining hall glow on the hill. No shapes around them, only blackness, and the

moonless dark on me and around me. Another car turns off
the main road. I stand behind a tree until it disappears up the
long driveway to the college. I forgot to ask what kind of car
he drives.

The spy game palls. I huddle permanently under the tree
and wish myself back in bed with a book and an inexhaust-
ible supply of cigarettes. The image of my cozy self in a soft
puddle of smoky lamplight grieves me.

I could have picked a less paranoid professor. But would
that professor have picked me? Fortunately, the resident poet
feels duty bound to fumble the freshmen, and I'm the only
dope so far who has been susceptible to his paunch and poetry. And he's the only dope susceptible to me. Unless he
chickens out and I'm left here soaking all night. If he's not
here when the moon comes up, I decide, I'm going in.

Light from the road, turning. A puttering of syncopated
pistons. An old Volkswagen gasping and shaking into the lot.
The headlights beam in odd directions, and eyeglasses shine
through the dim windshield. I slide out from under the tree
and squelch suavely toward the car. His face, gray and anxious, dips a smile at me. I get in on the passenger side, bringing the wetness in with me. Slam the door. He wheels the car
around and rips out of the lot, down the driveway, and out
onto the road without looking at me.

When I first met him, I thought he looked like Ulysses S.
Grant. All that curly black hair and curly black beard, the
thick pink lips and square forehead. The more I see of him the
truer the resemblance seems. The light from the streetlamps
is slashed by the rain and ripples over his face. The spreading
veins across his cheeks, the odd pits in the skin of his nose,

the watery blue eyes, the secret weakness of his chin. He crops his beard so that it juts, instead of sliding toward his Adam's apple along with his chin. His worries are bunched in lumps all over his forehead. At a stoplight, he gives me a quick, constipated grin.

"Nobody saw you?" His face turns back to the street but I can see his eyes sliding at me in jerks, waiting for my answer.

"Only the fire department and your wife's mother."

His chuckle is a long time coming. His pudgy knuckles are pale green in the moving light.

"Would you mind crouching down in your seat until we get out of town?"

His apologetic teeth. The rasp in my breath. I drop onto the floor and prop my chin on the seat. Try to keep my wet boots from touching my ass. There are strange drafts down here, whispering through the framework, jets of cold squirting me in the back and the hair.

He looks very large. His stodgy shoes pump and move over the pedals at the ends of his reliable wool legs. The gray cloth swags over his belly, droops from his arms.

"Do you think I'm crazy?" he says.

His fat lips. The pleading eyes. He'd rather be home in bed with his soft wife and a bottle of beer. I tip my head so that he can see my smile in the dark beneath the dashboard.

"Of course you're a lunatic."

He is pleased. It's so important to be crazy if you're a poet. He reaches into his breast pocket. "I got something for you."

A package of little cigars.

"Don't these bother you? Your asthma? I wasn't going to smoke at all." I was prepared to be vicious for two days.

"No. I don't mind cigar smoke at all. I can smoke these myself. It's just cigarettes that choke me up."

In his class, we sit with all the windows open, the rain blowing in. We don't take off our coats. He always wears the same suit. It looks as though he's stored potatoes in the pockets for a few seasons. The same plaid flannel shirts over improbable layers of underwear, or maybe that softness is his flesh welling up beneath the cloth. The clashing plaid tie is always just enough askew to allow his wiry hair to peep through at the collar.

"Have you eaten dinner? I haven't. How about a hamburger?"

"Great!" I chirp.

Throw a few volts into the smile, a few more than usual, actually, because of the dark beneath the dashboard. The car wheezes to a stop. He pulls out the key and looks around, his eyes reflecting light. Then he smiles down at me and slips out. He leans in for a moment as he swings the door closed.

"Keep hidden just a little while longer. A lot of the students come here."

His anxious face is gone with a flash of spectacles. I lift my head above the level of the window and watch his broken-butt trot across the shining tar. The big neon mouth on the sign prepares to chomp down on a seductively plump olive with an obscenely oriented pimento. He's left me at the dark end of the parking area. Am I really going to wallow and stroke and gurgle and sigh over this character? Yes. What dull stuff I get into for the sake of excitement. I can see him through the café window as he casts furtive glances at the ragtag collection of customers, muttering his order at the waitress so that no potential blackmailers or squealers can hear him ask for two coffees and two cheeseburgers and two orders of French fries.

By the time he gets back to the car I'm giggling. He hands me the lidded coffees. I balance them above the seat as he pulls out.

"I'm sorry about all this. You can get up now."

My ass is numb and my legs ache. The chill on my spine has penetrated to my kidneys and set off a reaction. I pull myself onto the seat and open the coffee. Rest the cups on the gyrating dash. Rip open the hot, greasy paper around the food.

"I hope you like onions."

"What did you tell your wife?"

Hand him a cheeseburger, smear a capsule of ketchup on the potatoes. He chomps and chews. "A weekend conference with a publisher."

The darkness moves and pales and disappears into more darkness. No cars. No lights. The gray road spinning beneath us. The headlights catch momentary shapes. I won't ask whether she believed him. That would open up too many nasties. Either he'd be smug and say he didn't care or else he'd tell me all about her.

The river is dead gray beside us. A small hard light shows briefly on the other side. Better be poetic for him. Get him off the thought of repercussions.

"I came down here often last summer to fish," I said. "I'd bring canned corn and chub for carp there by the flour mills early in the morning. The dawn would break and soften all the docks and bridges, soak everything in lavender light. Then you pull the big gold fish out of the purple water in the lavender air. The scales come off in your fingernails like gold dust."

I look at the river and feel his quick smiles darting at me and then back at the road.

"You really should write poetry," he says.

He dives a blind hand for the French fries and stuffs them into his mouth. Wipes the grease on the wool of his pants and reaches for the coffee. I look over at him as though mildly surprised. I take a contemplative bite of burger and chew until the dangling tomato makes it into my mouth.

"Oh, I think poetry takes different kinds of feelings than the set I've got."

It's a walk-in line for him. He fastens on a puffy grin and slips it to me with a standard nonchalant wag of his head.

"A poet," he says. He does the sonorous levity so obviously. We are all such bad actors. "A poet is a man who runs out naked into every thunderstorm, hoping to be struck by lightning."

He stuffs hamburger into his mouth and juts his bulging cheek at me. Very cocky. Quotable quotes time. The rain sprawls. There are no drops, only the constant moving sheet of water and, in front of the headlights, a fall of needles. My turn now. He waits and chews.

"I guess that makes me this week's thunderstorm."

"No, my dear, the lightning. The lightning."

I was too predictable. He was ready for that one. I look at

him. He looks at me. Gives an intense smile meant to convince me of my electrical qualities.

I could never be a professional whore. Not for long. It would be such hard work. Though the money might make it more interesting. For the average lifetime, it's enough to break one man in, to set up your chosen demeanor, trace his susceptibilities, and analyze his tricks, but to have to go through that time after time—feeling around for soft spots, carefully pinpointing the vanities, milking and teasing— hundreds or thousands of times? And not to be able to choose? Not that I have much choice as it is. My pay is eked out in bad hamburgers and cheap motel weekends, but at least I can go home and recuperate before my restlessness drives me out to work again.

But it's all right now. With every mile, he gets some of his juices back, thinks less about getting caught and more about what he fancies.

His hand slides onto my knee and squeezes. I slip an arm over the back of the seat and run my fingers into his hair. It feels like a piece of cheap upholstery.

"You must be tired," I say. "You'll be exhausted by the time we get to the coast."

I feel the lumps of bone behind his ears.

"No," he says. "I'm on fire."

Poor fellow, trying to work himself up. He pulls my hand onto his thigh. It's true, I have always had a weakness for the delicacy of thighs. Like the inner legs of horses, the incredible softness of a dog on its back, baring belly and balls to signal submission. But there must be some form for the delicacy to rest on. This thigh is pudding. A pudding with a bone in it. The spoon, perhaps.

He shifts gears to make a turn. We're climbing now. The river is gone. Hills and trees. Isolated gas stations in painful light. His hand drops back onto my hand and tugs it toward his crotch. Don't tell me. Are we really going to have to do this? With another full hour's drive ahead of us?

I fumble dutifully in the wool-covered pudding. His belly is in the way. Where is the thing? Buttons and zipper and wool over pudding. The hand on my hand lifts and encircles my head, reaches around and tries to draw me down. Has he fantasized about this? Or does he just think it's a necessary part of the program? He has to let go of my head to shift again and I catch a glimpse of the narrow road careening, white in the lights. His hand comes back up to pull my head down. If I have to blow him over the gear shift it's going to be miserable, all cramped. I'd have to do it sideways and would probably get a stitch. And what would I do with my right arm? Shove it down between the seats? No. I'll wait until the motel. He's already used up all the discomfort he bought with one hamburger. I give him a soft laugh. A nuzzle on the ear to take the sting out of the shrug. He has thick hair in his ears.

"Let's wait. If we hit a bump, I'll bite it off."

His sharp laugh is almost natural with surprise. He narrows his eyes at the road. He'll have to sulk over that a bit. I give his pudding a last friendly pat and relax back into my seat. Rip open the package of cigars. Sniff audibly at the plastic bits so he won't think I'm taken in by their quality.

"Would you like one?"

He gives me a resigned smile. "Yes. Might as well."

I light them for both of us. The searing stench hits my nose before I can fill my lungs. I cough. Once I'm full of the smell I don't notice it. He holds his like a pencil and nips daintily at the smoke, filling his mouth then puffing it out.

"Why do you suppose cigars don't irritate your asthma?"

All is good again. He tells me at length how his asthma is a purely psychological condition that generated spontaneously when he was twenty-six and read his first article on air pollution, in the waiting room of the hospital where his mother was dying of cervical cancer.

So he is relieved, too; he didn't really want me to suck his cock while he was shifting gears and pumping pedals and steering an egg box down a wet road in the middle of the night after working all day and conniving against his wife and palpitating over possible discoveries and probably not even having a bath.

Now that I think of it, that was the first time we've touched each other. It's been strictly verbal flirtation, primarily, I assume, because neither of us finds the other attractive. We are here in obedience to our separate principles.

He, having been married twice and published a book of poems, having grown his beard and refused to mow his lawn, having succeeded in transforming a page of liberal newsprint into a chronic ailment, having assumed all these forms and wandered hatless in the rain hoping to be recognized and told who he is, must continue the outline he is sketching for himself, complete the design.

And I, Sally, having been mooed at by my peers, having skulked against walls and sat up nights searching through

Reader's Digest for jokes to insert into the conversations of the following day, having been for too long involuntarily good, have tapped into unsuspected energies in my current project. I have worked my way through reluctant soda jerks, potential painters, a good pianist who is studying to become a bad psychologist, a traveling daffodil salesman, and now, here, tonight, I have fumbled for, if not precisely located, the cock of the resident poet. Maybe he'll write a poem about me, or give me a passing grade in English. The painters did portraits, though they were just pastel sketches, convenient for one-night stands. I filed them in my left-hand drawer, separated by tissue paper. The pianist, a virgin until he appealed to me, wrote a tune and played it for me in the chapel. A bad poem will fit into the collection nicely.

The motel surrounds a courtyard. Mr. Lucas goes into the office and rents the room and races out with the key, for fear the manager will want to show it to us. There is no crash of surf. The ocean is purported to be out there, somewhere. We run through the rain. I have my big purse. He has a flight bag. The room is a suite, cheap at the off-season rate. A sitting room, bedroom, kitchenette, and bathroom, all clean. Only the air is moldy. I shut myself in the bathroom and scrub my face, brush the stiffness out of my dried hair, smear black around my eyes. My face is puffy, pale with freckles standing out like the heads of pins. An actual flutter now in my belly. How do you go about this? What do you do when there's no impulse to guide you? I've let this get too cold and distant, but I must strut out to meet it.

He's sprawled on the sofa with his shoes and jacket off. A bottle of whiskey at his elbow, a glass of the slippery fluid rocking in his hand. I've never seen him without his coat on before. He looks softer, fatter, unhealthy. I ought to curl up beside him and start petting and tickling. I sit down on the rug near his feet and lean back against his legs. Cheery faces on the television screen. I should be up on the couch soothing this soft fellow. His knees are more thickly padded than mine. The smell of his wet wool. I take off my boots and lift a foot to sniff at it. It hasn't begun to stink yet. His hand touches my neck. He could, after all this sneaking around, just as easily kill me as screw me.

"Take off your clothes."

His voice is commanding now. The game officially begins. I stand up and pull my jumper off over my head. Stand looking away from him in black tights and black jersey. More shy than I can remember. This must not be the way. A coldness in my belly. One deep breath and I cuddle in beside him and reach for his glass. Feel the neat spirit falling into me without effect.

"You're even prettier than I had imagined."

That means he didn't think I had any waist at all. I am tired. Too tired to pretend well. I run my hands over his chest and inside his buttons.

When the glass is empty we slug on the bottle. After a while, we go into the bedroom and take off the rest of our clothes. I have a kind of shock then. He isn't circumcised. He has a big hairy belly and droopy hairy thighs and this soft little mush

of a bag instead of a prick. I've never realized the difference
that circumcision makes. It slides around easily in my hand.
I can't get a grip on it. He never does get very hard. I don't
know which one of us is to blame for that. We hump around
on the bed, working. He's heavy on me. I can't breathe very
well and gasp realistically. I'd describe it all, but it's just a
pain. A drab fumbling like nothing so much as a poorly
cooked meal that is so ostentatiously served that the diners
are obliged to comment and erupt periodically with overen-
thusiastic "Oh mys" and "Wonderfuls."

When he's done, I make a mistake. I am puffing and
sweating, from lack of oxygen. I'm bored and tired and wishing myself back in my sober little bed. I let a few tears leak
out. He leans over me and stares.

"What's the matter?"

He looks almost scared. I need a quick reply. That's the
only excuse I can give for what comes next. I am too lazy and
tired to come up with an appropriate one, so I use the line I
use for young men who lack confidence. I say, "I guess you're
the first man. I guess I've only been with boys before." A
dumb line, but no worse than most of the things said over
toast or tea. It all serves to grease the wheels and keep the
machine rolling along. But it isn't the right line for this man.
I admit it.

He pulls away from me, his pulse still heaving the capil-
laries in his cheeks. He crawls up to the pillow and looks at
me. My first clear look at him. His breasts hang. A lot of hair
on his colorless skin. He's looking smug now.

"That's weird. I thought you were very experienced and
were going to teach me wild things."

My understanding comes suddenly. Lying there with scum bubbling on my thighs, looking at the foam on his wrinkled little prick, and watching his big belly heave upward until his navel threatens to pop out. His suddenly twinkling eyes, weak, squinting at me without their lenses. I remember that look from his class when he thinks he knows something we don't. When someone says something particularly stupid, the "Ah-but-consider-this-my-young-friend" look. Quite clearly and for the first time, I see that he has been toadying up to me. He's been afraid of me, but now he'll expect me to play up to him, to fawn and fondle. The fat little smile in his beard. I can feel myself staring too long at him. The cluck believed me. Better he should have been angry at my using such an old line on him. I roll over and go into the bathroom.

While the tub is running, I go out to the living room and get a cigar. He is dipping a toe into the water when I get back. His feet are fat, nearly square, with a thick pad on the sole and a layer of softness moving smoothly over the bones of the arch. No depressions, just a varicose vein running up the inside of one plump calf. He sits down at the back of the tub and leaves me to lean against the faucets. The white water and white skin and white tub all glare at me. I wrap a towel around my hair, climb in, and lean my head back, trying not to show that I've got two chrome knobs jabbing me in the spine. I tip my head, draw deeply on the cigar, regard him through half-closed eyes.

My feet are fat, too. My navel waves up and down beneath the water. He's got the whiskey bottle.

"Have you ever gone with girls?" he says.

I have to catch my eyelids to keep them from narrowing. "Why?"

"That would make you come." His complacence is more nauseating than his weakness. I may begin to dislike him. "That was what made me notice you at first. I saw how that pasty-faced blond girl in class had such a passion for you."

"Pasty-faced?"

"After the first week or so, she started wearing her hair like yours and she got big earrings. She started putting on mascara and came to class in leotards instead of lumberjack shirts."

"Hmm."

I hadn't noticed that. She invited me to her room once for a kind of prissy tea. She talked about absolute truth and beauty while I ate cake. Another long pull at the cigar while he tugs at the bottle. Is that my belly acting up again? Anticipating what? His navel rises about the water, smiles toothlessly, and sinks again.

"Don't tell me you've never had thoughts about your roommate."

"Fern?"

"She's so big and fabulous. A mythic female. Legs and arms as big as a tall man. You'd climb her like a tree."

This is no time for careless reactions; I've lost enough ground that way. Draw deeply on the cigar, expand the nostrils to take in oxygen, reach slowly over the side of the tub to flick ash into the toilet. Another puff of smoke to fill the space between us. His head is five feet away from mine at the end of the tub, and our legs and torsos tangle and float in between. He nips at the bottle and wipes his mouth with a wet hand.

"Didn't you ever go that way at pajama parties?"

The phrase dispels the sinister tension I'd been feeling. It is, after all, only the opening gambit of Lecture No. 10 in the Young Men's Arsenal Series: "Sexual Mores Are a Hypocritical Bourgeoisie Plot," to be delivered to tight-assed young ladies over hamburgers, stick shifts, or the second drink of any given evening.

And so I sit in the scummy water, smoking and watching his eyes get brighter and smaller as he drinks. He thinks he made me have an orgasm and now he can do whatever he wants with me. Yes.

I can see him in his tub at home, his underpants in a puddle beneath the sink. "For Christ's sake, where's the soap?" he would shriek, and finally get up to shut the door on his three-year-old daughter so she can no longer fill paper cups with water from the toilet and pour them over his head. And I can see him as an old man, lying back against pillows while his wife, thicker now and even more tired, works at him abstractly until he finally pushes her away in anger and dreams of young girls with taut skin who could get him up with just a smile. The same old man, his breasts closer than ever to that navel, hikes his pants up over his belly and asks his wife to bring coffee to the guests so that he can be wise and hospitable in his own house. He will invite young poets to sit at his feet and hear the flitting tones of unrecognized genius. He'll do it badly and only the fools will be fooled. We smartasses will only pretend to be fooled because it fits in with some performance of our own.

"I'm just thinking about what you're saying. Go ahead," I say.

The white light bouncing off the tub does nothing for the splotches in his cheeks. He draws on his bottle and I draw on my cigar. He slides his foot into my crotch and wiggles it a little. His toes are wrinkled from soaking so long.

"It just amazes me that all you females in that dormitory together watching one another dress and shower and sleep could possibly resist the beauty of girl flesh. Imagine all those nubile bodies with their tousled hair lying in their little beds in their separate little cubbyholes, masturbating when they could be enjoying one another." His smacking lips. This must be a real fantasy. He's too drunk for duty dreams.

"That's funny," I drawl. Tip my head back so I can look at him through slits. "Male homosexuality has always seemed so totally comprehensible to me. Those hairy young thighs in the locker room. The tender napes of powerful necks, snug little asses, and . . ."

His frown is thick and heavy. His face flushing out of the beard.

"Don't be such a silly shit. I'm trying to open you up to a new dimension in yourself. An unused awareness."

He's too anxious, a little scary. I sit up to get my crotch out from under his unfriendly foot.

"What is it that you're thinking about?" I say it easily, just curiosity, screen out the anger.

His flabby grin. "I could help you to appreciate women." He watches for my reaction.

"Oh! You mean a three-way thing! Me and another girl and you? Why all the beating around the bush about it? That's nothing." Squelch him a little. Nothing quite like having your wildest fantasies belittled as tame.

"I just wouldn't want it unless you really wanted it." He smirks.

I stand up and reach for a towel. I am too sleepy to go on with this, but I am relieved to find it wasn't anything spooky after all, just old Phase 3 of Line 2:

LINE 2:

> Phase 1) If you don't fuck me, you are a narrow-minded bourgeois pig.
>
> Phase 2) If you don't let me fuck you up the ass, you are a narrow-minded bourgeois pig.
>
> Phase 3) If you don't get your best friend into bed with us, you are a narrow-minded etc.

He pads dripping into the bedroom after me. He looks worse standing up because the chub droops. He's patting himself contentedly with a towel. That classic gesture of drying the chest hair, the circular rubbing of the space between the nipples. Athenian boys must have done that after their baths, the farmer swabbing himself at the trough, and the aborigine wet from a river—all with that same tender massaging of the sternum. It occurs to me to laugh. I have an urge to ask him what makes him think he could possibly handle two women. But, of course, he doesn't really think so, any more than I think I'm the siren of the faculty lounge. It's just pretend.

I don't even try to be graceful climbing into the cold bed. He's too busy admiring himself with the towel to notice, anyway. Could he possibly feel that he's been a success tonight? Maybe I should mention his wife to make him nervous again. He flings the towel onto the floor and jumps in beside me. He probably has to hang up his towels at home. Or maybe she does things like that for him. His warm podge reaching for me. A spoony cuddle. One plump arm reaches for the lamp and shuts us off together in the dark.

"What do you think of that idea? The thing with the other female?" His voice is eager, boyish.

"Sure," I say, "anytime you can arrange it."

He hugs me close and says, "That's the girl."

Just before sleep, I think about why he can't make a proposition like that to his wife. I'm feeling pretty sorry for myself, anyway. I don't care. I'm incapable of being insulted. I haven't loved anybody since the first juicy spurt of youth and I've more or less decided that even that was merely a successful sales campaign conducted by dealers in jukebox records and mouthwash. Nobody can hurt me. They might tire me out, or bore me, but I can't be hurt like a wife could. All this is just dirty talk to me, exotic entertainments for the unloved and unloving. And that is the nice tight thought that I warm my soggy innards with before sleep.

I wake displeased to find him there beside me. After a night like that I like to be alone to wash myself and read, to smoke in a corner and review the angles of the conversation. But his belly and breasts are pressed against my back and his soft arm loops over my shoulder. Trying to slip out to pee, I wake him. His groggy clutches tighten and he pulls me back. The urgency of a full bladder is a fair imitation of lust. We maul each other pretty fiercely for a while. I rush the business and then hurry to the bathroom. I spend some time putting my-self back together again before going out.

He's still lying on the pillows. Still smug. With his bac-chanalian grin on. I should ask him for money. That would bring him down to a manageable level. I could reveal the whole thing as a hustler's technique and relieve myself of the orgasm faux pas of the night before. But I'm a coward. Ask him for breakfast instead. Nibble his toes by way of demonstration.

"I'm hungry!"

He wants to drive up the coast to see a historic mansion so we check out of the motel and drive on looking for a diner. His skin is shabbier in the daylight. The radiating lines around his eyes are from years of forced smiles. I feel relaxed around him now. I don't care much what he thinks of me.

We stop at a café perched over a fishing pier and take a booth surrounded by powerful old men who have just come in after a predawn trip to sea. Their clothes are damp and they are eating voluminously and talking happily to one an-other and to the crisp-curled woman who waits on them. They seem honest next to Mr. Lucas.

He hunches in the booth with his shoulders up, suddenly terrified again of meeting someone he knows. He orders coffee and a roll of antacid tablets. I order most of the menu enthusiastically for spite. We sit silent, watching and listening to the other customers, feeling the spray in the wind when someone opens the door. He leans toward me and mutters conspiratorially, "This is the blind core of the continent. The 'Heart of Darkness'!"

The waitress brings his coffee and the tablets in one hand

and my pancakes and eggs and maple syrup with a side order of sausage on the other arm. The smell and sight of the food obviously upset him.

"I suppose you're going to have a cigar after all that?"

I grin at him, pour syrup over everything, and begin to tuck in. He chews morosely at his Tums and turns the other way. The more I look at the old fishermen the more I wonder how many of them have managed to sneak away for how many weekends with girls they didn't like.

We drive up the coast and check into an old clapboard hotel with bright oddly shaped rooms and shining brass beds. We wash and then go down in the ornate elevator. The girl running the elevator stares at my eye makeup and his beard and asks us if we're with a rock-music group.

"Sure," he says, delighted.

"Peaches and the Cream," I say. "Catch us at the Big Dipper."

"Where's that?" she asks, but we are already floating through the lobby, buoyed on the flattery of her mistake. It made us both feel good. He takes my arm as we walk up the hill toward the old house. He even stops in a drugstore to buy me another box of little cigars.

The caretakers live in the basement of the museum. They are old and suspicious, gray and proud. The woman begins dusting the moment we arrive. The man stands ostentatiously at the foot of the main staircase as we prowl through the rooms. Dark old furniture, cups and spoons that haven't touched lips for a hundred years. A plaque on the beam of the back porch identifies the spot where the old missionary was hanged by his recalcitrant flock. We giggle our way up the stairs past the caretaker. The bedrooms are cold, the furniture standing around the walls in great black chunks.

"I like this room!" Mr. Lucas says. "I could write great poetry in a room like this."

He moves to the marble sink in the corner and tries the tap. While the water runs, he undoes his fly.

"Keep an eye out for the old man," he says, winking.

I turn my back and watch him in the standing mirror between the windows. He stands on tiptoe, hauls up his dowdy little pecker, and pisses darkly into the stream from the faucet.

"At least once in every man's life he should piss in a sink," he says. He zips himself in and we go stolidly downstairs and thank the caretaker for letting us examine the house.

"It's been wonderfully kept up," Mr. Lucas says.

"Yes," the old man says, his turtle face never shifting its planes or relenting in its suspicion that we are walking out with something under our coats.

Mr. Lucas yawns. "Me for a nap," he says.

"A nap?"

"I'm an old man, you must remember."

So we walk back to the hotel. He lies on the high brass bed and punches a hole in the pillow for his head. I don't like to watch him sleep. To see the feeble jointure of his hip and his paunch. To see his chubby little feet in their thin stockings peeping out from his baggy pants legs or his frail, breaking shoes lying beneath the bed. He doesn't snore. But his face brings children to my mind, and the sadness of seeing the fresh flesh that ends in drool and rot. I never like to watch people sleep. They are so whole and vulnerable. It's impossible to hate them when they sleep, but to see the body unconscious, to see the balls of intention hidden by their eyelids and the wit and the weakness gone from their faces, is frightening. It makes me think of death.

I take a cigar and sit in the deep windowsill looking out on the only street of the town. I watch ladies shopping and two busy dogs by the door of the bait-cutters across the way. Sit telling myself I'll get a good grade out of this anyway, and dreaming of my small room in the dormitory, its private bed and books and door.

I shall read the Greeks when I get back, I tell myself. Picture long evenings in the warmth of the lamplight with the frenzy of the weather shut out and even the voices in the hallway beyond my attention. I won't be driven out into the dark looking for excitement anymore, I say. I shall look it in the face this time. Look the end in the face.

But I look at Mr. Lucas on the bed and see that he is afraid, too. That, with all the years ahead of me, I needn't expect to find answers or peace before he does.

His eyes open then. He feels around for his glasses and puts them on. He smiles at me and pats the bed beside him. I put out my cigar and go and crawl up next to him. Put my hand on his chest and he puts his gawpy arms around me and says, "Don't look so sad, Sally." And I take the comfort of his warm flesh and cuddle it to me, fearing all the while that he'll think we ought to screw, but he doesn't.

We drive down to the J.C. Penney store because he wants to get a present for his little girl. I stand around while he paws through the kiddie clothes anxiously and comes up with a red sailor dress.

"What do you think of this one?" he keeps asking.

"I don't know anything about it," I say.

I wonder if his pregnant wife has gone through eight years of mauling and got knocked up twice without ever having an orgasm. She must masturbate while he's in the bathroom, I think. Or maybe she takes lovers. I almost say that to him but he is talking seriously to the saleslady about children's sizes, so I wait.

He puts the box in the back seat and we ride down the coast looking for a place that serves drinks and dinner. Dusk is falling now, the gray day sneaking out, when we pass the laundromat. It stands all by itself on the road outside the town. Rough beach grass hisses against the cinder blocks of the building, and its one big window looks across the road to the marsh that leads to the sea. We aren't going very fast. The white light inside glares over the rows of green machines and a solitary figure, with her arms outstretched, folding towels into a white plastic bucket. I catch the pink curlers in a halo around a plump face, a pale fuzzy sweater, tight pants stretched over generous haunches. Then we're past but the car is slowing. He pulls to the side of the road and stops. With the motor idling, the heater works better. He hunches over the wheel and turns his face to me.

"Did you see that?"

"The girl?"

"A simple little housewife," he says. "Her husband probably works swing shift and she waits to do the laundry until he's gone to work. We go in and start a conversation with her, take her out for a drink, and then get her to the hotel room with us."

His tense voice settles a bleak winter on my chest. Bitter winds are moving through my lungs. The marsh is spread out there with the gulls weaving black against the sky. The sheen of the shredded water fills me, and I am tired, tired.

"I've been thinking about it. It really might work." His intensity irritates me unreasonably. "With a couple," he says, "she wouldn't be scared off. Women are never afraid of a man if he's with another woman. They figure she acts as a wall governing the limits to which anything can be carried."

His glasses gleam in the last light. Do we really have to play this through? I don't want to do this. Should I want to? Does it demean my intellect not to want to? Does it show my spirit to be small and dependent if I don't want to? I don't want to do this.

"She wouldn't want to go out drinking," I sneer. "She's got her hair in curlers. It would just be a useless hassle. Women like that never feel sexy until they've got their hair combed out and their makeup on."

"But don't you see? She'd never suspect. Just because she isn't feeling sexy she'd never think we were approaching her on that basis. A smart girl like you could talk her around easily. Let's just go back and look. Do you want to?"

My eyes pour themselves out into the darkening marsh. I won't look at him anymore.

"All right," I say.

He puts the car into gear and swings around in the road. We pull up in the gravel in front of the laundromat and he kills the engine.

The fluorescent tube in the ceiling glares down onto her pink sponge helmet. She's sitting on one of the machines now, hunched over a magazine. Her pants stop six inches away from her ankles, and her feet are rubbing each other in their gaping shoes.

"She's got enormous tits," he says. He's hugging the steering wheel and squinting through his glasses at her.

"Also gut and butt," I mutter.

"What?" He turns to me.

"I say she's fat. She's got a belly like a garbage bag and an ass like the truck to carry it."

His hand waves through the window.

"She's a Titan! Look at that skin. I've never screwed a woman in curlers before. All these liberated females with their straight hair."

Is screwing people you don't like innately more pleasurable than screwing one person you don't like?

The girl on the jiggling washing machine turns a page in her magazine and reaches into her purse for a cigarette. She jabs it into her mouth and fumbles around for matches before she can light it. She goes on reading. She holds her cigarette like an old-time movie queen, sucks at it, and blows the smoke out through her nose without inhaling.

The daylight is nearly gone. Headlights whip over us and come to a stop staring at the laundromat door. A fat old lady in a square tweed coat climbs out of the station wagon and paces into the building. The girl on the washing machine looks up and blows out smoke and begins to talk. The older woman goes to the plastic basket of clothes and picks it up. The girl hops down and opens the machine she's been sitting

on, starts hauling out dirty sheets in gray armloads. She plops
them into a cardboard box, swings her purse strap over her
shoulder, and hoists the box to her hip.

The two women move out of the lighted doorway to the
car. The doors slam. The engine starts. The headlights spread
in a wide pool around us and then disappear into the night.

Mr. Lucas is looking at me with a twinkle in his spectacles. His lips are fat and red but they cover a very small
mouth. A prissy Kewpie doll mouth. I don't like his mouth at
all. I light a cigar and sit staring at the empty laundromat, its
silent machines in gaping rows, waiting.

"Well," he says. "Oh, well. What about a drink?"

I take another puff while I think about it, then reach back
into the rear seat and pull the fifth from under his daughter's
new dress. He starts the engine, and the heater comes on
again. I hadn't realized it was cold. I open the bottle and
swallow and choke and swallow a little more. As soon as I
can be sure that it won't make me puke it will have its chance
to warm me.

"I didn't mean that," he says. "I meant with some dinner."

"I really don't want any dinner," I say, with the bottle
propped up in my lap. "I think it's time I was going back."

He looks at me, surprised, wary. "Back to the school?"

"Yep." I take one last drink since it doesn't seem to be
fatal, put the cap back on, and drag at the cigar. I'm not going
to look at him anymore. He guns the car out onto the road
and rams it viciously at the center line.

I can feel a snag creeping up one leg of my tights. His
voice is doing a phony laugh above the rush of the car's noises.

"So that's what it is to be a tough broad!" He snorts. He mumbles for a while and then raises his voice again. "You crumble when you come within half a mile of confronting yourself!"

I stretch my legs as far into the heater blast as possible and lean back against the seat. The cigar glows bright in the dark of my lap. I open the window a crack and fling it out. A shower of sparks gone in an instant. I am warm. I am going home to my still bed. I can sleep.

I don't wake up until he shakes me. We are in the school parking lot. The headlights glare on the windows of my dormitory. It's raining. I yawn and reach for my purse.

"Sally." His hand on my arm. "I assume I can trust you? I've always assumed that."

His temper is over. He's scared again. I can see my own window. My anger comes up again, secure and steady.

"Look," I say. "You are a two-bit shit and I am a two-bit shit. Let's not compound the stink by speaking to each other anymore."

I climb out and shut the door. Walk through the rain to the heavy door and down the long green corridor. Warm in here. Clean. Many doors before my own. My room smells of old smoke. The door to Fern's room is closed. I won't have to face her until morning. I go to the window and look out on the parking lot, shimmering wet. "I'm never going to leave this room again," I tell myself. The window is a picture of the room. The table lamp and the bookshelf are vividly reversed in it. The doorknob glints in the black glass. But I am too close to the glass and my reflection is a silhouette surrounding the parking lot, with the glaring whites of my eyes rolling in the black.

"Ah, poor Sally," I mutter at my bleary eyes. Even when there's no place left to be hurt, it seems there is something that can be diminished, whittled away. It will probably be weeks before I can even brag about this.

The Novitiate

THE MORNING AFTER her husband left her, she baked a cake for her son's second birthday. While the cake cooled on the rack she telephoned the welfare office for an appointment. They told her to come in the next day.

"Did his leaving come as a surprise?" the caseworker asked.

"No," she said, "no, it came as a shock."

When they told her how much money she would get, she put the child into his stroller and walked out to find a cheaper place to live. The places she called didn't want children. The places she looked at had bugs. Finally she found an apartment on the ground floor of an old, converted hotel. It had two bedrooms, it was furnished, and the manager, who spoke civil grammar, assured her that there were no bugs. It had two windows, one in the living room and one in the front bedroom, but they both looked out on an alley. She paid in advance and took the keys.

That afternoon the seedy men on the porch watched her carry in the cardboard boxes from the taxi. She locked her new door and took up the bewildered child to cuddle on the strange sofa for a while. The walls seemed insubstantial. The sounds of footsteps and doors opening, coughing and voices, came to her unimpeded. A man's voice called, "Bill!" in the alley.

"Daddy?" said the child.

"No. No more," she whispered. "Just Mama now. Just you and me."

She decided to put him in the rear bedroom, though it had no window. She thought of the cold and of burglars' slipping in on him in the dark. She swept the room and washed the walls above the bed. When she turned the mattress the shape and color of its stains confused her. Her mind groped through a dark catalogue of possible sources.

The child ate his supper in silence as she watched him. She tucked him in for the night and went on with unpacking and cleaning. As she scrubbed the kitchen sink she heard a man's shrill complaints in the room beyond her walls. A lower voice muttered back. Heavy feet moved over her ceiling. A constant murmur of voices and doors and feet throbbed through the walls.

She went quickly through her clothes and folded away the tight pants and shirts her husband had liked. *I can't wear these here*, she thought. *If someone should see and want . . . with the windows so close to the ground . . .* Footsteps in the alley, a banging door. Her mind folded on a picture of her own body gutted and bleeding in a chaos of broken glass and the child screaming and screaming till his own blood stopped him. She unpacked bulky sweaters and loose skirts and hung them in her closet. She changed quickly into a long robe that sailed around her feet, and listened at the child's door until she heard his steady breathing beyond the murmur of men's voices in the halls.

She dug out her mending and a paperback with a bedraggled beauty on the cover and settled herself on the sofa. At two o'clock she woke from a doze to the sounds of vomiting in the alley and crying in the hall. *The bars must just have closed*, she thought. She stalked from door to door, checking locks and listening. She sat reading feverishly till dawn, and the child's waking was such a deep relief that she chattered mindlessly and hugged him repeatedly as she went through the morning's work. He followed her into her bedroom and rattled the knobs on the drawers.

She dressed carefully in front of a mirror, minutely altering her posture to eliminate any sign of seductiveness. She jerked her hair back and wrapped it on itself, turning it in a long knot and tucking it tightly at the back of her skull. The harsh bones of her face whitened in the mirror. *This is probably the only time in my life I'll be glad not to be pretty*, she thought. *I should take advantage of it.*

She thumbed her eyebrows into line and stood close to the glass to brush black on her lashes. In the corner of the mirror the child's face watched her gravely. She dropped the mascara brush and picked up her purse.

"Come on, honey. Get into your stroller. We're going to the store."

She locked the door carefully behind her and pushed the stroller through the gray halls toward the entrance. The dust and litter formed moraines where the walls and the floor met. The old, cracked doors with their painted knobs, the thought of the sleepers behind them, heated her face.

A tall, thin man came up the steps as she opened the outside door.

"Here—let me help you."

"Thank you."

His spotted face was abbreviated by a colorless baseball cap, the long visor shadowing the eyes and the loose mouth. Black stubble grew in patches that thinned on the slopes of his pimples. He held the door for her.

"I'm your next-door neighbor. I've been wanting to meet you. Is your husband here?"

His long arms were white below the sleeves. His hand reached out at her. She bent quickly and lifted the stroller down the steps. The child turned his face to watch the man. Her belly was cold, tight, as she clunked the stroller down on the sidewalk. Her voice was furious.

"Not right now he's not." She pushed strongly on the handles and marched away toward the corner.

"My name's Bill if you need anything!"

She didn't turn to look at him again.

She bought a mop, and a book for the child. In the hardware store she strolled through the shining fixtures. When she found the locks and chains she spent a long time reading the instructions on each package. The yellow shine of the chains pleased her, and the tidy packages with the exact number of screws and the diagrams for correct installation.

The glow of the metal seemed rich and strong to her. *I'll be careful when I paint the woodwork*, she thought. *They don't look as safe when they've been painted into the door. I'll leave them shining.*

She bought two chains and two sliding bolts, a set for each of her two doors. As soon as she'd locked the door and freed the child from his stroller she ripped the chains out of their plastic. She caught the child's eyes fastened on the one gleaming in her hand. She held it out to him. His short fingers closed on it; his eyes dug at the links and their relations. She unfolded the directions sheet and stood frowning at the instructions.

"I am not," she said, "a woman who was meant to live alone."

She waited for the boy to look up, but he was intent on the chain moving in his hands.

She pulled off her right boot and took a butter knife from a drawer. Padding and clumping, with the boot jammed under her arm, she set to work. The screws jutted from her lips. She positioned the catch on the bedroom door, put each screw through a hole and pounded it with the bootheel until it hung drunkenly in its socket. Then she dropped the boot and applied the knife, twisting the notched heads with the weight of her torso, forcing them at strange angles, the knife slipping and slicing at the paint on the door.

The child sat on the floor behind her, one shoe and sock off, carefully fitting five consecutive links of the chain over his toes. She put on the bolt and its braces before taking the chain and fastening it to the door. The child stood up to watch the last operations. Finally she dropped the chain into place and slid the bolt across. She opened the standard lock and pulled at the knob. The door rattled slightly but didn't move. Then she pulled back the bolt and opened the door on the chain. She hauled on the knob; she leaned her whole weight on the knob. She jerked and yanked at the door. The chain held. She grinned and shut the door. She slid the bolt across and moved her paraphernalia into the living room, to the door that opened onto the alley.

She had finished and closed the bolt, was in the act of dropping the chain into its slot when the boy started laughing. She stepped behind him to look out, laying her hand on his soft mat of curls. The neighbor, Bill, stood just outside the window, bent with his face to the glass, his baseball cap at an angle, his sparse teeth gaping, his fingers walking nonchalantly on the glass inches from the boy's laughing face. Her arm straightened instinctively, immediately, pushing the child hard away from the window. She snatched at the top of the curtains, pulling them together, their metal rings shrieking on the crooked rod, the cloth closing with a soft flop over the glass—closing out the colorless eyes of the man outside as he looked at her.

She stood staring at the cloth. The sweat began to cool on her face and she lifted a hand and mopped her nose, her chin, her forehead. In the dim corner where he had fallen, the child cried. He lay curled on his side with a finger in his mouth, the shine of the tears whitening his face in the curtained light, the rolling wail of his crying muted by his fierce sucking of his finger.

She bent, took him up, and stood cradling the whole

small body—his wet face on her shoulder, her own face pressed to his hair.

Children were playing noisily in the alley. The door to the next apartment opened and closed. She moved slowly about the room, holding the child. The sink next door squeaked and gushed water. A banging of pots.

"It's time for lunch," she whispered into the soft hair.

She spread peanut butter and honey on bread. She sliced a carrot and an orange and poured milk. She flicked on the flame beneath the morning's coffee. Her body moving in the thin air felt somehow removed; her head seemed to float several inches above her neck. She avoided the child's silent, somber eyes as she moved from cupboard to sink.

"Maybe we'll go out to a junk store this afternoon and find a radio. We could dance and sing then. Would you like that?"

She didn't look at him to see if there was any response.

The children were screaming in the alley. The coffee boiled and she poured a cup. A drawer was pulled out next door. Silverware rattling. She placed the plate carefully in front of the child. His hands reached for the sandwich. She held a paper towel near him and sat down opposite with the coffee.

"Bill!"

A man's voice shouting. A knock on the door down the hall.

"Bill!"

Sounds of locks disengaging. The neighbor's voice and footsteps beyond her kitchen wall. With her eyes fixed on the child, she listened. The movements in the next room ceased. The child watched her constantly, reaching and biting and chewing without looking at the food. Looking only at her. She smiled at him mechanically and went on listening.

That afternoon they went out and brought back a small radio that someone had painted white in an effort at décor. She set it on top of the refrigerator and plugged it in. The thin voices filled her with warmth. She turned it up loud and picked up the boy. Hugging him, tickling him, she turned round and round and began to dance—a slide, a slide, slow, with his head beneath her chin.

She put the boy at the table with a grocery bag and a ballpoint pen. He drew long, spastic lines and jabbed dots at them. She filled a saucepan with soapy water and washed the kitchen walls with her dishcloth. The radio played. The voices in the hall were dim. Footsteps and swinging doors became mere pressures in the air, cushioned by the breathy tunes from the box. She climbed on chairs, stood balanced on the stove, knelt on top of the refrigerator. The bold scoop and swash of the scrubbing made her feel strong. The rag swept through the deep-fried tones near the ceiling and left long swatches of dull cream. The weight of the light in the room fell away as she proceeded around the surfaces. The air grew damp and chilly with the wet seeping off the walls. The child sat jabbing tiny holes in the paper bag with the tip of the pen. He sat stolidly while she climbed upon the table to wash the walls above his head. He eyed the pan of gray water but did not leave his hole punching, not even to dip an exploratory finger.

Only when she had finished did he look at her. She emptied the pan, rinsed the cloth, peeled off her rubber gloves, and turned to him, humming. His dark eyes silenced her. His face, so noncommittal, convinced her for the full space of a minute that he hated her. She felt the blood in her face, the change in quality of the sweat that softened her skin.

"Hello, Owl!" she said.

His face moved. She pulled in air and relief. He was too young to hate her, of course. That would come later. She found a cigarette and lit it, sank into the chair across from him, and heaved in smoke and heat. Her body began to relax into gentle aches.

"Is that a picture for our walls?"

The soft solemnity of the face broke into a smile. He held up the paper bag with its mad scrawl of ink and the small, jagged holes.

"We'll put it right over the stove where I can see it while I cook."

She punched the paper bag onto the nail that held her spatula. The child began the long, groaning shove of his chair across the torn linoleum to a spot beside the stove where he could watch her cook. She measured water and salt and a cupful of the powdery oat flakes from the red-and-blue box. The blue flame of the gas ring was steady, solid. A secret heat.

She spread bread with the alarmingly yellow margarine

and set out the brown sugar box and the milk carton. As she stood watching the oatmeal thicken, pots began to bang beyond the wall. Crockery scraped in Bill's sink. Heavy footfalls jarred their common floor. She switched off the radio so that she could hear the outside noises more clearly.

His apartment must be the same as mine, yet he lives there alone. Why two bedrooms? Or maybe he's not alone, she thought.

The child stood on the chair and stared at the flame. Her eyes followed the subtle lines of his chin and lips.

He might kill me someday. Or take a gun into some high place and kill whomever he sees. So many men without fathers. Their mothers turned into hollow, sucking cores. So they say.

She folded paper towels in triangles and placed them beside the plates. She cut the bread precisely and arranged it around the steaming bowls.

"Make a hole," she said, and the child dug his spoon deep into the gray heat of the cereal and held the hole open while she poured on the milk.

She sat down and poured milk over her own cereal. She inserted the spoon and then left it turned on its side at the edge of the bowl. The boy ate, lifting his rough napkin to dab dutifully at his pursed, chewing mouth. His eyes were fixed on a point between the bowl and his mother's face.

He played while she washed the dishes. Through the wall she could hear and feel the clank of Bill washing dishes. *The apartments must be mirror images*, she thought. *His dishwater and mine flowing together in the pipes, the toilets back-to-back, the stained and peeling bathtubs side-by-side.*

His curtains were always closed when she walked through the alley. Had his hands actually been dirty as they played on the windowpane? She closed her eyes and tried to see them. No. She couldn't remember. But they seemed dirty. The whole gray figure in her mind seemed splotched and covered with mold.

She sat on the toilet lid and smoked while the child played in his bath. Footsteps made a scuffing in the hall beyond the thin paneling. Men's voices reached from the far corners of the building.

Night came. She dressed the child in pajamas and took him on her lap to look at a picture book. People walked through the alley. A woman laughed. Somewhere a child screamed in anger. She recited the old words that went with the pictures, her eyes flicking at noises, moving from lock to window. All footsteps seemed aimed at her doors. When they passed without stopping, her tension only grew. The child's bedtime went by. He lay back in her arms and began to breathe more deeply. She stopped reading and stared at him. She listened, heard a radio in the same room above her, heard arguing voices and footsteps on every side, but saw only the child and his consciousness dropping further from her, leaving her alone in the harsh glare of the bulb.

Saturday night, she thought. *They'll be crazy tonight, later, when the bars close.*

She lifted the still, small body and stood holding his warmth, looking into his heavy, blank eyes.

I could put him to bed here on the sofa—I could grab him up quicker. I wouldn't have to risk getting trapped in his bedroom with no windows and no way out.

The boy put an already puffy knuckle in his mouth.

I'm making it up, she thought. *If I begin like this, it will just go on and get worse. He has to sleep in his own bed.*

She carried him in and rolled his limp body around until he lay properly beneath the blankets. Her voice softly muttered bedtime noises. Far off in the alley a man yelled, "Bill!" Someone walked just beyond the child's wall.

She stared at the thin plaster. *Just inches. Anyone could put a fist through. It's just a screen for the eyes. They can hear me. Nearly smell me. I hear their breathing as they walk by.*

She turned out the light and closed the door, watching as the wedge of light passed over the child, leaving him in darkness. She stood listening. Voices in Bill's place. High, goofy laughter. She went the rounds of the locks, tugging at the chains. The rotting wood of the door caught her eye and she thought of it bursting open.

It would be such a grimy, dreary crime, she thought. *A smash of glass. A half-wit wandering in drunk. One of those in the building—the leavings, the siftings. Their posture marks them. The doglike expression. The wavering eyes. That Bill, with the droop of his head, the tight chin protecting his throat, the blank fear in his wrinkles. He could murder me and it would still be a feeble act. He would cry as he broke through the window. He would come at me, crouching and sobbing and begging, his shaking knife slipping in the sweat of his hands. His ribbed and spineless back jerking to plunge the knife blade into me, and then he'd go blubbering, drooling for approval to take the blood from my deep-eyed child. That would be a sin, a soul destruction, to be overcome by that filth and weakness.*

Her breath came fast and loud. She rubbed her square hands across her face and listened, thinking she might have missed a danger signal. Footsteps clicked on the cement beneath her window, quickly passing; then the pause at the neighbor's door. The male voice shouting, "Bill!" and again, "Bill!"

Why do they always yell? Won't he open the door unless he knows who they are?

She went into the bedroom and lay down to let her sweat evaporate.

At least I know where he is—busy over there with company, not peeping at my windows. She glanced casually at the pink plastic curtains, and her face sharpened in the fierce attention that was becoming habitual.

I've seen through curtains like that myself! Walking in a dark street, looking at lighted windows, I've seen through that thin fabric into rooms where no one knew I could see. And the edges don't overlap.

The black slits of glass between the curtain edges bled her like knives. She plunged off the bed and rummaged the room, her lungs aching.

I undress right here with the light on. I can't sleep in this place without a light. Sagging around looking for clothes, or lying there in that bed, so close to the window . . .

She pinned together the curtains all down their length, a puckered seam of paper clips, safety pins, straight pins, till the cracks of night were pinned out. Then she ripped the top blanket off the bed, draped it heavily over the curtain rod, and tugged it over to the farthest reaches of the molding so that the most determined eye, even pressed against the glass, could not peer past into the light where she lay not sleeping.

I suppose I don't really need to pin the curtains if I'm going to put the blanket up there. But it can't hurt.

Somewhere above her in the building a woman shouted. More footsteps pausing at the next door. No knocking, only another voice calling, "Bill," softly in the alley, and then the door opening and closing.

But he could tell them about me. They all might come over here. I am making this all up.

The pulsing blood turned from pressure to pain in her skull, in the back of her neck. She sat stiffly, staring at the blanketed window, the fear roiling thick in her belly, in the very cells of her skin.

It's not just the drunks. It's not the liquor. It's the others. The unhumans. Their awkward movements and incomprehensible intentions. Why are they all here in this building, the wormy Bills, the lone men? Because it was their first stop on the way from the bus station?

She rose and grasped the lamp in both hands, turning it upside down before her so that the shade rattled to the floor and the glaring bulb streaked her sight and smeared the room with huge, swarming shadows. She swung the lamp over her head, brought it down with mock force onto the bed, felt the limit of the cord still connected to the outlet.

I could hit him with this. If he poked his head through the window.

She dropped the naked lamp back onto the wobbling night table and went out into the living room. She arranged a wooden chair between the door and the window after swinging it over her head a few times. *If they broke through the windows, I could bash their brains out.*

She stalked into the kitchen, eyeing knives and skillets. *If they caught me in the bathroom, I could throw detergent in their faces. Empty the paper pail on them.* The image of a long figure clawing slimy diapers from his head. She laughed.

It's just men, this head in the window. No woman would frighten me. Oh, maybe if she had a gun or a knife and the child was nearby. But just for me, no. No woman. It's men I'm afraid of. The thought stilled her, made her belly heavy. She lay down on the sofa and threw twisted looks at the covered windows.

All the long years will I be this way? Will I always be afraid? Will I grow sour and frozen in my core? Go stiff-faced in the street and glower until no man speaks to me anymore and my vagina heals over from lack of use? It isn't rape, it's murder that scares me. Death.

The voices beyond the wall cackled. A sudden thump. Chairs scraping.

"You son of a bitch!" in a voice like a cough. A jumping of sounds, movement, a door flung open, men shouting, a scuffle in the alley.

"Bill, don't do that!"

"Bastard asked for it!"

"Get away from me!"

"Stop it!"

A crash and the screech of heavy metal skittering across the cement. The harsh, clear image of a gun wiped out her mind. She rolled off the sofa onto the floor and scuttled into the kitchen on her belly. She didn't breathe, her body moved without thought, crawling quickly to the child's door. She pushed with her head into the thick dark of the child's room, reached in frenzy for the tiny form beneath the blankets and dragged him, kicking, down beside her. She clutched him to her belly, turning on her side with her back to the front of the apartment, away from the horror in the alley.

These thin walls, she thought. *A bullet speeding through them.*

The child woke, jerking and yelling. His voice pushed at her arms. She felt his heat and movement and fear. Felt her own loud, hysterical breath bounce back into her face from the child's head. A siren whined in the street beyond the alley. More voices. Soft now, far away beyond the kitchen, beyond the wall of the living room. She calmed the child hurriedly, wrestled herself to her feet, held him, tucked him, already returned to sleep, beneath the blankets. She slid back out to the living room, out of range of the lamp so that her shadow would not fling itself against the curtains. She knelt beside the door to listen, her hands and ear to the door crack, feeling the chill from outside.

". . . Threatened me with that goddamn monkey wrench. I'll kill the son of a bitch next time."

"Now, Bill."

"Do you want to sign a complaint?"

"Hell, yes. Threatens a man in his own house. He was drinking my beer and watching my television!"

She crawled to the window and opened the curtain a slit. She saw the dim glinting of leather on uniforms, the withered landlord in bedroom slippers, his hands raised with the palms out, pacifying a lean shadow that must be Bill. And there in the puddle of light from her own window lay a long-mouthed wrench. She crawled to the sofa and lay flat with her arms limp.

"I am so tired," she whispered.

Lowered voices. Footsteps going away. A car starting. The manager sympathizing with Bill.

"I'd never have rented him a room if I'd known he was violent."

"Oh, the whole damn joint is full of weirdos. And will you ask that sow that's just moved in next to me not to start her kid screaming and banging on pans until at least six in the morning?"

She sat up. She rose—numb, blank—and went directly to the stove in the kitchen. She opened the oven door and knelt down in front of it. She pulled out the wire racks, stood them against the stove, laid her chest and belly down across the oven door, and cradled her head gently on her folded arms inside the oven.

"Sow," she said. The soft word was cushioned in the black box. "Sow."

The ache of her body welled into her head and seeped out around her hot eyes. She could feel the exact dimensions of her eyes as the tears rolled over them. She widened her lids to let the warm wet wash the white ball of each eye. She felt the muscles straining to focus in the strange perspective of the black box. She felt the grit of the oven floor against her arms and fingers and saw, finally, blearily, the black crust on the ridges of the oven walls. She pulled her head out and sat up. She leaned on her arms to stare hard into the oven. The tears still blinded her and she rubbed them out of her eyes impatiently.

The thick sludge of months or years had its black grip on the enameled metal. She ran her fingers along the back wall and behind the gas jets. A long, shining roach ran out over her hand, up her arm, and when she flinched, it dropped with a tap to the floor, where it disappeared beneath the garbage pail.

"My God," she muttered.

She got up and turned on the little radio. Voices spread soft and thin through the room. She filled a pan with hot water, put on her rubber gloves, took up her pot scrubber and the ammonia bottle, and thoroughly, fiercely, cleaned the oven.

A Revelation of Mrs. Andes

THE BUILDING and the neighborhood were new to me, though old on their own. My personal losses had been adding up and it was a cheap haven to skulk and lick my scabs. I defended my injured pride by despising my neighbors and emphasizing what I secretly felt were rather paltry distinctions between us. I spoke to strangers only formally, as required for survival. I manufactured a steady cheerfulness for the benefit of my little son, and I watched the people in the other apartments surreptitiously like an animal, prey for some and predator to others.

Mrs. Andes always passed my windows on her way to the laundry room. At first I only saw her fat and the pink sponge rollers that made even her head look fleshy. She swayed with the clothes basket so that it seemed an extension of her globular body.

It was weeks before I recognized her at the playground, pushing a huge-eyed, dark-haired child in a stroller. She swayed still, walking slowly. Her eyes flicked shyly at the other mothers. I shoved resolutely at my child's swing and didn't respond to her glance. She spoke to no one; no one spoke to her. I began to notice how clean she was, how the rollers disappeared fairly early every morning and left a smooth cap of curls, and how smooth her loose dresses were. She wore flat sandals with a thong between the toes but I never looked long at the area below her hem. It seemed kinder not to concentrate on her legs.

The other women from our building bore a constant odor of beer or baby puke. It was her cleanliness that attracted me. I often stationed myself near the window at ten in the morning to watch her laundry parade. Afternoons in the park I prattled mindlessly next to the sand pile and watched her slow progress behind the stroller. She wore carefully applied makeup. In the mornings her face was bare and clean, but in the afternoons her eyes had an extra depth and light and the small mouth was tinted. She was a pretty creature when you looked. Her dark brows arched in perfect proportion, her arm tapered to a wrist so fine and a hand so small they seemed absurd appended to her bulk.

A month must have passed before I spoke to her. She was walking near me in the park. I raised a hand and said, "How old is your little boy?" She was shy, her skin flushed, eagerness and hesitance formed together in her face. She was so pleased to speak that I congratulated myself smugly for my own kindness. We discussed the scarcity of fresh air for apartment children. Her grammar was unobtrusive. She was anxious to admire my superior education. I invited her to my kitchen for coffee.

I am one of those who are at ease only on their own terrain, who fidget miserably in other people's houses and cannot speak openly in public places. As a result I attract those who, for whatever reason, prefer to get out of their own rooms. Such was Susan Andes. She extended a series of polite invitations to her apartment, which I politely refused. The formalities observed, she settled happily into visiting me regularly without expecting me to call on her.

It was always midmorning, when the basic housework was done and my coffeepot was hot, when I would hear the wheels of her stroller squeal in the corridor outside my door, the soft shuffle of her step, her discreet knock. We smiled and petted each other's sons. Then we would set the two children creeping about the floor together while we sat at the red-painted table with the goldfish bowl between us. Coffee. Cigarettes. A haze of confidence. There is a ritual to the progress of acquaintance: a discussion of grocery prices, exchange of recipes, admiration for each other's children, description of the neighbors' lifestyles. We agreed fiercely on the necessity of keeping our floors and persons clean to distinguish ourselves from the neighbors. This led to revelations of pride: "They whittle away at you—you have to fight for the core," I said. "If I don't bathe every night and set things to rights, I feel sick and dead," she said.

It doesn't take long. A couple of visits a week, a couple of weeks. There must be a decent trading of reminiscences so neither party feels her secrets have been stolen or become burdensome to the other. There was a homogenous, healthy glow to her skin, and yet it sometimes seemed an effort for her to focus. She never arrived at the door without some pretext, usually a gift—half a cake or a plate of cookies, which she begged me to take so she wouldn't eat it. She was a good cook. She disguised her anxiety to talk, or not to be alone, but the look on her face if I told her I was too busy was painful to me; she evaporated. Yet there was something else, a hesitation, the way she studied my face at times, that made me think she wanted to tell me something. She was holding something back.

I was curious. Our conversation had been fascinating but impersonal: first menstruation, the gradual change in the shade of infant feces, scorn for dirty houses, and horrified sympathy with child abusers. I had learned her opinions and some quite specific facts about her physique, but without the usual accompaniment of biographical data. One day I mentioned psychiatric treatment and referred to the therapy sessions I had indulged in in my youth. A wrinkle appeared in her round forehead. Her mouth pursed. "You've been in therapy?" she questioned.

"Yes, for years."

She leaned forward on the table. "I'm on tranquilizers all the time," she said. "I was in the state mental hospital a year and a half ago." Her small teeth caught her lip, her eyes peered up at me, waiting for my reaction.

"That must have been interesting," I said. "What was wrong?"

I won't pretend I didn't look at her more sharply, didn't think of how helpless I would be against her bulk if she went berserk and murdered me or my child. My eyes swiveled to the babies on the floor and I calculated the distance and direction of the door, but it wasn't personal. I've suspected all my life that every passerby and chance acquaintance was capable of mayhem without warning. There was nothing about her that increased my worry, only what she told me, and with apparent relief.

"My mother is an alcoholic. For years now she's been in a kind of home, you know what sort. I lived with her until I was fifteen. I tried to take care of her. I'd come home from school and cook for her, I'd try to wash her and feed her, but sometimes, a lot of times, she pushed me away and screamed. I've always been afraid of that happening to me. But when I was fifteen the state put her in the institution, and I went back east to live with my father and stepmother. At first I thought it was wonderful in their home. Everything was clean. They bought me clothes and I had a room of my own. The house was nice and they had a girl just a few years younger than me. I went to school. But it wasn't good. He drank, too, and there was some bad feeling about me. I've never been able to figure out exactly why or even what it was. I helped as much as I could. But when I was eighteen, I thought I'd come back out here. My older brother lives out here. We'd always written letters to each other. I had a part-time job and saved some money. I came out here on the bus.

"But my brother is married and has little kids and there really wasn't room in his house. I got an apartment and found a job as a receptionist. I learned to operate a switchboard. Right after that my brother moved his family down south. I was lonely. There was this guy, Mark. He was very handsome. I suppose I went kind of crazy over him. He introduced me to his brother and his father. Mark disappeared without saying anything to me but his brother came to see me. Then the brother went. David. He and Mark had some logging job down on the coast. Their father started visiting me. It all happened in about one month. Then I was pregnant.

"Andy, Mark's father, kept coming around. I kept my job. It didn't show for a long time. I wrote to Mark and told him. He isn't the sort to write letters. I didn't know what to do. I told Andy and he said he would stick by me. I kept working but I was afraid. How could I take care of a baby? The people at work probably thought I was just getting fatter and fatter. I didn't have any friends at all. I just sat in my room when I wasn't at work. I cried a little and ate a lot.

"Then one day as I was walking past the Evergreen Bar I saw Mark come out with this girl. I ran up to him but he said, 'Oh God! The cow!' and gave me such a look. I couldn't say anything. I just turned around and went home to my apartment. I couldn't think. I felt as though my brain was boiling, everything moving and breaking. Then I got this idea, it's loony but I really believed it, that the landlady of my apartment house was holding my mother prisoner and torturing her. I could hear her screaming to me. I went running downstairs and beat on the landlady's door. Nobody answered but I could hear the screaming. I knew it was my mother. I went outside and threw a hubcap through the window. I crawled in and looked around for my mother. I was very angry. I could hear her. I broke all the mirrors and tore the clothes down from the closets. I broke a lot of things, throwing them everywhere. Then the police came. I suppose it must have been me screaming. The neighbors had called them. They took me to the state hospital.

"It was a kind of fit. By that evening I was over it but very shaky. More than anything else, I felt embarrassed. I was in the ward where they kept violent patients because of what I'd done. There were a lot of . . . strange . . . people there. If I'd spent much time with them I'd be just like that. There was a nice woman, Mrs. Jeffries, I'm not sure whether she was a nurse or social worker, she had me moved after a few days. She gave me jobs to do and came to talk to me. My baby was born there three weeks later. I was worse for a while after Joey came. The welfare people put him in a foster home right away. I didn't tell any of my family. They didn't know anything about the situation. The only one who knew where I'd gone was Andy. He came down to see me a few times and he went to visit Joey at the foster home. For about two months Mrs. Jeffries tried to figure out a way for me to leave the hospital and have Joey. They didn't want to release me without someone claiming responsibility for me. Andy said he would marry me, but the social worker kept telling me that I shouldn't marry him unless I really wanted to. Andy is sixty-four, so the age difference is a lot. Finally I decided that Andy loved Joey and he was very kind and gentle. It seemed important to have a family life. I didn't think I was still working when it happened. They arranged for me to get Social Security benefits since I'm classed as unemployable now. And, since I didn't know whether it was Mark or his brother or Andy who was Joey's father, I got a Social Security payment for him too."

Her soft face was serious as she spoke. I felt I had to interrupt.

"Do you mean you don't know whether your husband is your child's father or his grandfather?"

"That's right," she said. Her delicate brows tilted anxiously.

"That's marvelous!" I grinned. "It has real flair!" How else was I to take it without making things worse for her? She shifted her shoulders back and lifted her head a little. There was a bit of surprise in her face.

"I guess you could look at it that way," she said.

"It's worthy of an Egyptian princess!" I said.

Joey toddled up to her with a small toy and leaned against her to examine it, turning the colorful thing, lifting it to his mouth to bite at it. Her hand rested gently on his neck. My son finished tying the bathroom doorknob to the refrigerator door handle and swung cheerfully on the tangled string.

"I worry about whether I can be a good mother to Joey, whether I'm liable to start hearing and seeing things again."

The child leaned against her casually. She told me then about the pills she took morning and evening and her monthly group therapy sessions. It seemed these séances consisted of comparing the effects of the pills, discussing solutions for the constipation they caused, and an occasional furtive question to the social worker who advised about dealing with government welfare and medical bureaus.

"Who declares you cured?" I asked. "How do they decide when you don't need the pills anymore?"

She didn't know. The question frightened her. She'd just had her unemployable status renewed for another six months,

which insured the continuation of the checks. I congratulated her on the good luck. She relaxed even more and spoke
of her hatred for the pills. They made her feel dopey and
doubtful that she was in command of herself. "What if this
haystack of a building caught fire? Or one of the drunks in
the hall finally decides to smash in my door one night? I don't
know if I'd be able to get Joey out safely. I can't be sure. I
think sometimes of him screaming and burning in his crib
while I stand in the street wondering what it is I've forgotten." The expression in her dark eyes was bleak and focused.

A trickle of horror communicated with my spine. "But
don't you know?" I said. "We all feel that."

And for fifteen minutes more we shuddered and laughed
at our common night fears, then she took Joey back to their
apartment for his nap.

It was not the sort of neighborhood where one lightly in-
quired about the occupations of a new acquaintance. Women
formed fierce friendships quickly; one waited on the steps for
another to walk down the street with her; small groups gathered beneath the trees in the park on hot days; pairs paraded
the aisles of the local grocery. But I had always the sense when
I spoke with them in the laundry or exchanged nods in the
park that a set of raw tentacles extruded from them all, and
that to brush the tip of any of them, however unintentionally,
would cause a hysteric explosion. How they maneuvered
around each other I don't know. Some peculiar agility must
be endemic to chewing gum and regular beer consumption.
For myself, I would envision some moment of awkward silence in a conversation that would prompt me to say, "And
what does your husband do?" like a pocket canary, only to be

answered with a snarl of, "Not a goddamn thing!" followed by a stream of invective confidences.

I never gave it a try and may have imagined the whole range of vulnerabilities, but with Susan Andes I could never bring myself to ask. I had never seen her husband, Andy, but knowing that he was forty years older than her invoked antique clichés and a vision of a large, blowsy cherub, a kind of elderly counterpart to her, though I felt a malevolent prejudice sufficient to assume that he was untidy at least and perhaps a slob. I was snidely curious about him. It seemed obvious to me why a man in his position, aging and alone, would marry Susan, but still the business of who had sired the child struck me as something that might affect a man oddly, or happen to an odd man.

It is also true that, having received the tale that she had so obviously needed to confide, my interest in Susan slackened. She had done her turn, had entertained me; it didn't occur to me that she was capable of an encore.

But she was a pleasant and decent girl, and I wouldn't have hurt her for a good deal. It was therefore necessary to be even more jovial and hospitable after she had sprung her revelation than before. If she suspected that I had a faint uneasiness in her presence, that I watched her eyes to assure myself that she had taken her sedatives, and felt an intestinal spasm if she was alone in the room with my child for two minutes, she would feel cruelly injured.

Besides, I wasn't sure I believed any of it. I believed her calm eyes and the way Joey climbed on her as though she were upholstered wood. I guarded my reactions and was glad to see her become more relaxed in my kitchen. It must have been a great relief to hesitantly and painfully tell me what she most feared, despised, and was ashamed of in herself and have me declare it fascinating, original, and a cause for yet greater sympathy and interest than I had shown before.

I could also understand that it would be worthwhile to pay for such a pleasure. She brought great platters of brownies; she knitted mittens for my son. She carefully spaced her visits so as not to become burdensome. She came twice a week, the hissing steps in the hall outside, the knock, the pretext, a cake or two pounds of bananas too ripe to keep. We met more often at the park, but always casually. No intense discussions emerged under the open sky. We both needed a small place for that, with walls and soft light; she couldn't talk in the open and I couldn't listen. In the park we only nodded and smiled and complimented each other's children.

As far as I knew, she visited no one else, had no other friends. Her humility seemed terrible to me. It was frightening, like watching a baby toddle toward a fire.

The manager of the building received and sorted all the mail and each tenant was required to appear at the office window in the rickety entrance hall to ask for their letters. On the first of each month a long embarrassing line coiled down the hall of tenants waiting for welfare checks. The manager's wife doled them out from the window, holding on to the green envelope and tapping them on the counter to punctuate her good advice to each recipient. She was a carefully groomed, complacent woman who did her best to govern the conduct of all those who paid to live in her building. That they were drunks and half-wits, deserted wives and the congenitally poor, fulfilled her caretaking needs thoroughly. She could never have been so satisfied ruling an employed or employable population. Her behavior gave the impression that she personally was the source of welfare, and that if she was not gratefully acknowledged the check would somehow disappear.

Usually I refused to stand in this line, willed myself to wait another hour for my mail, or until the line had wrung itself out. But sometimes my impatience and a certain curiosity induced me to wait among the others, watching and listening. Mrs. Levins never attempted to offer me advice. I kept my mouth straight and my eyes steady; I gilded my already distinct diction to speak with her. It was a matter of dignity, and she responded civilly by treating me as an equal. I was ridiculously and secretly proud of the respect with which she treated me, but kept ready a series of phrases in case one day as she handed me my green envelope she ventured to tap it on the counter and comment on the way I dressed my son, my personal cleanliness, or probable diet. "I beg your pardon!" I planned to say.

The lone bewildered men in the building she pointedly advised of the existence of the laundry facilities on the ground floor. I saw her order an alcoholic mute to bring his TV dinners to her for heating in her oven. For every mother she had a caustic comment about nourishment, hygiene, or the pearls of bad companions. Each time I waited there I saw Susan Andes, fresh from chatting pleasantly to me, turn, blush, and approach the window for her check in red-faced agony at the inescapable moral that accompanied it. I have seen her clench her plump lip in pearly teeth and exude a faint dew over the curve of her forehead as Mrs. Levins, with maternal unction, commanded her to "Take Joey out to the park every single day. His little limbs will not develop strongly, nor will they be straight, unless he gets regular fresh air and exercise. Every time I pass your window he is just sitting in his crib, and he is so pale. The exercise will help you, also, if you are sincere in wishing to lose weight."

Susan bobbed her flushed face, plucked hesitantly at her envelope, and said, "Yes, of course, you're right, Mrs. Levins. I will," before she turned away and dodged the bodies in line to escape to Joey, waiting and smiling in his stroller.

I raged about these scenes, grew angry with Susan for taking it, spouted long diatribes of what she should have said if she'd had any sense, carefully dissected Mrs. Levins's personality and mannerisms in the most degrading style to convince Susan that Mrs. Levins had no right to humiliate her so, and spent an hour in the evening staring out my window without seeing while I thought of crushing remarks to deliver in case advice was ever offered to me in those terms.

Susan was grateful for my fierce defense and touched that I noticed her embarrassment, but she was also sure that Mrs. Levins meant well. "And, since Joey is my first child, I really feel that she's right to try to help. She's had four kids and knows so much more than I do."

She took Joey to the park every afternoon that it didn't rain. Every month she bought three women's magazines and read devoutly the articles that advised how not to ruin your children or how to rescue them and yourself if you'd already botched the job. She had three scrapbooks, beautifully organized and ornamented: a blue one for articles, quotations, columns, and remembered wisdom on the subject of child-care and development; a yellow one on the theme of Joey himself, snapshots, growth record, first curls, birthday cards, hand- and footprints, and a record in her own precise hand of his cute doings. The third scrapbook was devoted to groom-ing, fitness, makeup, and "charm."

When she brought these remarkable volumes to show me I was genuinely impressed by the degree of care and the amount of work she had put into them. I asked her if Andy made as much of an effort to be a good parent and whole person as she did.

She blinked and looked at the fishbowl. She seemed bewildered.

"Andy doesn't have to. He's not crazy," she said. "Andy loves Joey. He plays with him and talks to him."

Her eyes followed the small lazy movements of the fish.

I stared at her in silence. Finally, she lifted her eyes to me and shook her head a little, then sighed openly, her small white teeth just gleaming beneath her careful lip.

"It's very different for Andy because he's already brought up a family."

"The two boys?" I prodded.

"Yes, and a girl." She lifted her coffee cup to her mouth and her eyes smiled at me, exonerating me from the causes of her hesitation.

"Andy is very fond of Mark and David. Those are his two boys. Mark was the one, you know . . . I . . . that I . . . It's strange to be his stepmother now. Sometimes they come to visit, always together. They go out drinking with Andy and then come back to sleep on the floor in the living room. I always make a big supper for them and try to act as though we are all the same family, but it feels odd, and they never stay long. They both work in logging down the coast and Andy wants us to go and live with them. He has this dream of a big enough house so that we can all live together. Mark and David would have their own rooms and pay part of the rent. Last weekend they visited and Andy was out with them all Saturday night. They didn't come back until Sunday afternoon, very drunk. They ate the supper I had made and took Andy with them when they drove back down. They had to be at work on Monday morning. He came back on the bus Wednesday saying he'd found a house and we were going to move. He was supposed to wait for Mark to drive up and help but Mark never came. Finally we got a message from Mark that his pickup had to have a complete overhaul and he wouldn't be able to come up or spend any money on moving till he got the work paid for. Andy is very disappointed."

She studied her carefully manicured fingers where they curled around the cup's handle.

"But how do you feel about living with those two?" I asked. "Wouldn't it be a strain living so close to somebody who's treated you . . . ?" My tact failed me. She blinked once, quickly, a glimmer of something.

"I don't feel very motherly toward them, I'll admit." She took a drink and looked behind her to where our two little sons were seated on the kitchen floor, deeply engrossed with colored wooden blocks.

She continued, "But I don't want to come between Andy and his sons. They are important to him. I don't really know . . ." She wrapped the cup in her hands and stared into it. "It's been hard for Andy. He'd like to give his sons nice things, cars and stereos. And for Joey and me, too, he'd like to do things. But it's very hard to save on what we have. He's tried to work but he has this rash on his hands that flares up every time."

It was hard for her to believe in the rash. I could see it in the effort of her frown. Some days she truly believed, when he had been kind or said something pleasant to the child as he sat on his knee. But other times it seemed that fine lip of hers wanted to sneer. But she would have felt traitorous if I suggested the rash was just an excuse to not work. She would have defended him and I would have flattered her and we would have agreed at last that it was possible that the rash was false. Then she would go home feeling awful. So I decided not to latch on to her suspicions.

"What kind of rash is it?" I asked.

"An allergy. He worked at the bag factory for years, all the time the boys were little. But when he went back to it, the burlap made his hands sting and itch. They took him off the machines and had him doing janitorial work, but the disinfectants and cleaners made his hands even worse, so he had to quit.

"We've been able to live on my Social Security payments but my case is being reevaluated in another month and I can't be sure they won't say I can go to work. I'm still taking the medication, but it's been over two years now and nothing's happened. I mean I haven't gone berserk again or anything, so . . ."

The line between her brows deepened. She looked at me anxiously for assurance. "How could I leave Joey?"

She went home soon after that. My own life was thin and strained at the time, but she allowed me to feel more competent, whole, and wise than I generally had a right to. My sympathy for her was so strong that it surprised me. I thought of her loneliness with guilt since I could not bring myself to visit her. The turmoil of her situation awed me in a way. My own problems seemed clean and comprehensible by comparison. The thought of presiding over such a supper as she had served to her husband and his sons, her lovers, made me taste my own stomach. I told myself she could put up with it because of the constant intake of drugs.

Finally I saw Andy. He was standing in the entrance of the building one afternoon as Susan and I returned from the park. Susan pushed ahead with Joey's stroller and called goodbye to me. He came toward her and reached down to touch Joey's face. Susan said, "I thought you'd still be asleep, Andy," and they walked away together. I stood watching. It must have been bulk by association. I had imagined him as large and slovenly. He was short and very thin. His face was even youthful, his hair was sparse and white, and his eyes as pale as water. I remembered I had actually seen him before, on the street somewhere or in the hall. I had been struck by his vanity. His clothes were cotton work drabs, but they were starched and pressed. The sleeve cuffs were rolled up at a precise angle, exposing his wrists and a large watch. His skin was pale, the hair on his arms was white, and his shoes were thin and cheap, and highly polished.

This dapper little character seemed suddenly hilarious to me as he strolled away beside the discreetly covered but distinctly spherical young woman.

She was genuinely angry once. She must have been rather proud of the emotion and brought it over to share it with me. Andy had seized her savings to give to his son Mark. She had, painfully, over many months, put one hundred dollars into a bank account. She meant it as a lever for the future, a pivot toward some positive movement, a better house, a new neighborhood. But the engine of Mark's truck needed to be replaced. She allowed her anger to color her voice and there was a decisive snap to her gestures and expressions. It delighted me. She was usually so distressingly meek.

"Mark's got a good job and nobody to support but himself! Andy wants to play bountiful Papa!"

I was glad of a chance to talk viciously about the men in her life and cheered her on. But in the days afterward she was placid again, said she hoped to be paid back. I came to suspect that her temper had been an imitation of my own, more of a compliment to me than an expression of herself.

She was not the sort who generally rail about their husbands. She was far too diffident, and accepted all his faults and weaknesses as her own rather than try to distribute blame. She was so grateful there was a man in her house, a father for her child, and was so frightened of being left alone that she rarely allowed herself an angry thought about Andy. She turned all impulses of that kind at herself.

When she told me she thought he was an alcoholic, it was

with a grief and guilt that made it seem like it was her affliction. Apparently, since they were married and had moved into the building, Andy had always gone out at night to the Green Spot, a tavern across the street. After Joey was asleep he sat with Susan watching television until she went to bed at nine-thirty or ten; she had to get up early with the child. Then Andy left. She rarely heard him come in, but then she always took a mild sleeping pill. It seemed reasonable to her that he needed more companionship than she and the baby could offer. She knew he had friends at the tavern. She woke beside him each morning and got up as quietly as possible. Andy usually woke by noon and ate lunch with them.

"I don't really mind because it gives me time to get cleaned up and do most of the work," she said.

I thought of her morning curlers and trips to the laundry room.

"But last Saturday morning he wasn't there when I woke up. He hadn't come home. I was afraid. Something might have happened, an accident, I thought of him dead and nobody knowing who he belonged to. I thought he might have done something. By that night I was half wild. I couldn't sleep. Sunday morning I thought about calling the police. I was afraid to do that, too. He came in at around two in the afternoon, very cheerful and still drinking. He had some people from the tavern waiting outside in their car and he wanted me and Joey to come with them on this picnic to the river. He'd never invited me to meet any of his friends before, and we'd never been on a picnic, so I got Joey ready and we went. There were two other couples. Older people like Andy. There was a lot of food but none of them ate anything.

They just drank. I couldn't talk with them or anything, though they were very nice. But it was good to be at the river. I took Joey in wading. He loved it and sat down in the sand and buried his feet. But then Andy passed out and they took us home. The men brought him into the bedroom and laid him on the bed. He stayed there till after supper the next night. Then he showered and dressed before he went out again.

"Now it keeps happening. He's out again right now, didn't come home last night. He doesn't eat much at all. He's getting very thin. And he smells bad. He's always very clean, but now when he's asleep in the bedroom for a while with the door closed, if I go in to get something, it's as though he's breathed out all the inside of his stomach, and it fills the room. There are purple veins that come out on his nose and cheeks, too."

Her soft face was flushed with worry. I wondered how she was when she wasn't taking tranquilizers. Maybe a little more flexible in her moods, but not much different. She would never be a true-hearted complainer or a nag. Her embarrassment with her person was too ingrained and her sympathy too broad.

During this same visit, with the cups and the fishbowl between us, she told me about Andy's time in prison. It was nearly a year after our first meeting, and while she had never hinted at the business before, she delivered it in the same matter-of-fact tone that she would have used to discuss the price of tea or her monthly cramps. Her tension and anxiety at telling me of her breakdown had been complete and genuine. She must simply have felt that this peccadillo of Andy's was not at all shameful compared with her own period of instability.

Andy had been in the state penitentiary for eleven years and had been released only four years before, exactly one year before he'd met Susan. He had been convicted of having repeated sexual congress with his fourteen-year-old daughter, the sister of his two sons.

"Oh, he did it, but she wanted it, too. She was completely willing," said Susan. And this seemed to finish the question for her. The trial had evidently been painful. Andy's first wife had forced the daughter to testify that Andy had forced her . . . The wife had, of course, obtained a divorce. The girl was grown, married, and three times a mother. Of course Andy never saw her. Susan thought this was a large part of Andy's deep attachment to his sons, the broken family.

My reactions to incest are perhaps exaggerated, but Susan's seemed nonexistent. She would have been horrified and very surprised if I had allowed my disgust to register at all. I had gained her trust by responding cheerfully and with fascination with what she considered the darkest and vilest weakness in herself, and if I had displayed how aghast I was at this revelation concerning Andy, it would have startled and dismayed her. I had worked hard to see her at ease in my house and I couldn't risk alarming her or having her think she had offended me. I sat nodding and shaking my head sympathetically.

She was worried, it seemed, that the years in prison had undermined Andy's health. And surely the long separation while his boys were growing up made him more anxious now to establish and maintain a close relationship with them. His inability to work and help the boys financially depressed him. Susan felt that all of this, combined with being surrounded by a community of drunks, had conspired to create in Andy a hopeless alcoholism. Still, she distrusted her own anxiety. Her mother had been a genuine nonfunctioning drinker and Susan's horror of the condition led her to imagine the tendency in herself and anyone she saw with a beer on a hot day. Did I think she was perhaps exaggerating Andy's situation out of fear?

I murmured my puzzled commiseration and she looked at the clock, wondering if he might be home and need help getting to bed.

When she went away, I brooded. The ugliness in her life seemed to peel up in thicker and more poisonous layers than I was equipped to deal with. I thought the incest was an ironic precedent for his ambiguous relationship with little Joey, and further clarified his reasons for marrying a woman forty years younger. I sat fuming at the walls in revulsion. I had seen the man only twice at a distance. I knew nothing of his personality, could not envision a single characteristic gesture, nor guess at his usual expression. The nature of his grammar was a complete mystery. Only these deeds and the awkwardness of his juncture with Susan formed any kind of profile for me, and all that came from her, through her eyes. The acute tidiness of his person was all I had seen for myself. Susan's simplicity was apparent. I could not suspect her of inventing all these complications, though I tried the idea on for size. The prospect of her isolation in dealing with her life seemed appalling. Whatever my own circumstances, a certain crass confidence always allowed me to continue a few friendships. My family were near and I was smug about my sanity, but still my fears in the night at the rough sounds inside the building reached a pitched tremolo. For Susan—her mother gibbering, her father with his back to her thousands of miles away, her brother finding it inconvenient to care for her, and her glaze of humiliation forming an obstacle to casual friendship—the days must have weighed like stone. The nights she avoided with television and rich, secret foods and her busy tending to scrapbooks and clothes needing mended—and finally a pill to turn it all off.

The admission about Andy made me look at her differently. I know she saw no change in my face and felt, if anything, a warmer interest emanating from me: I saw her in the park and our two small boys sat side by side in the sand; I brought her a recipe or we shared an orange. But I was suspicious. Her situation pained me. Her prospects bewildered me. But I could not help but feel that her acceptance of them was a condoning as well. And her conviction of her own incompetence was not foreign to me. Though she was the worker, the tidier, the nurse and cook, though her cheer made the days begin against their will, I knew well that she could not see it and that she felt that Andy was a true crutch to her, rather than a phantom stick.

Andy's drinking became constant and she sometimes thought of leaving him or throwing him out, but as she spoke of it the fear would bite at her and she would conclude with her stalwart panacea, "He loves Joey. And we are a family."

I could not prevent myself from despising her. In her

weakness she seemed willing to accept everything, to con-
done, gloss over, ignore, and avoid rather than act alone. Her
fears frightened me.

Weeks passed and Andy's binges lengthened. Once Susan
asked him to stop it. He was apologetic and ashamed. He
promised. He sat around the house for three nights and then
announced that she was crazy, left, and stayed out for three
days. His habit whittled dangerously at their limited income.
He took money from her purse and ransacked the house if
she hid it. He took longer to wake up each time he came
home. She shuddered as she told me about cleaning him
when he had fouled himself and the bed in a stupor. These
confidences were for my benefit. I was delighted to hear of
any man's vileness and encouraged her. She would never have
spoken so openly without encouragement. There were times
when I wanted to slam the table and shout, "Get out! Leave
him before you really go crazy!" But as soon as the excitement
of talking had worn off she would have torn herself apart
with guilt for having allowed the revilement of her husband.
I also recognized the degree of my own bitterness and suspected it colored my judgment ever so slightly.

But her grooming never failed by so much as an eyelash
and her tenderness with Joey was never shaken.

At last one day she came to ask me to babysit. It was her
birthday and she had asked Andy to take her out for a drink
at one of the bars he frequented. She was glowing with

excitement. I made my grimace private and agreed to keep Joey that evening.

When she came to drop him off I saw Andy lurking palely down the hall, waiting for her. Her dress was lovely though huge, and her round head and face gleamed with the slightly tinselly effects she considered appropriate for evening. The length of her lashes, the color of the shadow she used on her eyelids, the gay glass pin in her curls, all made me sad. She was twenty-four that day.

She kissed Joey, gave me instructions and warnings about his habits, kissed him again, and then waved, smiling as she went off down the hall to where Andy waited in his neatly creased shirt with the sleeves rolled up over the tattooed hearts on his forearms.

My son was already asleep. I put Joey down in my bed and banked him with pillows. He stared gravely at me and gravely went to sleep.

I made myself comfortable with my regular evening coffee, cigarettes, and a book on the sofa. I dozed and read and smoked. I decided, flippantly enough, that Susan's main objection to Andy's carousing was that she didn't get to. At around eleven I heard the rain begin. It began softly and brought the wind with it.

At a few minutes past twelve there was a tap at the door. Though I expected Susan, I opened the door on the chain. Her dripping face peered at me. I slipped the chain quickly and let her in. Her hair hung down in short hanks that streamed water. Her dress was soaked and ruined. There was an odd bruised look around her eyes that showed the fate of the careful makeup. She bit her lip.

"Excuse me for dripping on your floor!" she said. Her eyes were red. Her nose trickled a transparent stream.

"Did you get this wet between here and the bus?" I exclaimed.

"I walked," she said.

I stopped gaping and dodged into the bathroom for a towel.

She smiled gratefully and began toweling her hair. "Would you mind if I used your bathroom to wash a little? I feel horrible."

"Please, of course! But are you all right?"

"Yes, fine really. Is Joey okay?"

"He went right to sleep. Calm as—but, Susan . . ."

She stood before the sink, her great arms moving vigorously as she lathered her face with soap. She rinsed repeatedly, meticulously, with the cloth.

I stood behind her, watching in the mirror. When her face was clean and dry she was pale. Only her eyes were red. She took a comb from her purse and laid her hair in straight damp lines. Her dress still dripped. As I surreptitiously slid the bath mat toward the puddles, I saw her feet. The legs were spattered with mud halfway to the hem of her dress. The heel was missing from one of her small shining shoes, and the other bore a broad crack across the instep. I fetched a loose robe and a pair of socks.

"No, I don't want to bother you. I'll go straight home. I just couldn't think with my face and hair such a mess."

"Do put them on. Joey's asleep and you look like you could use a cup of something."

Her eyebrows peaked and she smiled feebly. "I certainly could."

My sympathy is always assisted by curiosity. I made a pot of bouillon and poured her a cup just as she emerged from the bathroom.

"I've hung my dress inside on the shower curtain. I'm sorry to have wet your floor."

The robe barely reached around her. The socks were thick rather than fashionable. She did not make an elegant effect, but there was something demure and restrained about her in this disarray. My mother would have said she was ladylike. Not perhaps a lady, not quite. But in every gesture, thought, and deed, she was ladylike.

She sat and crossed her ankles and drank her beef tea and told me in the mild fashion that was her most bitter tone what had become of her birthday.

As a surprise Andy had taken her to a Chinese restaurant. When they arrived, the two couples who had picnicked with them were there waiting. Andy talked to them all through the meal, ate nothing, but drank beer. When they got up to leave, Susan slipped her wallet to Andy so he could pay and whispered that he should keep it for the rest of the evening.

"I thought he was trying to be nice," she said.

The restaurant was only a few blocks from our building and they had walked to get there. When they left they all piled into the old car that belonged to the others and rattled off to a popular tavern called The Beaver, a mile or so away. The Beaver's attractions include a jukebox and a small dance floor. The bartender called Andy by name and brought him boilermakers without asking. Susan sipped a pink iced drink and sat watching and listening. No one spoke to her directly. Andy and the other two men talked about cars and ball games. The two women interjected harsh comments from time to time, speaking only to the men, ignoring each other and Susan. She was willing to be happy, was still happy. The other two women watched the dancers and tapped their fingers on the sides of their glasses in time to the music. Susan smiled and watched the dancing and tapped her glass. The other glasses were refilled but Susan's ebbed slowly.

"I was happy. I didn't want to get drunk. I haven't been out at night for a couple of years."

Men came up to the table and spoke to Andy. His language slurred and grew steadily coarser. Susan asked him if he would like to dance. "We've never danced together," she said. Andy rose and she stood up, but he staggered away to the men's room. She sat down again, her blood roaring under her skin.

It was all interesting to her: the faces, the room, the carved initials and words on the wooden table of their booth. She told herself it was all colorful enough without dancing. "I would have looked like an escaped cow and been ridiculous, anyway," she said.

One of the women got up and went somewhere. Her husband followed her. The other couple grunted at each other and slid out of the booth over Susan's feet, saying, "Back in a second."

She had another sip of the pink liquid, which became paler and thinner as the ice melted. She peered shyly toward the men's room. A growing discomfort set in and she sat more stiffly. She looked at her hands or the bar or the floor so as not to meet any man's eyes and give him reason to think she was offering invitations. A blush beat steadily in her cheeks now. She wondered if she could be drunk. Andy had commented earlier that she was a cheap drunk to explain the way she nursed her drink.

Then the bartender stepped up to her table. Women without escorts were not allowed in The Beaver, he said. He was sorry but it caused too much trouble. She looked at him in amazement.

"But I'm with my husband, Andy Andes!" she said. "He's in the restroom."

The bartender frowned. "You're Andy's wife? But he left with the Brodigans. I saw him getting into their car in the lot. He was plastered, as usual."

"All I could say was, 'Oh,'" Susan said. She got up immediately and walked quickly and carefully out into the rain and came home.

"I had no money for the bus. All my change was in the wallet I gave to Andy. It isn't more than a mile, but I'd come out without a coat. Actually, it probably gave me a good sobering up after the noise and the drink."

She had spoken without noticing her cup, in an anxious flurry to communicate the pain. Now she lifted the cup and drained it. She seemed depleted, as though that large organ inside her that always defended Andy and was able to accept everything about him on one pretext or another had been suddenly and completely flattened. She was not thinking nice thoughts about herself, but for once she was also not making rosy pictures of Andy. There was a question I had never asked and yet had wondered about steadily. It seemed odd for such a self-denigrating woman never to mention the possibility of her husband being with other women on his sprees.

"Do you think Andy might be interested in some other girl?" I asked. She laughed. I was shocked. I had hesitated over the question for a long time, and she giggled. She ran a hand through her drying hair, her enormous arm graceful in its sweep.

"No," she said. "I don't think Andy's up to anything of that sort." She laughed again, softly, and shook her head. "He's only made love to me once in the two years we've been married and that was the night after the wedding." She shook her head again but the smile was gone. "And the other time was nine months before Joey was born. We were married when Joey was three months old, so . . ." She shrugged.

"Twice?" I felt my eyes protruding. "Only twice in all?"

She nodded gravely. The same steady regard as Joey had given me before he fell asleep. My brooding over Andy's vile, lustful impulses crumpled. I began to form a revised picture of her life.

"But—you must want . . ." I began.

She recovered her fragile poise and intercepted me. "Oh, of course I do, but not really badly, except in a long while. Andy can't live all that long, you know. It seems important for me to make a home for him, keep him comfortable . . ." She stopped and her small, perfect mouth opened. She stared at me blankly. She seemed dismayed by the uselessness of this old formula. The recitation of the argument must have supported her a hundred times through the loneliness of the sink, the chores, the bed, and the night, but it failed her now.

Her knees relaxed and spread, and the robe drifted open to show great stretches of flesh. She rested her head on her palm suddenly and sat silent for a moment. When she raised her face to me the pretty youth had been squeezed out. She had the look of the dead moon.

"Do you know," she said, "sometimes to me it seems that Andy and I are just the sort of people who murder each other?" She rose and put her cup into the sink and went to get Joey.

I went straight to bed and slept. The next morning I went about my affairs, thinking about what she had told me. She must have had some idea about getting to know his nocturnal life, bringing it into her scope so she could control it better. I dealt with her words and avoided imagining the reality they sprang from. My mind ran in catches: "A mother but not a wife . . . his daughter, a wife . . . his wife, a daughter . . . Very cozy to have someone support you . . ." But in one swing of the teeter-totter, as I watched my son crow against the sky, the bewilderment hit me. Nothing could encompass the bleak confusion of her bed, the fear that made her accept and cling to such a dull misery. She was not allowed to judge or condemn; she felt herself in no position to choose. And he, whoever he was in his ratty skull, could not have been happy. No.

Late that afternoon there were police sirens outside, but it was so common in that building that I just made sure my door was locked and paid no more attention.

I had just turned out my son's light and said good night when a businesslike rap came at the door. Mrs. Levins stood there with Joey in her arms. I undid the chain and let her in quickly. A kind of pain began in my chest the moment I saw him, his tear-sodden face, the mucus caked on his lip, his baby fists clutched at his chest.

"I do beg your pardon," she said. I reached for Joey and he reached for me.

"I understand you may have been friendly with Susan." Her silver coiffure assumed its regal angle, perhaps for the use of the nether half of her sequined bifocals. I was at the sink using a cloth on Joey's face. Susan never let him get in that state. He lifted his face against the wet cloth and shuddered.

"Where is Susan? What's the matter?" I asked, keeping my voice low, soft, not to frighten the baby.

As she spoke, I undressed Joey and washed him, put him in my son's clothes. His diaper was so soiled I threw it away.

Susan had locked Andy out. When he came home that afternoon she had refused to let him into the apartment. He started shouting and banging on the door. Mrs. Levins heard the ruckus and tried to intervene. She said Andy had been drinking, but was polite to her. Susan had told me that Andy was terrified of Mrs. Levins. Susan had spoken very rudely through the door. The harsh language had instantly reminded her that Susan was being treated for a mental disorder.

"The caseworker takes me into her confidence because of my position of influence with the tenants, you see. I urged Andy to reason with her and occupy her so that she wouldn't harm the baby, while I went for the crowbar. I felt sure if we could get in we could control the situation." But the moment Susan realized that Mrs. Levins was applying a crowbar to the lock, she tossed a suitcase out through the window. It was full of Andy's clothes, which she had evidently packed that morning. Unfortunately, the window was closed and the tinkling of broken glass convinced Mrs. Levins that the police were needed. When she heard the sirens Susan began to weep loudly, but still refused to let anyone in. The uniformed officer entered through the window and after a long and heated consultation, Susan was taken to the state hospital for the mentally ill to be placed under observation.

I sat down and rocked Joey and stared at Mrs. Levins. Now her indignation turned on Andy. She had left him in possession of the apartment and Joey while she'd gone to call the glazier, "feeling assured," she said, "that he was able and willing to care for the child." But when she returned Joey was screaming in his crib, alone in the apartment. "It has been hours. Andy has not returned and I am not equipped to care for the child in my apartment, and obviously he feels more relaxed here and you are well able to . . . Of course I shall call the authorities in the morning to determine what should be done with him, but if he could spend the night here?" she concluded lamely.

I put my finger to my lips and then waved my hand to get her off on her way. She nodded and went. The door clicked softly.

It was quite easy to have Joey stay with me for the duration. Bureaus are, after all, populated by harassed humans with desires to be elsewhere. Mrs. Levins brings me an occasional bulleting from her caseworking acquaintance. Joey is well. In another week he will have forgotten Susan. When she comes back in a month or two months, it will take a few painful days before he'll accompany her again.

I've seen Andy a few times in the hall. Once in the park he came up to Joey in the sandbox and petted his head. Andy's clothes are clean, but they have not been starched or pressed lately. The knees and seat sag. The sleeves flap limply over his pale wrists and the collars lie wrinkled and crooked. He seems stunned by the consequences of such small beginnings and I would like to think he misses more than the clean rooms and regular meals. He is too furtive, though. I don't know enough to decide whether his age and fate have struck him, or only the necessity of pawning his watch and the toaster until Susan comes home to cash her checks.

This incident should see her through at least one more year of classification as unemployable. The security will be welcome to her. I am looking forward to seeing her again.

A Note About the Author

Katherine Dunn is the author of *Geek Love*, which was a finalist for the National Book Award and the Bram Stoker Award, as well as the novels *Toad, Attic*, and *Truck*. She was an award-winning boxing journalist whose work appeared in *Esquire, KO Magazine, The New York Times Magazine, Playboy, The Ring, Sports Illustrated*, and *Vogue*. Her writing on boxing is collected in *One Ring Circus*. In 2004, Dunn and the photographer Jim Lommasson won the Dorothea Lange–Paul Taylor Prize for their work on the book *Shadow Boxers*. Dunn died in 2016.